# *boy, snow, bird*

**Center Point
Large Print**

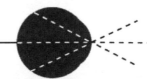

**This Large Print Book carries the
Seal of Approval of N.A.V.H.**

# boy, snow, bird

## HELEN OYEYEMI

CENTER POINT LARGE PRINT
THORNDIKE, MAINE

This Center Point Large Print edition is published in the year 2014 by arrangement with Riverhead Books, a member of Penguin Group (USA) LLC, a Penguin Random House Company.

Lines of verse on page 213 are quoted from *Selected Poems of Antonio Machado* translated by Betty Jean Craige, published by Louisiana State University Press, 1978.

This is a work of fiction. Names, characters, places, and incidents either are the product of the author's imagination or are used fictitiously, and any resemblance to actual persons, living or dead, businesses, companies, events, or locales is entirely coincidental.

The text of this Large Print edition is unabridged. In other aspects, this book may vary from the original edition. Printed in the United States of America on permanent paper. Set in 16-point Times New Roman type.

ISBN: 978-1-62899-160-4

Library of Congress Cataloging-in-Publication Data

Oyeyemi, Helen.
 Boy, snow, bird / Helen Oyeyemi. — Center Point Large Print edition.
 pages ; cm.
 Summary: "A reimagining of the Snow White story set in the United States during the 1950s and 1960s"—Provided by publisher.
 ISBN 978-1-62899-160-4 (library binding : alk. paper)
 1. Fairy tales—Adaptations. 2. Large type books. I. Title.
PR6115.Y49B69 2014b
823'.92—dc23
                                                    2014011787

For Piotr Cieplak

# boy,
# snow,
# bird

Wake, girl.
Your head is becoming the pillow.

—*Eleanor Ross Taylor*

*one*
*two*
*three*

# 1

*n* obody ever warned me about mirrors, so for many years I was fond of them, and believed them to be trustworthy. I'd hide myself away inside them, setting two mirrors up to face each other so that when I stood between them I was infinitely reflected in either direction. Many, many me's. When I stood on tiptoe, we all stood on tiptoe, trying to see the first of us, and the last. The effect was dizzying, a vast pulse, not quite alive, more like the working of an automaton. I felt the reflection at my shoulder like a touch. I was on the most familiar terms with her, same as any other junior dope too lonely to be selective about the company she keeps.

Mirrors showed me that I was a girl with a white-blond pigtail hanging down over one shoulder; eyebrows and lashes the same color; still, near-black eyes; and one of those faces some people call "harsh" and others call "fine-boned." It was not unusual for me to fix a scarf around my head and spend an afternoon pretending that I was a nun from another century; my forehead was high enough. And my complexion is unpredictable, goes from near bloodless to scalded and back again, all without my permission. There are still days when I can only work out whether or not I'm upset by looking at my face.

I did fine at school. I'm talking about the way boys reacted to me, actually, since some form of perversity caused me to spend most lessons pretending to absorb much less information than I actually did. Every now and then a teacher got suspicious about a paper I'd turned in and would keep me after school for questioning. "Has someone been . . . helping you?" I just shook my head and shuffled my chair sideways, avoiding the glare of the desk lamp the teacher invariably tried to shine into my eyes. Something about a girl like me writing an A-grade paper turns teachers into cops. I'll take the appraisal of my male peers over that any day. Four out of five of them either ignored me or were disgustingly kind, the way nice boys are to the plainest Jane they know. But that was only four out of five. Number five tended to lose his balance for some reason and follow me around making the most extraordinary pleas and offers. As if some kind of bug had gotten into him. Female classmates got "anonymous" notes that said things like: *So—I fall for you. Probably because I can see and hear. I see you (those eyes, that smile) and when you laugh . . . yeah, I fall. I'm not normally this sincere, so you might not be able to guess who I am. But here's a clue . . . I'm on the football team. If you feel like taking a chance, wear a blue ribbon in your hair tomorrow and I'll walk you home.*

The notes I received were more . . . tormented. More of the "You've got me going out of my mind" variety. Not that I lost any sleep over that stuff. How could I, when I had a little business going on the side? Boys paid me to write notes to other girls on their behalf. They trusted me. They had this notion that I knew what to say. I just wrote whatever I thought that particular girl wanted to hear and collected dollar bills on delivery. The notes my friends showed me were no work of mine, but I kept my business quiet, so it stands to reason that if anyone else had a similar business, they'd have been discreet about it too.

When my hair started to darken, I combed peroxide through it.

As for character, mine developed without haste or fuss. I didn't interfere—it was all there in the mirrors. Suppose you're born in the Lower East Side of Manhattan in the year nineteen hundred and thirty-something. Suppose your father's a rat catcher. (Your absent mother is never discussed, to the extent that you nurse a theory that you're a case of spontaneous generation.) The interior of the house you grow up in is pale orange and rust brown; at dawn and sunset shadows move like hands behind the curtains—silhouettes of men with Brylcreemed waves in their hair gathered on the street corner to sing about their sweethearts in

15

seven-part harmony, the streetcar whispering along its track, Mrs. Phillips next door beating blankets. Your father is an old-fashioned man; he kills rats the way his grandfather taught him. This means that there are little cages in the basement—usually a minimum of seven at any given time. Each cage contains a rat, lying down and making a sound somewhere between twittering and chattering: *lak lak lak lak, krrrr krrrrr krrr*. The basement smells of sweat; the rats are panicking, starving. They make those sounds and then you see holes in their paws and in their sides—there's nothing else in that cage with them, and all your father does to them at first is give them water, so it stands to reason that it's the rats making the holes, eating themselves. When your father's about to go out on a job, he goes to the basement, selects a cage, and pulls its inhabitant's eyes out. The rats that are blind and starving are the best at bringing death to all the other rats, that's your father's claim. Your father puts three or four cages in the trunk of his car and drives away. He comes back late in the evening, when the job's done. I guess he makes a lot of money; he does business with factories and warehouses, they like him because he's very conscientious about the cleanup afterward.

So that's Papa. Cleanest hands you'll ever see in your life. He'll punch you in the kidneys, from behind, or he'll thump the back of your head and walk away sniggering while you crawl around on the floor, stunned. He does the same to his lady friend, who lives with you, until he starts going for her face. She'll put up with a lot, but not that. One day she leaves a note under your pillow. It says: *Look, I'm sorry. For what it's worth, I'd say you deserve better. Take care of yourself.*

You don't get too upset about her departure, but you do wonder who's going to let you bum Lucky Strikes now. You're all of fifteen and you're a jumpy kid. You don't return people's smiles—it's perfectly clear to you that people can smile and smile and still be villains. One of the first things you remember is resting your head against the sink—you were just washing your hair in it, and you had to take a break because when your hair's wet it's so heavy you can't lift your head without your neck wobbling. So you're resting, and that clean hand descends out of nowhere and holds you facedown in the water until you faint. You come around lying on the bathroom floor. There's a burning feeling in your lungs that flares up higher the harder you cough, and the rat catcher's long gone. He's at work.

Where does character come into it? Just this: I've always been pretty sure I could kill someone if I had to. Myself, or my father—whichever option proved most practical. I wouldn't kill for hatred's sake; I'd only do it to solve a problem. And only after other solutions have failed. That

17

kind of bottom line is either in your character or it isn't, and like I said, it develops early. My reflection would give me a slow nod from time to time, but would never say what she was thinking. There was no need.

A couple of teachers asked me if I was applying to college, but I said: "Can't afford it." Actually, I was pretty sure that the rat catcher could, but I didn't want to have that, or any, conversation with him. He hit me when one of his caged rats bit him. He hit me when I pronounced a word in a certain way that made him think I was acting stuck-up. (He told me that the difference between him and other people was that other people would only think about kicking me in the shins whenever I used a long word, but he went ahead and took action.) He'd hit me when I didn't flinch at the raising of his arm, and he'd hit me when I cowered. He hit me when Charlie Vacic came over to respectfully ask if he could take me to prom. I seem to recall he began that particular beating in a roundabout way, by walking up to me with a casserole dish and dropping it on my foot. There was almost a slapstick element to it all. I got a sudden notion that if I laughed or asked "Are you through?" he'd back off. But I didn't try to laugh, for fear of coming in too early, or too late.

There were times I thought the rat catcher was going to knock me out for sure. For instance, the morning he told me to run downstairs and blind a couple of rats real quick for him before I went to school. I said NO WAY and made inner preparations for stargazing. But he didn't really do anything, just pointed at my clothes and said: "Rats paid for those," then pointed at my shoes and said: "Rats paid for those," and pointed at the food on the table and said: "Rats . . ."

He imitated them: *"Krrrr. Lak lak lak lak."* And he laughed.

The unpredictability of his fist didn't mean he was crazy. Far from it. Sometimes he got awfully drunk, but never to a point where he didn't seem to know what he was doing. He was trying to train me. To do what, I don't know. I never found out, because I ran away almost as soon as I turned twenty. I wish I knew what took me so long. He didn't even hit me that night. He just sat in his easy chair snoozing after dinner, like always. I watched him and I woke up, I kind of just woke up. He was sleeping so peacefully, with a half smile on his face. He didn't know how rotten he was. He'll never know, probably never even suspect it.

My feet walked me into my bedroom while I thought it over. Then I gave my mattress a good-bye kick. I didn't pack much because I didn't have much. There was only one really important thing in my bag: a flag that Charlie Vacic had wrapped around my shoulders once when we were watching the Fourth of July fireworks over

19

at Herald Square. He said it was a loan, but he never asked for it back. Ever since he'd started at medical school people talked about him as if he'd died, but he was the same old Charlie—he wrote to me from upstate, and he mentioned the flag, and that night. I'd written back that I was still looking after the flag for him. It took up a bunch of room in my bag, but I couldn't just leave it there with the rat catcher.

I did look for the key to the basement, but I couldn't find it. Hard to say how much of a good turn it would've been to set those rats free after standing by while they'd starved, anyway.

Three times I opened and closed the front door, testing the depth of the rat catcher's sleep, trying to make the softest click possible. The third time I heard him shift in the chair, and he mumbled something. The fourth time I opened the door I didn't have the nerve to close it behind me, just ran. Two girls playing hopscotch outside Three Wishes Bakery saw me coming and hopped right out of the way. I ran six or seven blocks, the street one long dancing seam of brick and bicycle bells, hats and stockings, only stopping to turn corners when traffic lights wouldn't let me pass. I ran so fast I don't know how my pumps stayed on. A crosstown bus, then a subway ride to Port Authority. "Nervous" simply isn't the word. I stayed standing on the bus ride, stuck close to the driver, looking behind us, looking ahead, my heart stirring this way and that like so much hot soup, my hands stuck deep in my pockets so my sleeves couldn't be grabbed. I was ready for the rat catcher to appear. So ready. I knew what I'd do. If he tried to take me by the elbow, if he tried to turn me around, I'd come over all tough guy, slam my skull into his forehead. I stayed ready until I got to Port Authority, where the priority shifted to not getting trampled.

I really wasn't expecting that kind of hullabaloo. If there'd been more time I'd just have stood stock-still with my eyes closed and my hands clapped over my ears, waiting for a chance to take a step toward the ticket counter without being pushed or yelled at. Folks were stampeding the last bus with everything they had—it was as if anyone unlucky enough to still be on the station platform turned into a pumpkin when the clock struck twelve. I tumbled into the bus with a particularly forceful gang of seven or so—a family, I think—tumbled off the bus again by way of getting caught up in the folds of some man's greatcoat, and scuttled over to the ticket counter to try to find out just where this last bus was going. I saw the rat catcher in the ticket line, long and tall and adamant, four people away from the front, and I pulled my coat collar over my head. I saw the rat catcher get out of a cab and stride toward me, veins bulging out of his forehead, looking like he meant nothing but Business. I whirled around and saw the rat catcher again, pounding on the bus window, trying to find me among the passengers. Okay, so he wasn't really there at all, but that was no reason to relax—it'd be just like him to turn up, really turn up, I mean, a moment or two after my guard came down. I saw him at least twenty times, coming at me from all angles, before I reached the counter. And when I finally did get there, the guy behind it told me it was closed for the night.

"When do you open up again?"

"Six in the morning."

"But I've got to leave tonight."

He was basically a jerk. "Jerk" isn't a term I make free and easy use of. I don't go around saying *He/she/it is a jerk.* But this guy was something special. There I was, looking right at him through the glass as I wept desperately, and there he was, petting his moustache as if it were a small and fractious creature. He sold me a ticket five minutes before the bus left, and he only did it because I slipped him an extra five dollars. I felt a bout of sarcasm coming on when he took the money, but made sure I had the ticket in my hand before I said: "My hero." I was going to the last stop, on account of its being the farthest away— the ticket said the last stop was Flax Hill, and I'd never heard of it.

"Flax Hill? Whereabouts would you say that is?"

"New England," my hero said. "You're gonna miss that bus."

"Where in New England? I mean . . . what state? Vermont, or what?"

He studied me with narrowed eyes, selecting a nerve, the fat juicy nerve of mine he'd most like to get upon. "Or what," he said.

He drew the blinds down over the counter window, and I ran. There were only two seats left on the bus—one beside an elderly man and one beside a colored woman who was sleeping with her head laid up against the window. The man smelled somewhat urinaceous, so I sat beside the woman, who opened her eyes, asked me if she should get up, nodded, and fell asleep again when I said no. She looked just about worn-out.

Across the aisle, a baby started screaming, and its mother bounced it up and down on her knees, trying to soothe it into good behavior. But the shrieking went on and on, primal, almost glad— this protest was righteous. I couldn't make up my mind whether the baby was male or female; the only certainties were near baldness and incandescent rage. The kid didn't like its blanket, or its rattle, or the lap it was sat on, or the world . . . the time had come to demand quality. This continued until the mother, who had been staring into space, suddenly came to and gave her child a particularly vicious look, along with a piece of information: "I don't *have* a baby that acts this way." The baby seemed taken aback, hiccupped a few times, and fell silent.

I held that talisman ticket of mine smooth between my hands right up until the bus pulled out of the station, even though deep down I knew there was no way the rat catcher could have figured out where I was. It wouldn't have occurred to him that I'd leave the state. Maybe he wouldn't look too hard. Maybe he'd just shrug and think, *Well, that's cut down the grocery bill.* (Actually, I knew he would be murderously mad—I could almost hear him bellowing: "I'm a RAT CATCHER. No two-bit wretch runs out on me, even if she is my daughter!") *Don't think of his face*—Flax Hill, Flax Hill. With a name like that, it was probably the countryside I was going to. Moonlight, hay, cows chewing cud and exchanging slow, conversational moos. It was a scenario I felt doubtful about. But I was game. I had to be.

As pillows go, my bag served pretty well. I listened to the drumming of the bus wheels on the road, made a note that running away from home was as easy as pie once you'd made your mind up to it, and fell asleep with my limbs carefully arranged so as not to touch my neighbor's.

# 2

*i*t was snowing when I got off the bus at Flax Hill. Not quite regular snowfall, not exactly a blizzard. This is how it was: The snow came down heavily, settled for about a minute, then the wind moved it—more rolled it, really—onto another target. One minute you were covered in snow, then it sped off sideways, as if a brisk, invisible giant had taken pity and brushed you down. Next, just as you'd caught your breath, a boomerang effect made a snowman of you all over again. I could only see a few steps ahead of me, and about one step behind me. When a pair of headlights slid past my elbow, I got out of the road and began following the voices of two women huddled under a broken umbrella, mainly because I heard them mention their landlady. I had to find a landlady. Any landlady would do. I stuck close to the umbrella girls, even when the snow hid them from me for seconds at a time and I began to doubt that they were real, even when they took what they called "the shortcut" across abandoned railway tracks overgrown with grass and through a pitch-black tunnel—I retched and retched again at the smell of it. Dead things and rotten eggs. Insects dropped onto my shoulders, tentatively, as if wondering whether we'd met before. More than once I became certain we were being pursued by the very darkness itself. But if the umbrella girls could take it, so could I. A couple of times they stopped and called out: "Hey, is someone there?"

I hung back, kept my mouth shut, and thought: *This landlady had better be great.* Once we were out the other side of the tunnel, the umbrella girls giggled and accused each other of being nervous Nellies. Of course that got me thinking about times I'd been in the dark and felt that someone else was there but convinced myself that I was wrong. Probably nine times out of ten there really had been someone there.

When the umbrella girls finally went in at the door of a prim, skinny, redbrick building, I walked up and down in front of it for a few minutes after the door had closed, wondering what story to tell. But I didn't know the landlady's name and it was too cold to think. I knocked at the door and managed to walk in and ask for the lady of the house without shivering too much. She had steel gray hair, an elegant figure, and a "Honey, I've seen it all" expression that served as the basis for all her other expressions, from amusement to annoyance.

I said: "I heard you're a landlady. Please don't tell me I heard wrong," and then I ran out of vocabulary. She sat me down on her own personal sofa, piled cushions onto me until only my head stuck out, and called for soup and blankets. Her name was Mrs. Lennox, and she was Flax Hill born and bred—"A Massachusetts classic, you know." She told me she'd never lost a prospective tenant yet, and the girls who answered the cry for soup and blankets backed her up. "Doesn't get under your feet, either," one of them added. (That turned out to be correct. She wasn't someone that you just saw around, you had to make appointments with her.) The girls hadn't consulted one another, so there were four bowls of soup and seven blankets. I took that as a sign that I was welcome and said "Thank you" about fifty times in a row until someone laughingly pointed out that it was only soup.

Over the days that followed, I tried to identify the umbrella girls by the sounds of their voices, since it was all I had to go on. But fifteen women who live together get to talking alike. It could've been any two of them who'd led me in out of the snow.

As for Flax Hill itself, I was on shaky terms with it for the first few months. Neither of us was sure whether or not I genuinely intended to stick around. And so the town misbehaved a little, collapsing when I went to sleep and reassembling in the morning in a slapdash manner; I kept passing park benches and telephone booths and entrances to alleyways that I was absolutely certain hadn't been there the evening before. My boarding house room was the cheapest around, and truly, I got what I paid for. A narrow bed, low beams I kept knocking my head against, and a view of a bus stop with a hangdog air (its sign was illegible). There was no chair to sit on, and no mirror in my room, so I made brief consultations with myself as I washed my face in the bathroom down the hall—"I heard she's a gangster's moll," I whispered, repeating things I'd overheard while supposedly out of earshot. "Nah, she's an actress studying her next part. Trust me, I've seen this before." The woman in the mirror gave me a big wink, told me it'd blow over soon enough, and sent me to bed on my own.

I dreamt of rats. They spoke to me. They called me "cousin." And I dreamt of being caught, dreamt of sedative smoke, tar, glue, and strange lights the size of the sun, switching from red to green so fast that I had no time to react. Then the rat catcher held me by the tail. He exhibited me at a conference and answered questions on my habits. He was awarded a medal, and I was very much against the whole thing, but I was dead. I'd wake up with both hands covering my nose, which twitched violently and felt like the coldest part of my body after such dreams. I tasted salt, and that was how I knew I'd been crying in my sleep. I think I missed home. A lot. It didn't make any sense but I missed home a lot.

*three things were* unsatisfactory about me—the first, that I was from Manhattan.

("What could a girl from *there* be looking for around *here?*")

The second problem was my name.

("It's Boy."

"Oh, sure. Very cute. And what's your government name?"

"I already told you: Boy. Boy Novak."

"Wow . . ."

"Wow yourself.")

The third problem was that I hadn't brought any skill with me. Flax Hill is a town of specialists, and if someone turns up in that kind of town with nothing but a willingness to get their hands dirty, that someone had better forget about being given a break. All anybody ever seemed to want to know about me at first was *how come*. How come I wasn't good at anything? I went on a lot of double dates with a girl named Veronica Webster who lived on the floor below me. Like the other tenants, she carried her pawnshop tickets folded up inside an antique locket around her neck. Unlike the other tenants, she had a nice room with a fireplace, and she hosted hot chocolate parties, but you had to bring your own hot chocolate. Webster was seventy percent all right and thirty percent pain in the neck, one of those women who are corpselike until a man walks into the room, after which point they become irresistibly vivacious. She wore her hair like Mamie Eisenhower's only with longer bangs, and she was out three nights a week, one of them with Ted Murray, her unofficial steady date. I kept feeling I should try to talk her out of her attachment to Ted. First of all he was a stingy tipper, just couldn't seem to make himself round up to the nearest zero, and that filled me with foreboding. The other thing was that we all met at his place for predinner cocktails once and he had this garish oil portrait of Lincoln up on a wall—the product of one of those mail-order paint-by-number kits if I ever saw one. Something came over me as I stood there looking at that noble profile reproduced in puce. I don't ever want to feel that way again. It's Lincoln. You can't do that to Lincoln.

Back at the boarding house I said to Webster: "So . . . how about that portrait of Lincoln in Ted's parlor?"

She shrugged. "Nobody's perfect. Anyway, I don't know about you, but a man who admires Lincoln is my kind of man."

I said darkly, "Ah, but does he . . . does he?" and left it at that. I wasn't supposed to rock the boat. It was up to me to try to keep Ted's friend entertained. The friend's name was Arturo Whitman, and he and Ted were a team—Ted sold the jewelry that Arturo made. I could see how Arturo might not be the best salesman; he was big and shaggy and not a little gruff. More often than not he knocked both our wineglasses over on account of waving his hands about too much while talking about the parallels between Robespierre and McCarthy. He had tawny, heavy-lidded eyes, and he wasn't very good at dancing, but I couldn't help liking it when he held me in his arms. One evening when Ted and Webster were playing footsie and talking about Guatemala (Ted was describing parts of it he'd been to, and Webster chipped in with "Sounds divine!" and "I'm awfully jealous!" and "I'd sure like to see that for myself someday, Teddy . . ."), Arturo and I just sat there watching the rain wrap the window round and round in a trembling veil. I heard the raindrops say, "I have a daughter. She wears red amaryllis blooms in her hair"; then I realized it was Arturo talking.

I looked across the table. He smiled. Not at me, but at the window, as if he saw her there. "Last month it was forget-me-nots," he said. "And before that, yellow everlastings."

"I bet she's pretty." The safest remark I could think of.

"Her name's Snow," he said, as if that explained it all. He checked his watch. "Her grandma will have put her to bed about ten minutes ago."

"It's early. How old is she?"

He frowned. "She'll be six tomorrow."

"Ah. Is it all happening too fast?"

"No, it's—fine. The birthday present she's asked for is a tall order, though."

"Lemme guess: a pony."

31

"I almost wish it was. Two more guesses."

"Uhm . . . an enchanted object. A lamp with a genie in it, something like that."

"Not exactly," he said, after wavering for a moment.

The next guess was inappropriate, I knew, but I was too curious not to give it a shot. "A mother."

He stared. "You're good."

"It's just . . . you said it was a tall order."

"Yeah."

He closed his mouth tight after saying that one word. I figured he only kept coming out on those dates of ours because Ted was blackmailing him—he always looked so relieved when it was time to go home. On the boarding house doorstep I halved a cigarette and lit Webster's half, then mine, so we could have a quick couple of smokes before going in for the night. Arturo's wife had died a week after giving birth to his daughter, Webster told me. Childbirth complications. He'd been a history professor at Boston University at the time. But he took Snow and went away, he still wouldn't say where. Wherever it was, he'd learned to work metal there; when he came back two years later, he set up a workshop in his home.

"What was his wife's name?"

"Julia, I think."

"You're not sure?"

"He doesn't really talk about her."

"And have you met the kid?"

I'd reached the end of my cigarette half before she had, and Webster grinned as she blew smoke past my ear. "Who, Snow? Sure. She's a doll."

There was a misunderstanding between Arturo and me. An unspoken one, and how do you correct those? It happened at Ted's place, when I was transfixed by that god-awful portrait. I stayed standing in front of it for longer than I actually looked at it. Time ticked by and I faced the portrait dead-on without seeing it at all. Had anyone asked me what it was that I could see, I wouldn't have been able to tell them. It was almost as if I'd left the room. I say almost because I could still hear Ted trying his best to wet blanket Webster's Halloween costume idea.

"This year—wait for it—this year I'm doing the telltale heart."

"And how do you propose to dress up as a heart?"

"Oh, I'll just paint myself red all over and wear a red hat, silly. And I'll tell *tales*."

"That's just plain cryptic. Anyhow, didn't the telltale heart throb horrifically loudly?"

"Oh, that's hardly difficult. I can throb horrifically loudly right now, if you like."

"Be my guest."

*"Buh-boom,"* Webster began, in a deep voice. *"Buh-boom, buh boom."*

I was smiling. My eyes came back into focus and that was what I saw—a face I recognized, smiling. I'd been looking at myself in the picture frame the whole time. The smile turned wry, I scanned the room without turning around, and there was Arturo Whitman. The left side of him, to be precise. The rest of him was out of the picture, but there was a look of steady dislike in that left eye of his. He seemed to think he'd caught me practicing being fascinating.

He was pretty sarcastic with me after that, when before he'd been almost kind; he took to replying to any little observation I made with "Indeed," and he got even worse a couple of dates later when I fell into a similar trance only to come to and discover that I'd apparently been contemplating my mysterious smile in the back of my dessert spoon.

Our misunderstanding worried me. I thought: *I should talk to him. I should tell him it isn't vanity.* If it was vanity, I'd have been able to disguise it, all this insipid smirking at myself. Other women did it all the time; it was just that they didn't get caught. No, the only behaviors we can't control are those caused by nerves. I rehearsed an offhand explanation. It began with the words: "Hand me some nerve tonic, Whitman." But I didn't know for sure that it wasn't vanity running the show. What I did know was that I wouldn't be able to stand it if I tried to explain myself in good faith and his only answer was "Indeed."

The other two date nights Webster and I spent

with bachelors eligible enough to stop Ted from taking her for granted but not so eligible that he quit competing. As for me, I knew I was onto a good thing. I was guaranteed three moderately fancy dinners a week, including dessert, and I was mingling with the locals. The only cost was a little of my pride. I had one dress that was fit for a dinner date, a deep red shantung number the rat catcher's girlfriend had outgrown. Each time I went to a restaurant, that dress came too. My dates cracked jokes about it, and I acknowledged the jibes with an affable but distant smile. Every other young person I met was an apprentice at this studio or that workshop. The potters scrubbed up pretty well but never managed to shed every last bit of clay; there'd always be just a little daub of it on their chins or wrists. My favorite potter, whose name I forget, said, "Awww, not again," when I told him there was clay on his forehead. He said: "You know how possessive clay is." His tone of voice made me wish I could agree with him. As far as he was concerned, he was talking about something as true as thunder, as true as his thumb. So clay leaves hickeys. Who knew . . .

I told Arturo Whitman about it, just to make conversation. He shrugged, and said: "You should go back to New York."

In my head I counted slowly to five before answering. "Oh, I should, should I?"

"Yup." He cracked his knuckles. Maybe he just

felt a little stiff at that moment, but as a gesture made while telling someone to leave town, I didn't like it.

"And just why is that?"

He finished his lunch and started on mine, methodically, without enthusiasm. He didn't seem to approve of lamb chops and spinach. "You must've thought you'd get an easy ride around here. You must've thought you could show up and say 'Hey, I'm from the big city' and everyone would just roll over—"

"Would it kill you to get to the point?" I inquired.

"All right," he said. "I'll keep it simple. People make beautiful things here. We're interested in the process, not the end product. Now, you—you don't have what it takes to start that kind of process, let alone see it through. So. There's nothing here for you."

I looked him in the eye and said slowly: "Oh, isn't there?" I wasn't referring to anything in particular—all I was conscious of was the desire to give him a gigantic scare, right there in the diner, with the rest of the Sunday lunch crowd all around us, happy young families and grandpas carefully chewing the pasta in their minestrone as they listened to the baseball scores.

Arturo didn't turn a hair. "What were you at home, a dressmaker's model?"

"No," I said, amazed that he could have got it so

wrong. That "big city" stuff too. New York wasn't a big city to me. It was no bigger than a Novak rat cage. The nearest of those blinded creatures always knew when I was nearby, and would turn their heads toward me if I made the slightest movement, just as if I'd called their names.

"Well, you could probably do that kind of work here. I know someone who—"

"I'll find my own job. Thanks."

That evening I told Webster she should find someone else for her double dates. It was just one of those things, I said.

I found it easy to disregard the suggestion that I didn't belong in Flax Hill. The town woke something like a genetic memory in me . . . after a couple of weeks, the air tasted right. To be more specific, the air took on a strong flavor of *palinka*, that fiery liquor I used to sneak capfuls of whenever the rat catcher forgot to keep it under lock and key. But now, here, clear smoke rose from my soul every time I breathed in. A taste of the old country. Of course I knew better than to mention this to anybody.

Arturo was right about the way Flax Hill worked, though. I swept the floors of European-style ateliers and watched luxury made before my very eyes. Brocade gloves in quarter sizes for a perfect fit, *peau de soie* slippers with a platinum sheen, hall-length tapestries woven from hand-dyed thread, wooden doorknobs shaped like miniature tigers midleap—the people of Flax Hill made all these things, packed them up in crates with no more emotion than if they were hen's eggs, and sent them to department stores and private clients across the country. The town should really have been called Flax Hills, since it was huddled up between two of them, but maybe that was the locals' way of instructing one of the hills to scram. The hills are ringed round with old, dark, thick-trunked trees. They're so tall you feel a false stillness standing under them; when you look all the way up, you see the wind crashing through the topmost branches, but you hear all the commotion only distantly, if at all. I met men out among those trees. Bearded men who carried axes, and drove carthorses, occasionally stopping to deftly bind logs of wood more tightly together. The woodcutters didn't seem surprised to see me. They'd just say hello and point, reminding me where north was so I wouldn't lose my way. Light fell through the leaves, liquid in some places, sometimes stopping to hang in long necklaces— but only for a second or two, as if aware it wouldn't get much admiration in Flax Hill.

There were houses along the road back into town. I hadn't taken much notice of them when I was walking toward the trees, but the closer it got to nightfall, the more those houses stood out. They were mostly basic, hutlike structures, and the majority of them looked abandoned, but I saw stripy curtains here and there, or a basketball hoop fixed to an outer wall with a freshly chalked scoreboard beside it. One of the bigger houses had brambles growing up the front of it in snakelike vines. The smell of baking chocolate-chip cookies aside, it looked like a house you could start fanciful rumors about: "Well, a princess has been asleep there for hundreds of years . . ." and so on. The front door was open, and the porch light was on, and a little girl came around the side of the house, singing loudly. I couldn't see her face properly—it was obscured by clouds of dark hair with big red flowers plaited into them—but she had a large cookie in each hand and more in the pockets of her dress, and I wanted to go in at the door behind her, sit down at the old piano I could see in the living room while she stood on tiptoes to retrieve the glass of milk set on top of it. Her voice sounded exactly the way I'd thought it would sound. For some reason that scared me, so I didn't stop at the gate to greet her even though I heard her saying "Hi" in a startled way. I just said "Hi, Snow" as if we'd met before, when of course we hadn't, and I kept going, kept my gaze fixed on the road ahead of me. "Scared" doesn't even really describe it. I almost crossed myself. It felt like the evil eye had fallen upon us both.

# 3

*i* became well acquainted with the Help Wanted column in the local paper. I read it in the mornings, lying in bed with my little wireless set on my chest, pouring piano concertos directly into my heart as I scanned job descriptions I couldn't answer to. I continued my reading at the Mitchell Street lunch counter, where Gertrude the waitress called me (and everyone) "schatzie" and kidded that I was cold-blooded because I drank my coffee without blowing on it first. One day I opened the newspaper to Help Wanted as usual, slumped for no particular reason, ordered a cream soda for a change, and started reading an article on the other half of the page. A "shy, quiet" girl of sixteen had been missing for a month and a half, and various developments had led to the police dragging the river. They'd found the remains of a young female, but apparently it wasn't the shy, quiet girl—this one was older, "somewhere between twenty and twenty-six years old, well nourished . . ." The police were looking for help identifying the body, and there were a couple of other details, but it was "well nourished" I got stuck on. How could they say that? How was that going to help jog people's memories? Were they calling her fat? I mean, being well nourished is good, it means you're healthy. But when you're dead and someone says that about you without any kind of modification to the description—I guess it's all wrong to describe a corpse as "well nourished yet slender"—I just wouldn't want that for myself. I pushed the cream soda away. *I should cut back on treats.* I pulled my cream soda back toward me, feeling as embarrassed as if I'd just said that out loud. What a way to be thinking when some poor girl had been murdered. I returned to the Help Wanted column and read it with extra attention to make up for the past few minutes' slacking. A company that specialized in cocktail mixers had put a call out for blondes (*lots of blondes, most shapes, shades, and sizes! Tell your friends!*) to act as hostesses for their Valentine's Day soiree. It was a one-off, an evening cruise on Lake Quinsigamond in a party boat, but the money was good, so I picked up the telephone around the corner from the soda fountain and gave my dress measurements to a decidedly unfriendly receptionist who instructed me to be at the club at four p.m. the following Friday. "You'd better not be lying about those measurements, by the way. This party is for the big-shot investors, and the bosses want to make sure that these investors like what they see. So if you don't fit into the dress we'll have ready for you, you'll have to go home."

Webster lent me bus fare. "Must be great being a blonde," she said. "Maybe you'll meet a millionaire!" I couldn't find any sarcasm in her gaze. I told her she could quit secretarial college and join "us" anytime she wanted.

I was one of about a hundred blondes who showed up at the dock that afternoon, and none of us got sent home—in fact, quite a few of us found that our violet chiffon dresses were too loose, evidence of the prune juice diets we'd been on ever since we'd heard the secretary's malignant warning. When we all stood in front of the event director, he rubbed his hands together and chuckled and announced that he liked what he saw. The boat would be sailing to Drake Island, where we'd continue the drinking and dancing begun on the boat before returning to Worcester. This was going to be the best party we'd ever been to, because this party was going to represent the spirit of Herb Hill Beverages—fun, accessible, yet exclusive, just like us lovely ladies. Accessible and yet exclusive? It seemed to me that a party could only be one or the other, never both, and I for one did not understand exactly what it was he expected of us. "Oh, and it's my birthday," he finished, and we chorused, "Happy birthday, sir."

He split us into groups. Then he and a few other suited men who never spoke to us directly gave us little tasks to do—walking up and down the subtly shifting floor of the cabin, with or without a tray that had glasses balanced on it, or saying "Hello" with a smile, or matching tickets to numbered

42

hangers. It turned out I had a genius for matching tickets to hangers, so I was one of ten coat-check girls.

"Not terrible, but not great," a girl in my group commented. "The hardest thing is staying awake long enough to give the coats back at the end."

"Yeah, I think I heard Mr. Ramsey say that this thing's gonna go on 'til six in the morning," someone else said. We were sitting in the belly of the boat, looking over the deck plan. We'd already padded around the velvet-draped suites making sure the fire extinguishers were where they were supposed to be. We'd already stood silhouetted by the sunset, letting the lake breeze blow our hair into a golden haze around our heads as we tested the outer railings on all three levels. We checked the escape hatches and made each other locate them blindfolded, because the two more experienced girls said that sometimes the lights cut before the alarm went off. "When rich folks get drunk . . ." Betty began, and Dinah finished: "They burn money. Handfuls of dollar bills."

I said I found that hard to believe.

Dinah sniffed, "Don't, then," but Betty said kindly: "Sweetie, I didn't believe it either until I saw 'em do it."

"Businessmen do all kinds of things we wouldn't be able to understand," Dinah said.

"It's all the pressure they're under," Betty agreed.

43

I listened in silence, hoping that they'd say more. They were women so determined to think well of people that they made it seem effortless, and I hadn't really come across their kind before.

"Baloney. We're all under pressure. If these guys really do set dollar bills alight, they're a bunch of devils," said the girl beside me. She put a napkin around her neck and another one on her lap, took a sandwich out of her handbag and sank her teeth into it. She was a tidy eater, and like me, she had very dark eyes for a blonde. I'd also noticed her looking exasperated when the event director said it was his birthday.

Her name was Mia Cabrini, and I was paired with her at the coat check; we were on for the first three hours. I'd thought there'd be a busy period of checking in coats and then a slow period until it was time to give all the coats back, but the coat check never stopped being busy. These big shots were indecisive; they couldn't make up their minds whether they were cold or not. Mia had a notepad and filled pages of it with shorthand. I didn't ask her why.

When our first three hours were up, we switched with Dinah and Betty and "mingled" with the guests. Well, Mia mingled. I went out onto the top deck and smoked my leisure time away. The boat was going pretty fast; the solid brick and earth of the waterfront lagged stubbornly, it seemed to be having a hard time keeping up. We left streaks of light on the dark water behind us. Canapés were brought around, but the girls with the trays didn't offer me any. The same went for wine; we weren't supposed to drink. I watched wealthy men and their wives and dates dancing and playing cards and making deals: *I will admire you exactly as much, no more or less, as you admire me. I will love you in the strictest moderation.* Some couples seemed pleased with their negotiations and others were in despair. They looked around with drained faces and drank less than their friends did, barely wetting their lips so as to keep their secrets. Merchant families, mostly, descendants of Englishmen who'd gotten rich trading with the tsars and sultans and rajahs of long ago, then come over to America because all their money didn't stop the aristocrats from snubbing them. Now their great-grandchildren just made a few investments here and there, and kept charitable institutions the way an average Joe keeps a pet. I'd read quite a number of lifestyle magazines over the years; you've got to have some sort of setting for your daydreams. At the end of the interview about the redecoration of a nursery or the refurbishment of a mansion, the reporter never failed to ask the price of a loaf of bread and a pint of milk at the nearest corner store, and the interviewee always knew the answer, down to the last cent—it reeked of research. So I got a kick out of seeing the stars of the show close up. Some of them even knew how to jitterbug. But I remembered my manners. I didn't let anyone catch me staring. I reminded myself over and over again that I wasn't at the zoo.

Mia came and found me when the band started playing "Pico and Sepulveda." She grabbed both my hands and I let her lead our quickstep, trying to match the swing of her hips as we mouthed the names of Los Angeles streets at each other, streets neither of us had ever been on. *Doheny* . . . *Cahuenga* . . . *La Brea* . . . *Tar Pits!*

The thing about dancing when you're hungry is that at the end of the song you find yourself sitting on the floor, or the nearest knee, whichever happens to be more readily available. I settled for a knee, and its owner got overfamiliar, put a hand to my waist, and said in my ear: "So she loves me." It was Arturo Whitman, got up in all his finery, managing to look both drowsy and savage at once, as a bear might if forced to wear a tuxedo.

I said: "Arturo Whitman, are you . . . rich?"

He held both hands up in the air. "I'm not. I swear I'm not. Ask the guys I came in with. I'm just here to amuse them." He gave me the once-over. "Same as you. What would you do if I kissed you right now?"

"Sock you in the solar plexus."

"Do you even know where to find the solar plexus?"

"No, but I'd keep going 'til I got there."

46

"Aw, she loves me not . . ."

I opened my mouth with that reckless joy that comes just before you give someone a genuine piece of your mind, but Mia pounced on us before I got started, crying, "Dr. Whitman!" They gave each other an odd, fleeting look with some kind of question in it. Arturo said: "Mia Cabrini. How the hell are you? Still involved in passionate love affairs with long-dead German philosophers?"

She glanced at me with a smile. "Mind if I hog this old man? He taught me history a million years ago, and I need to tell him all about how a guy called Mr. Friedrich Nietzsche and I finally split up for good."

I said: "What do I care?" at the same time as he said: "Why would she mind?"

He found a table inside for the two of them, and a dish of ice cream just for her, and I took a sudden interest in "mingling," passing them more often than was strictly necessary. "Do you want this ice cream?" he asked her, whisking the dish all around the tabletop. "I mean, do you truly want it? Would you fight for this ice cream? Would you bear a deep wound in order to possess this ice cream completely? How deep a wound? What if it was as deep as the grave? What does this ice cream really mean to you, Miss Cabrini?"

They looked good together. They were what society columnists called "a striking pair." I don't say this maliciously—at least, I don't think

47

I do—but it was only when I saw her with him that I fully realized I was younger than she was. She pulled a face and whacked him with her spoon. Not gently, either. "How's Snow?" she asked.

I didn't catch his answer. A few minutes later Dinah and Betty were back in circulation, and Mia and I were back on the coat-check desk. For almost an hour we hardly said a word to each other. Then she kicked off one of her shoes, placed her bare foot on the hem of my dress so I couldn't move away from her, and said: "Say, what's the meaning of this? Are we back at kindergarten?"

I said: "I don't know."

She narrowed her eyes. "You don't sound so sure." She moved her heel in a slow circle, dragging the material along with it.

"Okay, okay. I'm sure."

"Whitman and I are just good pals," she said. "Goodish—whenever I catch a glimpse of him, anyway. And yeah, maybe . . . maybe we were almost something more once, but it would've been a complete disaster. I don't know . . . he's a nice guy, but there are thoughts he doesn't allow himself to think. So you can't think aloud around him . . . it's too risky. You might accidentally hit a nerve. Did I already say he's a nice guy? He *is*, but you just stumble across one of those thoughts he hates to think and—it ain't pretty. When I die, they'll make me the patron saint of lucky escapes.

And that's all there is to it." She took her foot off the dress and we both checked for a print. Luckily there wasn't one.

"I don't know why you feel a need to tell me—"

"Because he says he can't stand you and you act like you can't stand him, and whenever a man and a woman behave like that toward each other, it usually means something's going on. There's a precious metal kind of gleam about you, and the man's a jeweler, you know. So look out. And listen carefully, Boy—we've got to start right. I'm talking about you and me. Kiss me now, right this minute, and I'll take it as a promise that the next time you get mad at me it'll be a fight that's actually worth having."

I kissed her cheek, and she kissed mine. "He said he can't stand me?"

She chuckled.

"What have you been writing in that notebook all evening?" I asked.

"I'll tell you later."

The boat docked at Drake Island and every one of us hired blondes temporarily became a coat-check girl. Afterward I stood on the middle deck and sipped a glass of water as I watched a crowd of fur coats with people in them tottering across the sand. I was one of the girls who had to stay on board with the guests who didn't want to go ashore, and my interpretation of "exclusive yet accessible" was to offer a smiling side profile to anyone who spoke to me. If my conversation partner moved to try to face me directly, I just turned my head again, and if they made another attempt to adjust our interaction, then so did I, and it was a merry circle that we walked until my opponent was defeated and either went away or settled for a cozy chat with a silhouette. It got so Arturo was the only man on board who'd talk to me.

"What are you playing at?" he said, taking my glass of water from my hand and tasting it.

"Keep it," I said, when he tried to hand the glass back. "I hear you can't stand me."

He didn't reply.

"You feel you've seen a hundred of me. You know how my tiny mind works. But maybe it goes both ways."

That tickled him. "I doubt it," he said, when he was through laughing. He wiped tears from his eyes—that's how tickled he was. "But Mia likes you, so . . ."

"I like Mia too."

"She's a sweet kid," he said, and I thought: *What?* You didn't have to talk to Mia for five minutes to get the message that she wasn't any sweet kid.

"Why'd you quit teaching?"

I felt him look at me, but I gazed steadily into the pastel pink dawn.

"I'm just trying to look busy, Whitman. I'm

throwing myself on your mercy here. If you don't talk to me, I might not get paid."

"Ha. All right, since you asked so nicely. Two reasons. First of all history got itchy. As a field of study, I mean."

"Itchy?"

"Yeah. I'm telling you it itched. I figured it'd pass, but it didn't. I'd sit in my office with my shirtsleeves rolled up, kind of clawing myself from wrist to elbow—my neck sometimes too. It got so bad I'd have to take my shirt off. I was terrified my wife would think they were love scratches, but . . . anyway, she didn't think that. No, don't look at me . . . stay just as you are, if you don't mind. Talking to you like this reminds me of confession."

"Well, go on, my child . . ."

"Thank you, Father. I think I got too close to the details of my era of supposed expertise. You lose certainty that anyone or anything is really instrumental; you know, maybe time just does all the deeds from great to despicable, and uses us, and we pitifully try to save face by pretending we were at the controls. From where I was sitting the whole thing looked and felt like a flea circus. Not entertaining, not illuminating, just endlessly pathetic. Why is this flea being made to carry that grain of rice across a stick of spaghetti? Sure, it's the strongest flea there, the strongman of the crew, but it's struggling . . . the rice is obviously

51

too heavy. The whole thing's kind of degrading to watch . . . I decided to quit, with no clear idea of what I wanted my new job to be. That wasn't as important as planning how to break it to my family that I was about to throw away a lot of work and a lot of sacrifice, theirs and mine. Snow was well on her way to being born, and my wife liked things the way they were; I think her favorite thing about our . . . collaboration was her actor and musician friends rubbing shoulders with my academic colleagues, she liked the atmosphere of challenge, the way anything that came under discussion could be claimed or rejected by either side. Time and time again the power of an idea or a piece of art was assessed by either its beauty or its technique or its usefulness, and time and time again my wife was surprised by how rarely anything on earth satisfies all three camps."

He rested an elbow on the top railing and stood at a slant that made me think of the crooked man who walked a crooked mile. How does the rest of that nursery rhyme go? Something to do with this crooked man journeying farther and farther along and coming across crooked things that he takes for his own because nobody else wants them, and then he finds a crooked wife and the two of them have a crooked whale of a time ever after . . . ?

It began to look as if he was just going to stand like that without saying another word for the rest of the boat trip, so I said: "I didn't know you had to change friends when you change jobs."

I think he smiled. "You don't, I guess. I don't know . . . I sometimes go to dinner with those same people now and I feel like a poser. I get what they're saying but I'm not as invested in their bickering. I'd rather talk metals. Anyway, back when I was still a professor, I think my wife got wise to me before I even said anything about quitting. She sat me down to tell me, quite urgently and emphatically, how proud she was of all my achievements . . ."

"I think I get the picture. But you said there were two reasons."

"Right. Good memory. The second reason is that I met a jeweler on the train from Boston to Flax Hill one evening, and we got talking. Making baubles wasn't something I'd ever thought about before I got talking to that man. Why feed vanity? He said: "Oh, come on now. What do you think you are, a Puritan?" He said any Puritan worth his salt knows that vanity isn't fussy; it'll eat almost anything. He said it's a matter of fact that there's no way to avoid feeding vanity, no matter what line of work you're in. He seemed to be doing okay, much better than I was. He was happy with his work. He mentioned that he'd recently left his wife, not for another woman, just for peace of mind, but he continued to look forward to the future and saw no reason why it shouldn't bring him good things. I picked up his briefcase by mistake as we were getting ready for our stop. We swapped back almost immediately, of course, but—his briefcase was so light. It was one of those cases that looked heavy—it looked like mine, which was full of printed matter—but its lightness was tempting. It made me want to walk away with it, walk all the way out of my existence and into his. He was going home to eat beans out of a can and sketch fractals into his design book. There were no flea circuses in his life."

"No Julia in his life, either," I said, wishing for a cigarette or something to do with my hands. I was learning the ways of the world; one of them being that the presence of a certain type of curly-haired man—your type—will cause you to fidget and fidget until the only way to reach some level of calm is to touch him.

"Right," he said.

I waited seven heartbeats and then I said: "Yeah, your kind isn't so rare. Spoiled brat. When he's a bachelor, life's tough because he has everything he needs except Miss Right, and when he finds a sweetheart with the full package—beauty, brains, sweet temper—she's too much, she's smothering him."

He poured the rest of the glass of water into the harbor. "Guess I wasted my breath, huh?"

"Guess you did."

*at seven a.m.,* as the three of us walked back along the dock in Worcester, the sun shone onto us through wooden slats and Mia pulled off her wig, ran her fingers through her bouncy black hair, and laughed at my expression. She was writing a piece for the *Telegram & Gazette*. She was going to call it "The Secret World of Blondes." I wondered aloud what she'd managed to find out.

"It's going to be the final nail in the coffin for blonde-brunette relations," Arturo predicted. "That or she'll win a Pulitzer."

"Very funny . . ." Mia blew him a kiss. She'd promised to give me a lift, so we climbed into her pink roadster and sped away. The road got brighter the farther east we went, and we passed trucks coming into the city. I think Mia wanted to swap some tales about the experience of being blonde, but I didn't feel like doing any more talking, so I pretended to be asleep. Then I guess I got too committed, because the next thing I knew we were parked outside the boarding house and Mia was tickling me under the nose with a feather.

*back in my room* I used the windowsill as a desk and wrote a brief and painstakingly breezy note to Charlie Vacic from home, just to tell him that I was still looking after his flag, and to give him my address in case he wanted to write to me.

*I'd appreciate it if you kept this address to yourself.*

I read it over through the steam from my coffee cup. Over the years there'd been long moments when Charlie and I had looked at each other without blinking, and I'd wondered what it was that was separating us and whether he or I could make it disappear. For my part I was always a little disturbed by him because I'd never heard him tell a lie. That was horrifying to me, like living in a house with every door and window wide open all day long. When I was in a reasonable mood, I knew Charlie wasn't for me. The note was only a few words long, but it took me the best part of an hour to get it written because I was aware of how closely he would read it.

The other girls were at work, so the bathroom was all mine. I ran a bath and walked back and forth before the mirror as I tugged at buttons, slowly removing my clothing piece by piece. The sight was unfamiliar, and I imagined I was watching a lover undressing just for me. My lover wasn't shy. Her motions were calculated, intent. Naked, I gathered the white mass of my hair up in my hand and turned my face from side to side, trying to see what Charlie, or Arturo, or Mia, or anyone saw. Then I moistened my lips with my tongue and walked toward the mirror, not too fast, giving myself time to change my mind, to stop if it felt too peculiar. But it was just peculiar enough. I kissed the glass with my fists against it, kissed wantonly until I felt an ache in my breasts and a throbbing between my legs. There was a taste of blood where my mouth met my mouth, as if our lips were blades.

# 4

Charlie Vacic's reply to my note contained a lot of guff about his sincere hope that I didn't consider myself under any obligation to him, not even as a pen pal. I happened to know that he'd soon be returning to the city from Albany, so I figured he was sweet on someone else. I considered all the girls we both knew and picked one at random—Jane-Ellen Nugent, she would do—and I wrote to Charlie that I didn't see what was so great about Jane-Ellen Nugent but I wouldn't dream of interfering with his happiness and have a nice life.

He sent a telegram: *Cut it out Boy you know where I stand when it comes to you—C.V.*

I didn't know, and said so by return.

His reply: *Can't believe you're making me say this am willing to fill any role required by you i.e. buddy best buddy laborer unpaid driver unpaid gardener unpaid father of your children coat etc just tell me which and how we'll manage come home will square things with your Pa—Charlie*

Alarmed, I changed my tune. *You really don't know that man at all let's stick to letters from now on you nut—Boy.*

He wrote letters, but I didn't reply. It wasn't a genuine attachment. We didn't even have photographs of each other. Charlie's telegrams were meant for the Grace Kelly look-alike in his mind's eye, and I—I had written a jealous letter directly to his freckles.

He kept up the letters for three months, then wrapped up his one-sided correspondence with a note that was so . . . like him that I had to show it to Mia.

All right, Boy. You win. I won't be bothering you anymore. This fella you've met out there, whoever he is . . . I was going to write that he's lucky, but actually I don't think he is. Because . . . with all due respect . . . I think you've got something that looks an awful lot like an attitude problem, and that's quite aside from the matter of whether or not you left the city with a roll of your Pa's cash like he says you did. Sorry. I had to be honest. Doesn't stop me wishing you were my bad luck, though.

So long,
C

We were having a little picnic at the park, Mia and I, wearing daring hats we'd made out of sheets of newsprint. Mia read the note slowly, placing a finger beneath each word, opening her mouth wide every now and again to indicate that I should place a pitted olive in there. That girl was suspiciously good at being waited on. I'd expected, even wanted, her to laugh at the note, but she didn't. She touched the letter C at the end.

"Huh," she said. "Did you really take the money?"

"It wasn't as much as he makes out. It was practically peanuts." She refused the next olive, so I ate it myself. "Also I'm going to pay it back."

"You're going to Hell, you dirty thief," she said, in a very mild tone of voice. "But this C—he's not like you?"

"No. He's just . . . Charlie."

"Charlie," Mia said, around a strawberry. "Charlie. Char-lie." She pushed her sunshades farther down the bridge of her nose so that I could see her serious eyes. "I think Charlie could really love you," she said.

"Oh, please," I said. "What do you think you know about him?"

"All I know is I'd think twice before counting out someone who could really love me."

"Yeah? Well, maybe you're a sap." I tapped a corner of her hat and it collapsed.

• • •

*i got work* as a telephone operator—they said they'd train me up because I had the right voice and manner for it. I counted myself lucky apart from the fact that I kept seeing Arturo Whitman on the way to work. He went running every morning, and I walked to the telephone exchange to save bus fare. Our routes coincided for about half a mile, along a road that swirled around one of the hills like a helter-skelter. That road was called Ivorydown, and I was always glad when I reached the turn onto Willoughby Street. Not just because of having to observe Arturo running up ahead or approaching from behind (there's something about being chased by a big strong man with yellowish eyes that makes you feel like an antelope in a bad situation), but because I've never liked roads that take you down from steep heights too quickly. Ivorydown was like that, the tyrannical kind of road that makes you take quick little step after quick little step until you're all the way at the bottom. Cars and buses flowed down the hill with ease, and the people in them watched you placidly through the windows. The road was lined with saplings, but they weren't there to help, they just stood there making pretty frames for the landscape with their branches. Arturo slowed down to speak to me.

"Hey," he said, as if he'd completely forgotten that we despised each other. "So when's our next double date?"

He may have been told that a rakish grin works wonders. If so, he'd been getting bad advice.

I became extremely conscious of the sound of my heels tapping on the concrete. I wanted to stop walking, but the road was forcing us both down it as fast as it could, and he was already a few strides ahead, looking back at me. And so, hurrying after him with only a bunch of saplings, a couple of cars, and a truck to see us, I told him I never wanted to see his stupid face again.

He said: "Oh," and continued his run. After that he'd pass me on the road without seeming to see me. And I went merrily on to the telephone exchange. I don't even know what happened to that particular job. I can't remember if I really tried at it. All those voices buzzing up and down wires, all those switches and dials, a single shift was like a long day out in dry rain. Of all the things that got to me, I never expected it to be that operator job. I couldn't work out why, either. It was just people saying hello to each other.

Then there was the usherette job—that one lasted three weeks and a day.

When the ax came, it was because I watched the movies too much. I'd already been given three warnings, two of them in writing. Then, half an hour after I'd received the third warning, the manager himself caught me sitting down and watching a movie like a regular audience member. To be honest I wasn't even really watching the movie. It was one of those ones they call screw-ball comedies, where people mislead and ill-treat each other in the most shocking and baffling ways possible, then forgive and forget about it because they happen to like the look of each other. Only they call it falling in love. Those movies are the equivalent of supernatural thrillers for me—if I watched them too closely, I'd shriek uncontrollably. So mainly I was just sitting.

The manager stood over me and asked me to explain myself. It wasn't that I didn't want to speak; it just seemed smarter not to. All of a sudden it felt as if I had far too many teeth, more teeth than it was decent to show.

"In that case I'm afraid we've come to the end of the road, Miss Novak," the manager said.

I was a little sad on my last day.

I wasn't going to miss being an usherette—the uniform itched, and identifying couples who were sitting too close together and assaulting them with a blast of light lost its charm surprisingly quickly. But I'd miss the cool, fresh, all-day darkness of the screening theaters, and the way light played across the screen with a staggering indifference. The men and women up there would speak, and laugh, and sing, and cry, walk away, stand still, and as long as the reel ran, all this would go on whether the audience was there or not, whether they watched or not.

I left the cinema with a tailor who took me to

dinner, then stopped me in the midst of some bushes in the park and pushed his tongue into my mouth. The weak wriggling made me so extravagantly sad that I gagged. He looked stricken, and I was sorry. I took an "Are you frigid?" quiz in a magazine once and got the highest score. *You are: Winter in Siberia. Few survive you, and those who do are . . . changed!* I mentioned this to my date, just to let him know he was dealing with a frigid woman. It wasn't what he wanted to hear; he left me at the front door of the boarding house and walked around the corner at a pretty fast pace. I'll bet he started running as soon as he was sure he was out of sight.

The following day Mia came over to the boarding house to celebrate the six-month anniversary of my escape from the rat catcher. Following an ancient Cabrini recipe, she filled a stew pot with cold champagne, stuffed in as many handfuls of chopped fruit as it would hold, and served it up. We clinked bowls at the dining room table, which was otherwise empty because it was eleven in the morning, and Mia said: "This, my friend, is champagne soup. Make a wish."

And I did.

It was standard-issue stuff. I wanted a family. But it was just as Arturo said—I didn't know how to start anything from scratch, and I didn't want to know. Getting pushed around as a kid had made me realistic about my capabilities. I know some people learn how to take more knocks and keep going. Not me. I'm the other kind. That's what stopped me from telling Charlie Vacic I'd marry him. See, I'm looking for a role with lines I can say convincingly, something practical. And I know Charlie, or at least I know that he's some kind of idealist. Charlie's woman probably wouldn't be able to complain that he didn't love her enough. She'd be getting his all. Not worship or anything weird, just a certain way he looks at her, something in his voice when he speaks to her, he'd let her know that he's ready to be asked anything, ready to ask anything. No games, no rules, no about-turns, no limits, by my side when rainstorms sound like serenades, by my side for flat hours of word tennis, each of us guarded, exchanging little comments that are so wretchedly banal that all we want to do is turn away from each other and throw up every single one of our internal organs. It'd be a love like the Siege Perilous. Nice work if you have the constitution for it, but otherwise the harshest of all tests, eliminating everyone who attempts it until the purest of heart happens along. And okay, it's just about conceivable that you could have a heart that pure and never suspect it until the crucial moment. Maybe I'd give it a shot if the conditions were the same as in the story: You sit in the chair and you die faster than your feet can touch the floor, and that's how you find out you're not the one. But in real life the finding out can really drag on, can't it? Mrs. Boy Vacic was a nightmare of mine. She hit her forties hard and fell to pieces. She had a gushing, anxious laugh that took a while to trickle to a stop (*krrr krrr*) and made her children ask her if she was okay. She babied herself, rewarding her own good deeds with candy and spoonfuls of grape jelly. That woman—the me that had married Charlie—had tried and failed to find a gap in all of this that was so ordinary, to take some instrument to the gap and shape it, widen it until it got big enough to slip through. She'd wanted to make a beautiful thing, like the Flax Hill natives did. But not a lantern or a bookcase, a life. Not to have what it takes, and to be surrounded by witnesses too. The man you tried with. The children. A boy version of you, or a girl version of him, or both, looking at you with clear, pitiless eyes. These are thoughts that come to you while you spend however long you spend holding icepacks to your eye, or tilting your head back against the wall to try to do something about the way your nose is bleeding, letting your mind work on the question: What reasons might somebody have for leaving her kid in the care of a man like Frank Novak? *Don't ever try to find her. Don't even try to find out if she's alive.* This way my mother's alive, she's dead, she's whatever she deserves to be on that particular day.

I was new to champagne, but as soon as I tasted

it, spark after golden spark, I thought, well, there's magic in this water, no wonder Mia said to wish on it.

"So when are you due to blow the secret world of blondes wide open? I keep walking into stores and waiting for some official-looking person to take me aside and inform me I'm not welcome in their establishment. It hasn't happened yet, but I can't go on like this."

Mia refilled our bowls. "You can't go on like this? I can't go on like this. This piece has me petrified. It's my first big piece after a year and a half on the 'cat stuck up a tree' beat. My dad's giving this journalism thing another three months to take off before he sends me to Chicago to run another one of his damn hotels. I keep telling him and telling him that I need more time, that it's not so easy for women in this field, but he just says: 'Don't give me that! You're a Cabrini! And this is 1953! Stop making excuses!' And I say to him, 'Yeah, it's 1953 and down South there's still a nice little system going, it's called segregation.' And *he* says, 'How about just showing a little gratitude that you're not colored?' "

"*One* of his hotels?" I said. "How many does he own?"

She shook her head. "Excuse me, but that's not the point. The point is I've been assigned a piece of froth—oh, look, it's a catty article about blondes written by a brunette—and I want to use it to pull the rug out from under their feet. But the more I write up my notes, the more it all just looks like a pack of playing cards."

"Well—show me what you've got."

She pulled a couple of typed pages out of her pocket. They had been folded into quarters. I opened them out and read.

You want the scoop, and I'm going to give it to you. But let's make a deal first. How often have you read an article all the way through to the end and said to yourself: "I don't know where this chump gets the nerve to show up for work in the morning!" I'll tell you how I get the nerve, and if you don't buy it, you don't have to read another word of it.

Here goes: I'm a brunette from a long line of brunettes. We've never really had anything to worry about. After all, gentlemen marry us. But something happened to me when I was ten years old. My hands began to draw distinctions between the sacred and the profane. I watched them and made notes. My left hand was part of me, it belonged to me, and it only consented to touch things I considered beautiful. If Peter Pan had visited me, I'd have given him a thimble with my left hand. I wrote letters to my best friend with my left hand. When I was reading a book and found that a line or paragraph moved me in some way, I'd touch the words with my left hand.

My right hand was an object, it belonged to the world, and I used it to manipulate other objects. Putting my clothes on, pulling my socks up, holding on to the standing pole in the bus, and so on.

I looked up from the page and said: "Mia, this is wacky."

"Oh, absolutely. But that's what happened." She had a little pot of nail varnish out on the tabletop and was painting the fingernails of her right hand blue. "I support you if you want to quit already."

"No, I'm in—I'm in."

It was around that time that my parents got divorced. My clothes and books and posters were divided up. Some were put into a room in my dad's new apartment and the rest stayed at home (which suddenly became new too, without him). My dad said: "Don't cry. Aw, what are you crying for? What's happening right now isn't a bad thing. It isn't good, either—it's normal. Okay?"

My mom said: "Yeah, listen to your dad."

That summer we had a heat wave that killed a lot of people. "More than a thousand?" I asked my dad. He said yeah. "More than TWO thousand?" He said yeah. I was chicken, so I stopped there. That summer Jesse Owens was in all the papers with that gold medal he won representing our country in the Olympics. That was the year the Abraham Lincoln Brigade volunteered to do the right thing by Spain and help fight Franco. And all the while there was the theater of my hands. It was theater, in that it was the performance of something that was true, and as such, I believed in it with all my heart but was also able to come to the end of it at a moment's notice. The whole thing was set up as a transaction: My hands were giving me a show. There was my left hand, dangling limp for most of the day—my parents took turns asking if it hurt—and there was my right hand, weary from gripping and pushing and pulling and lifting for two. When I asked my hands to end the show, they wanted payment. My right hand made me promise to "see far" and my left hand made me promise to "remember what is said."

I gave them my word. And I've kept it, partly from a fear of a repeated mutiny.

Add a third action: "Write it all down," and it seems to me you've got yourself a journalist of some kind.

All right, if you're still with me, thanks for staying. I write these words with a fifteen-dollar wig on my head. Wheatsheaf blond, that's what it said on the tag. So this is a bulletin direct from the secret world. The first thing you learn is whom to beware of. They're exactly the same people you had to beware of as a non-blonde. The kind who think they know what you are and don't mind telling you all about it.

I turned the page over, but there wasn't any more. Mia blew on her nails. "I guess I could start a hotel newspaper."

"No, you're going to do this. Got a pen?"

She handed me her fountain pen. "Finish that coat of polish," I told her. She still had three fingernails to go, but instead of doing as she was told, she read over my shoulder as I wrote.

Here's a story for you—the kind you find in an old library book with cobwebs between the pages. You know that book; you forget the title after you've returned it and over the years you try to look it up a few times, but you never find it again.

Once there was a pretty powerful magician. He spoke to the things around him, and as long as the thing he addressed had life in it, it obeyed him. "Barren tree, bear fruit," he'd say. And no matter what had happened to the tree, no matter how ravaged its roots, the tree flourished. "Horse, grow wings," he'd say, and the horse bowed its head as strong, finely plumed wings swept over its back. But that wasn't how the magician made his living. Mostly he improved women's looks for a fee. Women came to him themselves, or were brought to him by their ambitious mothers or diffident fathers. He'd look into a woman's eyes and say: "You are a beauty," and she heard the words and believed them so deeply that her features fell into either lush, soft harmony, or heartbreakingly strict symmetry—whichever suited her better. He'd say it to her only once, and it lasted the rest of her lifetime, so his fees were high. But the magician could also undo natural beauty, for a greater fee than the one he charged for beautifying. He sort of hoped the high fee would discourage people, but it didn't. It was well-known that if your wife or daughter was unruly or otherwise deserving of punishment you could bring

71

her to this magician, who would tell her, "Scarecrow, scarecrow . . ." He said it in such a way that the woman who heard him believed him, and the words did their work. It was a shame, and he didn't like to do it, but business is business.

Mia snapped her fingers. "I remember how this one goes!"

"Great." I was only too happy to push the paper over to her. I've always had a hard time figuring out what the moral of a story is supposed to be, and she was bound to know: She'd been to college.

Mia wrote.

One day a farmer came to the magician. "I've hesitated over this decision for many days, because my wife is very beautiful," the farmer said. "Possibly the most beautiful woman in all the world. Still, I think you'd better make her ugly all the same. She frightens me; she frightens everyone who goes near her."

"Frightens you?" the magician asked. "Frightens you how? And where is she?"

"She's back at the farm." The farmer shuffled his feet apologetically. "I tried to bring her with me, but she wouldn't come."

"Wouldn't come?" The farmer was big and tall, at least twice the size of the magician. He must not have tried very hard to persuade his wife to travel with him.

"Somehow I couldn't lay a hand on her," the farmer said, unable to hide his anguish. "I moved to seize her arm, and found I'd seized my own arm. I snatched at her hair and ended up pulling my ear. And if you want to know how I got this black eye . . ."

The magician was interested. He'd met several stunning witches, but none of them had married farmers, and none of them practiced this particular kind of passive resistance. He agreed to accompany the farmer home.

Mia dropped the pen and nodded at me to continue. "You do remember how it goes, right? I mean . . . we're not just . . . ?"

"Sure," I said. "I mean—no. Sure I remember."

I made my handwriting much smaller than usual, in case I was wrong.

The magician found the farmer's wife kneeling, planting cassava, setting the cuttings up inside little hills of soil. There's no use trying to describe her in detail; all that can really be said is that she had the kind of beauty that people write songs about and occasionally commit suicide over. The type who seems a very long way away even when she's right there in your arms. She wiped her hands on her apron, looked up at him, and said: "Hello."

As a test, he said to her: "Come, woman, be more beautiful." (Her husband groaned at that.) But nothing happened. The farmer's wife went on planting. The magician felt uneasy—was it really impossible for her beauty to be any greater? Could she really be first among women, hidden away here on this farm?— and so he told her, "Scarecrow, scarecrow," in the strongest tones possible. The woman didn't raise her eyes from the ground. Her hands continued to plant cassava, and she remained exactly the same. "Don't disturb my life, magician," she said. "Just leave me be."

The magician took her chin in his hand and turned her face up to his, though her gaze and the feel of her skin made his flesh crawl. "Scarecrow, scarecrow," the magician said again. The field itself heard him this time, and three scarecrows appeared at the perimeter. But the farmer's wife didn't change. She said: "All I've ever wanted is to make things grow, and to feed people. I've been doing that for some years now, and I've been happy. I don't want anything more or less than what I already have. I beg you: Don't disturb my life."

"But your husband is frightened of you," the magician told her.

"I've given him no cause to be," she replied.

"And yet he can hardly bear to look at you . . ."

"It isn't necessary for him to look at me."

Mia read that part over three times, and for a moment I thought I was busted. But she continued writing in silence, cupping her hand over the page as though she were the imposter and not me.

"Grow wings," he told her. "Bear fruit." She did neither. He pursued her for miles of farmland, got in the way of all her daily tasks, issued command after command, whatever came into his head. "Become a walking stick!" She didn't. His voice grew hoarse. At last he admitted that she was a formidable witch, and that he was willing to learn whatever she could teach him.

"It isn't magic," she said. "It's just that

I'm well dressed. You men who try to tell me I'm a scarecrow or try to grab my arm but can't manage it, don't you understand that you're not really addressing me? It's more as if you're talking to a coat I'm wearing."

She was sat on a low chair, shelling beans, and he sat down at her feet and began to help her. "I don't see what you mean," he said. "Teach me. Show me."

"What can I teach you?" she said. She closed her eyes and opened her mouth wide. She stayed like that for one minute, two minutes. He thought she was sleeping and forced himself to place a hand on her shoulder. A snake's head glided out from between her lips, bright as new chainmail; he saw that its golden coils wound down her throat.

"You're wrapped around her heart," the magician said.

"I am the heart," the snake replied.

He left the farm without looking back. There are few things in life more unpleasant than the laughter of a snake.

"Maybe that isn't the version you read," Mia said, watching me. She bit the end of the pen a few times. "I think I read it in Italian, so . . ."

"No, this is pretty much the version I read," I

said, because it felt too damn late to back down. I imagine that from time to time some similar situation has led governments to declare war.

I had to be up early for a trial shift at a bookstore, so I sent Mia home right after dinner.

"Hey," she said, on her way out of the door. "Maybe this bookstore job is the one."

I said: "Maybe!" But I thought: *Probably not.*

The best line of work for me would be roadside sprite. I'd live quietly by a dust-covered track that people never came across unless they took a wrong turn, and I'd offer the baffled travelers lemonade and sandwiches, maybe even fix their engines if they asked nicely (I'd have used my solitude to read extensively on matters of car maintenance). Then the travelers would go on their way, relaxed and refreshed, and they'd forget they'd ever met me. That's the ideal meeting . . . once upon a time, only once, unexpectedly, then never again.

# 5

*t*he next morning Ted took Webster on a trip to Wachusett Mountain. He said it was "just because," but we decided between us that he was either going to propose or he was going to call the whole thing off. I hoped he would propose. She'd been so sad that he hadn't proposed on Valentine's

Day. She'd asked me if I thought some women just weren't meant to be married. I said: "Yes. But not you." I meant it too.

She swung between hope and despair. She rehashed old conversations with Ted until I told her she had to stop it before she made herself ill or something. She was hopeful because she'd caught Arturo Whitman looking thoughtfully at her fingers, sizing them up, as it were. She despaired because long ago Ted had told her he didn't believe in marriage. She'd asked him how he could say that when there were so many real, live married people walking around, and he'd called her a wise guy. I told her she was born wife material whether Ted Murray realized it or not. She smiled at that. "And what about you?" she asked.

"Oh, I'm nothing but a pack of cards." I echoed Mia to protect myself. Not that it was necessary. Webster asked questions only out of politeness. Pursuing answers wasn't her style.

She knocked on my door just before Ted picked her up. It was six in the morning.

"Just wanted to say good-bye," she said, sitting on my feet. (When had we become friends?) "This could be the last time I speak to you as an unengaged woman."

I muttered, "Try not to break your neck on the slopes, Webster. I've gotten used to you," and I waved good-bye from my bedroom window as

Ted drove away with all their ski apparatus clattering away on top of his car. I even crossed my fingers for her.

*a couple of* hours later I emptied my purse out onto the windowsill and counted up my coins. I had bus fare, but only one way if I also wanted to eat lunch. I figured I'd take the bus back and began walking along Ivorydown, taking the route I'd so gladly abandoned a few weeks before when I'd changed jobs. It was a windy morning, and the wind pushed me, and the road dragged me, and the tree branches flew forward and peeled back and broke away, and their scrawny trunks hugged each other. I glimpsed—or more became aware of—someone walking on the other side of the saplings. She wasn't there at the beginning of the walk; I don't know when she caught up with me. This person was my height, her stride more or less the length of mine, smooth locks of her hair (blond) and flashes of her coat (navy blue) showing through the leaves. I was wearing a navy blue coat too. She had her hands in her pockets and I didn't want to speak to her, I'm not sure why, maybe because she was walking so close to me but didn't seem to notice that I was there. Or if she did, she didn't find it odd that we stayed neck and neck all the way down the hill. I tried to get a little ahead of her so that I could look back through the branches and see her face, but she chose the exact same moment to speed up and I began to feel as if we were running from somebody. Then she spoke. She said: "Hello? Hello? Is that you?"

My lungs kicked my ribcage, just once. I've never heard my own voice recorded, but at that moment I was sure it'd sound like that. It was me, but me played back out of some kind of machine, that was the only way I could understand what I was hearing.

"Hello? Hello? Is that you?"

We stopped walking. "I'm here, I'm here."

Shards of her face emerged through brown bark and greenish shadows. Her left eye was aligned with mine; we raised our left hands at the same time, and hers was bloody. She said: "I don't know what to do."

"Show your other hand," I said. She didn't move. "Show me!" She wouldn't until I raised my right hand too. There was a lot of blood. Dark, dark, red. She had done something, or something had been done to her. "I don't know what to do," she said, and took a step back, silently asking me to go to her there on the other side of the hill, but it wasn't clear what she was or what she'd done and I said, "I'm sorry, I'm sorry," and I walked faster than I had before, but with a weak feeling in my knees that almost threw me into the road with the motorcars and buses. A man with a ragged beard honked his horn and yelled that I ought to be ashamed of myself, drunk at eight in the morning. He couldn't see the other woman; she was well hidden from him. "Come here, come here and I'll tell you everything," she laughed, right beside me, not at all out of breath. I wasn't as scared as I could have been—the main thing was to get away from her—but my thoughts ran with me.

*What could you be, what could you be*

*Some future vision, will I go home this week, next week, the week after, strike suddenly, get the rat catcher back at last*

*What have you done Boy*

*Am I going to do the same, do I deserve her, whatever she is, did I call her to me somehow*

*Please go, go away*

The view through the saplings was so calm— miles and miles of crushed green-velvet valley behind her, and a line of telegraph poles marching out as far as the eye could see. And the wires ran between the poles, three lines, direct, direct. I became painfully conscious of my heels tapping the sidewalk a moment before I noticed she'd disappeared, a deafening solo drum roll, and at the bottom of that hilly road I placed both hands on the top of my head, to check, in all seriousness, if my head was still there. Then I buried my face in a handkerchief because my nose was running. I had that feeling that comes after days of fever— the beginning of recovery, the memory of how things worked before the cold flame ate away at you. The solution seemed simple to me. *Forget this road. Don't come here again. I never did like it.*

"You okay?" Arturo asked. He was sprawled out on a bench a few steps away, huffing from his run. I wondered what he'd seen, but not enough to ask him. I said I was fine and sat down next to him. He had a knife, a napkin, and a pear, and he was dropping peel for the birds, whose reaction seemed to be that he could keep it.

"Well, White Rabbit," he said. "Where do you lead me?"

"Who are you calling a white rabbit?"

"You can take offense or you can take it as a reference to your hair."

"I'll reference *your* hair," I said. Then I got mad at myself. I mean, I was two seconds away from fainting and "I'll reference *your* hair" was the best I could come up with. Meaningless. If you're about to fall to the ground like a frail creature in need of smelling salts, you owe it to yourself to at least say something fantastically vicious before-hand. But all I did was make him laugh. I pinched my temples, seeing the blood on her hands again. "Look—I'm going to have to ask you for a bite of that pear. I'm . . . dizzy. Think I'd better eat something."

"You didn't eat yet?"

I didn't have the money for breakfast, but I'd

rather have died than admit it. I said I was slimming. "Hmm . . . let's see . . ." He cut a slice of pear, the longest, thinnest shaving, near transparency, and he fed it to me bit by sweet, grainy bit, his thumb brushing tiny, wary circles across my cheek. I cut the next piece for him, and I held the knife until he'd eaten all the fruit off the tip of the blade. He licked the juice away afterward, and I kissed his mouth because of the way he drank down that one drop.

*i was an hour late* to the bookstore, and as soon as I stepped inside, Mrs. Fletcher jumped up from her seat behind the till with her hair all standing on end and yelled at me to get out. I didn't waste any time arguing and was halfway down the street when she bawled after me: "Just where do you think you're going?"

She prowled around the shop floor, slapping price stickers onto books, and I trailed her, removing duplicate stickers. Her prices looked very high to me and I didn't see how she made any money, but I quickly learned that there was no real point to her pricing her books—she preferred to haggle. Popular paperbacks and required reading for college classes were sold out front, but her main business was in the back room, where she dealt in antique books and first editions. She sent out catalogues and people drove cross-country to take a closer look, and even then she wouldn't let customers go home with the goods they'd paid for until they demonstrated an ability to open a book in the correct and proper way.

Three colored teenagers, two girls and a boy, came in just after lunch and stayed for hours, just sitting by the bookshelves, reading. After they spent four hours without a purchase, I was ready to kick them out and went to ask Mrs. Fletcher's advice, but she said: "Don't you bother those kids."

She didn't seem to care that they weren't buying anything, so I said: "They ought to be in school."

"That's your opinion," she said. "That's what you think."

"Don't blame me when it turns out some of your stock has been stolen."

She stared at me as if I had three heads and she was curious about which one was boss. "Just don't let the youngest eat apples around my books, that's all."

"How am I supposed to tell which one's the youngest?"

"Don't annoy me, Boy."

I thought she was terrific, and hoped she liked me, but she was clearly very precise in the allocation of her affections, so she probably didn't. At six-thirty, an hour after the store was supposed to close and only half an hour after the kids had put their books back on the shelves and sauntered out, I heard her hooting with laughter and put my head around the door of the back room, thinking I'd better take advantage of her good mood and ask if she wanted me to come back the next day. She was leafing through the obituaries section of the newspaper and wouldn't let me in on the joke, but said: "See you tomorrow."

I took a magazine quiz on the bus home, but I knew the result before I added the figures up. I wasn't in love with Arturo, and I wasn't going to be. You don't need a quiz to tell you these things; they don't escape your notice. The flag stuffed into the back of my wardrobe was there because someone had once draped it around my shoulders in such a way that the touch of his fingers made me feel like a million bucks. That's not how it was with Arturo. He held me so tightly that numbness stretched all the way down my arms and only let go a few minutes after he did. It wasn't as nice a feeling as the flag around my shoulders. But I felt more certain of it because it lasted longer.

# 6

People—well, Mia and Webster—told me I should make Arturo take me out more. Webster gave me lectures. "You don't seem to understand how quickly a man will stop treating you right if you let him. So when he gives you half-assed invitations like 'Hey, why not drop by for potluck tonight?' you can't stand for that, Boy."

(*Tra la la, I can and will.* She didn't know about his grilled cheese sandwiches. I'd asked him what made them taste so good and he'd closed my hand up into a fist, wrapped his own hand around the fist, and told me: "This much butter." Webster's lecture persisted, but my attention wouldn't stick. She had a lot of powder on, which made me think of geishas. She was probably right, though; she was wise in the ways of getting what you want; she was walking on air and sporting an engagement ring with a rock so notable that I and the other boarding house girls took to including it in our conversations, addressing it as "Gibraltar," demanding that it take sides.)

I made excuses. I was tired of my date dress. In fact I felt a little violent toward it. I'd open my bedroom closet and the red silk would shrink and shudder among the clothes hangers, as if it knew that I was on the brink of tossing it onto a trash heap. There was no need to go public with Arturo. I was happy to go to the Salome Club with Mia and a couple of her family friends, different ones each time. Her half brother came along one night too—her father's son, a gangly fellow with a passing resemblance to Frank Sinatra. His name was Rocco, and he knew how to lean in and light a girl's cigarette with a look and a smile that had me stubbing my cigarette out whenever his attention was elsewhere, just so he'd light up another one for me. It could have been the way he guarded the flame with his palm, the unexpected care with which he carried it up toward your lips; who knows what makes a man's gesture attractive?

If you're not afraid of a real night out, hit the town with guys who just got out of jail. They're the ones who can't be kept off the dance floor— they'll dance till they drop, and even when they're stretched out flat on the floor, they'll still shake their ankles. Sometimes our companions didn't speak much English and communicated with me through smiles and mimed gestures. It was nice. Their questions were some of the simplest there are. *Will you have another drink? Care to dance?* Simple to give clear answers to—*sì, sì.* I sat out the meaningful slow dances and sipped my sarsaparilla with closed eyes, trying to squeeze every drop of meaning out of the love songs. According to Kitty Kallen, little things mean a lot.

Mia's "Secret World of Blondes" had been the subject of enough letters to the editor for the paper to let her go ahead with a new piece. Her plan was to attend catechism classes with three girls and be an eyewitness to the preparations that led all the way up to each girl's Mexican, Italian, or Irish Holy Communion. By the time she'd attended one class with each girl, she already had a title: "Lucrezia Borgia Never Died."

So Mia was all right and I was to be one of Webster's bridesmaids. I'd become respectable overnight, was greeted on the street with cheery variants of "What's new?" instead of blank glances. Flax Hill had begun to see the point of me. Aside from bridesmaid duties, I was holding down a job at a bookstore notorious for having an owner who'd as soon fire her assistants as look at them. And I apparently had something to do with the renewed spring in Arturo Whitman's step, as well as his tone-deaf whistling of show tunes.

*I hear singing and there's no one there . . .*

All it would take was a single comparison to Julia Whitman and I'd be right back to square one. I didn't add up to much when placed beside old J. W. I couldn't think of many members of the non-movie-star population who did. I looked at photos of Julia, and listened to her voice on the vinyl recordings she'd made for her daughter. In a way they were practice for her. She was an opera singer; great onstage, but she'd signed a contract and was due to start work on her classical record once she'd recovered from having Snow. But in these recordings she didn't sound operatic—she was a mother singing her daughter lullabies; her appeal was for love, not for admiration.

She'd left notebooks filled with handwritten recipes for the wartime cook: four different kinds of butterless-eggless-milkless cake, tens of tips for stretching meat and sugar rations as far as they would go. She'd also left a list of all the names she'd considered giving to Snow. There were hundreds of them. She had wanted her daughter very much; anyone could see that. The multitude of names didn't seem like indecision—Julia Whitman was trying to summon up a troop of fairy godmothers. Somewhere in among the names of all those mermaids, warriors, saints, goddesses, queens, scientists, and poets I could see a woman trying to cover all the bases, searching for things her daughter would need in order to make friends with life. Conscience, resolve, loyalty, the kind of far sight that Mia wanted, the fearlessness to cross strange borders, whatever it was that gave Alice the guts to stick up for herself when Tweedledum and Tweedledee informed her she wasn't real. I sat with those names for hours while vaguely worrisome sheets of smoke poured out from under the door of Arturo's workroom. I've always wanted to know whether Boy is the name my mother wanted for me, and if so, what kind of person the name was supposed to help me grow up into.

Julia and I wouldn't have been friends. She looked like a bashful Rapunzel, dark hair pinned up high, doe eyes always downturned or gazing off to the side in every single photograph. I don't trust anyone who poses like that any farther than I can throw them. I think I know the drill: Mrs. Whitman only let down her hair when Mr. Whitman had been a good boy. He probably even thought their getting married was all his idea. These were things I couldn't really say to anyone. I'd have been able to say them only from a disinterested position. But I was grateful too, grateful to Julia in yet another way I couldn't tell anyone about. She'd left me her husband, who didn't expect much from me. He'd had his great love. And now he was willing, determined even, to be amused, to belly laugh at the slightest provocation, to appreciate heart-shaped pieces of toast as tokens of my affection. On our first night together I kept thinking, *Do I, do I, do I, do I . . .* then *Do I what?* Something to do with wanting, or daring. We sat facing each other, cross-legged on his bed, and the lamp light laid a strip of gold along his bare shoulders. I leaned forward so that there were mere inches between our faces and he could smell me. I smelt of soap and musk. I'd made sure of that. Not too animal, not too pure. The idea was that his reaction would show me what to do next.

He didn't move. He didn't even blink. We were both naked, and his arm was spread loosely across the bedspread; I'd moved so that his right hand was just behind me, less than an inch away. And he was aroused, he was visibly aroused. All he had to do to bring our bodies together was raise his hand to the small of my back. Instead of doing that he gave me this reserved but friendly smile. A smile from an official portrait—a politician's. *Vote for me.*

It felt like time to put my clothes on again, then add an extra layer of clothes on top of those clothes, for additional modesty. I used to make fun of women who ask men the question "What are you thinking?" but that night I got dangerously close to becoming one of them.

I asked: "Should I . . . leave?"

"Do you want to leave?"

"No," I said. "But . . ."

"Stay," he said, in a comfortable tone of voice, as if this was just the kind of conversation he preferred. (Later I asked him about this and he said: "I had a feeling it was your first time and I was trying not to rush you. I thought I was doing so well.")

I switched off the lamp and returned to the bed to find him stretched out on his back, breathing easily. I curled up beside him, found his ear, and whispered: "Tell me what you want me to do."

"Boy . . ." He stroked my cheek with the back of his hand.

I described the options to him one by one. I devised a minimum of twenty, each new configuration of body parts arriving in my mind with some kind of diabolical inspiration before I'd even fully dealt with the previous image. I used language that would have made Webster fall down in a faint. I promised him that he could have me in any way that he wanted, then I went on before he could choose. He nuzzled my collarbone a couple of times, and laughed at some of my more outlandish descriptions; because we were so close together and couldn't see each other clearly, it began to feel as if we were school friends plotting some ridiculous prank. He was a good listener. But I can't remember now exactly when he stopped listening and I stopped talking, at what point our breathing changed, fingernails dug into skin, and he covered my mouth with his so that I cried out into him. The whole thing kind of astounded me. I'd expected to have to explain to him about my being Winter in Siberia, but in the end I got to keep that to myself.

So there was the man (I began to think of him as mine when I told him about the rat catcher and he half seriously offered to drive down to New York, kneecap him, and bring me back a slice of pie from my favorite diner). And there was the home, with its long, low-ceilinged rooms. The floorboards were so snugly fitted that walking across them was like gliding across a bank of honey. There were no clocks, no real sense of time passing. It was the kind of house you went to in order to get well. Some nights I'd walk back to the boarding house from Arturo's house and see the stars through the tree branches, nestled in between the leaves as if they'd grown there. It wasn't just the man and the house, there was more. "I don't mean much to you, do I?" Arturo teased. "I'm just . . . you know, Snow's dad."

What was it about Snow? Some days she was just another little girl who considered the presence of green vegetables and the absence of a Fluffernutter sandwich on her dinner plate such a great tragedy that she'd cry until her face was swollen. She wasn't yet seven, but seemed a few years younger. Partly because she hadn't yet learned to smile even when she didn't feel like it, and partly because she was inattentive in the way that kids are when they're still learning to speak—always looking above or behind you while you're talking to them, their heads wobbling with concentration, as if they're receiving secret information that's much more important than anything you have to say. Her eyes were the shade of hazel that doesn't seem able to decide whether it's brown or green.

If Snow was ever worried, if any anxieties ever disturbed her for longer than a day, she rarely showed it. She was poised and sympathetic, like a girl who'd just come from the future but didn't want to brag about it. She'd pat your arm, and say, "Everything is okay. Everything is normal," and you took her word for it. Sometimes I think it was a trick of hers, deciding aloud what was going on so that everyone who loved her fell over themselves to make it so. Sometimes I think we needed her to be like that and she obliged. It's sad if that's true—I'm thinking of the time she crawled down the staircase on her hands and knees to announce that there was a troll in her room. Arturo asked her where exactly the troll was. Under her bed, in the closet? She said: "It is in all the room. Come see."

I would have gone with her, but Arturo got mad at her for not saying please, of all things, and refused to indulge her. *That's enough, Snow. Back to bed with you.* I added: "That silly old troll will be gone by the time you get back into bed. You'll see."

She said okay, and went back upstairs slowly, shivering. In the morning I asked her if the troll had disappeared like I'd promised. I asked real quietly, so Arturo didn't hear. She used a few spoonfuls of applesauce to draw a smiley face on her plate, and when she'd finished, she said: "Mmm hmmm, no more troll." She was lying, though; I could tell. As far as she was concerned, the troll hadn't gone anywhere, and would remain just as long as it pleased. All she could do was try to sleep in spite of it. I hate the thought of her trying, trying. Not just with her troll, but with me too, right from the beginning.

*there's something ominous* about being handed an ivory-colored card with scalloped edges that basically says *Hello, I'm your boyfriend's mother and I've heard such a lot about you and do please come to tea at half past five tomorrow.* I was in a terrible state about it, sweaty as anything. The general advice is always be yourself, be yourself, which only makes sense if you haven't got an attitude problem.

Olivia lived two doors down from Arturo, in a bigger house than his, a house full of playthings for her granddaughter. Skipping ropes, tin soldiers, all colors of crayons, and toy cars strewn everywhere. I wondered how many falls Olivia Whitman had had and was going to have just for the sake of keeping a little girl amused. Two other women joined us for tea, and I really felt that wasn't fair, especially since the other women turned out to be Arturo's younger sister and Julia's mother. Olivia really had summoned the committee. I wished I wasn't wearing violet eye shadow, which was funny, because just half an hour before I'd thought of the eye shadow as armor that I couldn't have stepped out of the boarding house without. It might have been the darkness of the room—they sat with the curtains drawn, and the only real light seemed to come from the silverware—but it was difficult telling the difference between the three women. Olivia and Agnes had a good excuse for sharing their style and mannerisms, in that they were both in their mid-sixties. Vivian was twenty-three. Twenty-three and wearing a twinset, with her hair in fussy curls. But she had Arturo's narrow amber eyes. She began by listing everybody she knew in New York and asking me if I'd ever met them. Her perfectly straight face threw me off at first. But by the time she'd got to the seventeenth name or so—"Fernanda Crackenbone. You've honestly never run into Fernanda? But she's awfully sociable. The most sociable girl I know. Goes every place there is to go"—I realized she was kidding around, and also that Olivia and Agnes had been holding their laughter in so that I wouldn't think they were laughing at me, which accounted for their strangely cramped expressions. When I said, with as much dignity as I could muster, that I didn't believe there was any such person as Fernanda Crackenbone, Olivia threw up her hands, let herself have a good roar at last, then said: "I'm only glad you don't think this girl of mine has a screw loose."

"I do have a screw loose, you know," Vivian said. "It's just that Mama doesn't want anybody to think so. More tea?"

I slipped up twice—once when Olivia talked about Vivian's progress at law school and what a wonderful singer Julia had been, a classical contralto, no less. Then she asked me what I wanted to do with my life. I said: "Oh, I like it at the bookstore," and Vivian and Olivia gave each other the briefest but most chilling glance, then changed the subject. Oddly enough, that was when Agnes, Julia's mother, smiled at me. Her smile was encouraging, though she shook her head a little bit, as if she thought I needed coaching. The second slipup was when Olivia announced that she wanted Arturo to return to academic life. "I didn't raise my son to be a jeweler," she said. "My husband didn't work all the way up from bank clerk to branch manager for that." When I forgot myself so far as to try to argue with her, she said "outrageous" and rattled the sugar tongs in a manner that was positively alarming.

Agnes took my mostly incoherent argument and rephrased it for me: "Livia, dear. Boy has got a point. Arturo is just as smart as he ever was—he's just making smart jewelry now. He's bringing ancient Egypt and Byzantium alive again in ways people can touch and wear. He always got so sore when people fell asleep during his history lectures, didn't he?"

I kept looking at the curtains and missing the sunlight. Maybe Agnes or Olivia had bad eyes. Even so, I didn't know how they could bear to sit here in this chintzy gloom. Agnes's neck was very thin. Swallowing tea seemed to cause her pain. There was a framed photo of Arturo's father, Gerald, on the sideboard, well-groomed white sideburns and all; his golf club was in midswing and his gaze was incredulous—I seemed to be putting him off his game. What would Agnes say, what would any of these three say if I began to tell them about Sidonie, the eldest of the colored kids who came into the bookstore day after day just to read? Sidonie, whose colored father had taken just one look at her Caribbean mother and fallen in love? "They're crazy," Sidonie told me, shaking her head. "She just can't seem to pick up any American fighting words, and he never learned any French ones. So they don't fight . . ."

I could have talked about how a photograph of Sidonie's mother had inspired a painting on the side of a fighter jet flown by colored pilots back in '44, and how Sidonie had inherited her mother's looks, and stayed away from school because she didn't want trouble. "White boys get stupid around this girl," her friend Kazim explained, and the couple of times I'd walked Sidonie halfway home from the bookshop, I saw what Kazim meant. Sidonie Fairfax had a goofy laugh, but when her face was at rest, it was imperious. There's a certain type of colored girl who speaks softly and carries herself well, but when you talk to her, her eyes firmly reject every word that comes out of your mouth, just as if she's saying: *Oh, come on now. Bullshit. Bull. Shit.* It had been hard to get her talking. She was often deep in conversation with Mrs. Fletcher, but when I said something like "It's a nice afternoon, isn't it, Sidonie?" she'd say "Certainly, Miss Novak." (Subtext: *If you say so.*) If I'd been a guy, I

98

wouldn't have been sure how to approach her without getting shot down, either. And so the jesters lined up to entertain the queen, scrambling up trees and trying to hit her with their satchels, starting impromptu wrestling matches with each other on the sidewalk at the very moment she happened to be passing by. One fool took it upon himself to turn a backflip and nearly broke his skull doing it. Those morons embarrassed her. She was only fifteen. At that age embarrassment is something you can actually die of, and avoiding it is more important than what your father will say when he finds out you've missed a month and a half of school. Someone had copied out a poem and put it in her coat pocket—*I would liken you / To a night without stars / Were it not for your eyes*—and that had been the last straw for her. "Miss Novak, I'm the only teenager I know who reads Langston Hughes. I mean, that note can't have come from a student. That's got to have come from a teacher, right? I'm not the one to get mixed up in that kind of nonsense."

What if I'd told that drawing room tea party: "Sidonie likes the bookstore too, because nobody gives her a hard time there. White girls don't spill ink all over her dress at the bookstore, and colored boys don't twist her arm behind her back, and nobody stands in her way just leering like crazy when all she wants to do is walk down the corridor. That's the kind of girl that exists out there, less than a mile away from those linen curtains. But if you saw her without talking to her, she'd make you paranoid in a way that only a colored girl can make a white woman paranoid. That unreadable look they give us; it's really shocking somehow, isn't it? Kind of like finding someone staring in at the window of your home, but not in a way that gets you scared you'll be robbed. No, it's a different kind of stare. A stare that says 'I don't particularly like being outside, but I don't want to come in, either.'"

"My, my," Olivia and Agnes and Vivian would have said. Or maybe just "indeed." Arturo must have learned his devastating phrasing of that word from somewhere.

I managed not to say anything about Sidonie Fairfax. I managed to drink my tea without slurping, and I passed the "Will you have another Fig Newton" test. (The correct answer was "Thank you, but I really think I'd better not. They're so delicious they could be my downfall!") I crossed my ankles and tried to settle, to be at peace. After a while Olivia asked if I'd met her grand-daughter.

I said I hadn't. The lady didn't need to know that I'd seen Snow once and been so spooked that I could barely remember what exactly I'd seen.

"Well—would you like to meet her?"

"Oh, is she around?" I'd assumed she was with her father.

Vivian lifted up the corner of the tablecloth that the tea things sat on and revealed Snow, curled up under the table, snoring. She'd crushed the flowers someone had carefully pinned behind each ear. A white petal fluttered on one of her eyelids, and with each snore her eyelashes swept the petal farther down, onto her cheek. I couldn't understand how she'd managed to sleep while we'd all been talking at full volume. I guess it was all just noise to her. I watched the women watching Snow. Their reverence was over the top. Sure, she was an extraordinary-looking kid. A medieval swan maiden, only with the darkest hair and the pinkest lips, every shade at its utmost. She was like a girl in a Technicolor tapestry, sure, sure, but . . . they'd had a while to get used to her, and acting like that every time they laid eyes on her seemed to me like the fastest way to build an insufferable brat. Vivian let the tablecloth drop, but Olivia signaled to her to raise it again and cooed: "Why don't you come out and meet Boy, sweetie?"

Five minutes later, Snow was sitting on the sofa beside me, swinging her legs and asking questions.

("Do you like cookies? Do you like cold water? Do you like elephants? How do you spell 'genius'? Can you jump rope? How are ya today? What does 'genius' mean?")

I was already halfway to smitten. Olivia looked

on and fanned herself with carded lace and smiled at us.

When I left, it was Agnes who saw me to the door. "Snow's the spitting image of Julia when she was a girl," she said, leaning close, as if she were letting me in on classified information. I knew what I should say next, so I said it: "And Julia was the spitting image of you when she was a girl."

Agnes gave me a little push. "Oh, you know what you're about. You'll get around Livia quicker than quick."

Olivia had already decided she'd put up with me. I knew it and so did Agnes. If Olivia had decided against me, I'd have finished my tea and been shown out without even beginning to suspect that Snow had been less than a foot away all afternoon. I doubt the kid would have come out before she was called.

It was all kind of irregular, but if that was how they felt about Snow, then that was how they felt about her. People insist that beauty fades. Take Webster and Mia—both of them older than I am but not by all that much. (Actually, I'm not sure. Maybe in the case of Mia and me, the seven years between us is a lot.) Webster often said things along the lines of "Hey, what we've got only lasts a minute, only one goddamned minute and we've got to make the most of it." Mia's view seemed to be that it wasn't a good idea to trade on your looks at all if you could help it. Not for ethical reasons, but because she was very protective of her future self—she called her "Mia the crone"—and didn't want her to get horribly depressed when people stopped letting her get away with things. But, Agnes's frailty aside, she and Olivia were pretty good examples of lasting beauty, right down to the creases that ran around their foreheads and lips, some soft, like folds in cream, others deeply scored. One frown or smile from either woman went a long way. If you'd just been smiled at, there was some dimension to the smile you couldn't quite get at. If you'd just been frowned at, the hint of amusement that came with the frown told you that all was not lost. Olivia's snub nose and wide mouth made her more minxlike than pretty, but whatever it was that her peers had gone nuts for was still there. She clearly intended for Snow to be part of her lasting-beauty club. And really, what of it? Most of the people who say beauty fades say it with a smirk. Fading is more than just expected, it's what they want to see. I don't.

# 7

*t*he morning I turned twenty-two I put twenty-two dollars cash into an envelope addressed to Mr. Frank Novak and mailed it to Mia's address in Worcester. It was the sum total of the money I stole plus interest. Mia was to mail the envelope to a friend she had in New York, who'd drop it into the rat catcher's letterbox and make him wonder if I was around. I didn't enclose a note, though there were a few things I'd have liked to say. Restraint is classier.

Over at the bookstore, Mrs. Fletcher asked me if I thought it was shaping up to be a good year for me. It was the closest thing to "Happy birthday" I was going to get from her, so I took it with a neutral smile. We were sitting in her office, dealing with her correspondence. She went through a folder of letters I'd already opened for her, scrawled responses at the top or in the margins, and I turned those responses into letters.

Thirteen-year-old Phoebe was crying next door, because she was reading *Les Misérables*—a trial for all of us, since it was such a long book, and she was liable to cry all the way through it. Sidonie was jeering at Phoebe for crying. "And just why are you weeping over a bunch of French people from eighteen hundred and whenever?"

"It's too sad," Phoebe sobbed. "I mean, it was only a loaf of bread."

"What's the matter with you? Are you stupid? It'd be less phony if you cried for every man who's been lynched in Tennessee or Alabama or South Carolina since eighteen hundred and whenever."

"Don't tell me who to cry for and who not to cry

for, Sidonie Fairfax. Dark girl like you talking as though you're the top. You've got a face like a bowl of goddamned molasses. Did you know that, Know-It-All?"

"Molasses is sweet, molasses is sweet," Sidonie chanted.

"Uh . . . where's Kazim?" I asked Mrs. Fletcher, preferring to ask that question rather than remind her that people were less likely to enter the store if they saw two colored schoolgirls fighting out front. I already knew how she responded to reminders of that kind: "Hm . . . I don't care." Besides, Kazim was my favorite of the bookstore gang—fourteen and tall for his age, his gaze vague behind the thick lenses of his eyeglasses. He drew comic strips about a boy called Mizak, and his card tricks went just a little bit beyond sleight of hand. He'd snap his fingers over a spread-out pack, say "Joker, fly," and the Joker sprang up into his hand. It had to be something to do with magnets. Still, we all exchanged glances. Because what if it wasn't?

"I suppose I'll have to be the peacekeeper today," Mrs. Fletcher said, and she went out front, yelling even louder than Sidonie and Phoebe. I looked over the letters I was yet to answer. I still didn't know Mrs. Fletcher's first name. It was beginning to look as if nobody did. Every letter came in addressed to Mrs. A. Fletcher.

Having sent Sidonie out to buy RC Cola, Mrs.

105

Fletcher returned and asked what she should bring to my dinner party that evening.

"Oh, thanks, but I can handle this."

She dealt with three letters in rapid succession, writing NO at the top of one, A THOUSAND TIMES NO at the top of another, and OKAY in the margins of a third. "I'm not asking to be helpful," she said. "I'm asking so as to make sure there's something there I'll want to eat."

I handed her the menu I'd been working on for weeks.

"'Pear spread and crackers,'" Mrs. Fletcher read aloud. "'Anchovy ham rolls. Stuffed tomatoes *ravigote*. Potato salad. Chicken à la King. Banana chiffon cake. Peach pie. Postdinner cocktail: Rye Lane . . . a stupendous blend of whiskey, curaçao, orange squash, and *crème de noyaux*, stirred, not shaken, as recommended by the International Association of Bartenders.'"

She leaned back in her chair. "Why on earth are you putting yourself through all this on your own birthday? And what's pear spread? Life has changed a lot, you know. You didn't used to get all this food inside food inside food when I was a girl. The other day I was eating a mushroom and found it had been stuffed with prawns. I've got so many misgivings over this craze, Boy. It's flying in the face of nature. A mushroom is a woodland fungus and a prawn comes from the sea. People have got no business stuffing one inside the other. Are the Whitmans treating you well?"

"What?" My mind was on the pear spread. I'd already made it the night before, over at Arturo's. It was sitting in a bowl in his refrigerator looking radioactive.

"The Whitmans. Arturo Whitman's family. Are they treating you well?"

"Oh. Yes. Gerald keeps issuing orders to Arturo not to let me get away and Viv's very sisterly and Olivia's very motherly and—it's nice."

She nodded. "Olivia Whitman looks so young, doesn't she?"

"Yup."

I typed *I hope this finds you well,* which was pretty high up on the list of phrases Mrs. Fletcher would never include in a letter if she was writing it herself.

She lifted a lock of her hair with a pencil and gave it a baleful stare. This was the first gesture of concern about her appearance that I'd seen from her. She cut her own hair carelessly, with regular kitchen scissors, and it showed. The ends looked like a bar graph. The hair itself was fine, though— rich brown streaked with gray. "I'm about the same age as she is," she said. "I just don't know how she does it."

Olivia made Mrs. Fletcher nervous. That was difficult to process. I'd recently come across a proverb about not speaking unless you'd thought of something that was better than silence. So I kept typing.

Mrs. Fletcher wanted to know if she could ask me a personal question. I gave her an "mmm hmmm" that Snow would've been proud of.

"Do you know what it is you want from Arturo?"

An impressive U-turn, but I didn't look up from my work. "You guessed right, Mrs. Fletcher. I'm a gold digger. If you know anyone richer and more gullible, let me at him."

The bell above the shop door jangled—Sidonie or a customer. There was a quiet exchange of words in the next room, followed by the sound of caps falling off soda bottles. Sidonie, then.

"Nobody's calling you a gold digger," Mrs. Fletcher said. "Let me explain myself."

"You don't have to."

She reached over and took my hand, patted it. "But if I don't, you'll poison me tonight, won't you? I want to be able to enjoy my cocktail, just as the International Association of Bartenders recommends. Listen—I'm not a Flax Hill original, either. I'm from a market town in the South of England."

"So that's why you talk like that!"

"Well, what did you think?"

"I thought you just went to one of those . . . schools."

"Oh, good grief. I'm not in the mood for this.

Don't interrupt me anymore. My husband died nine years ago, and I came here looking for some trace of him. He was my right-hand man for twenty-three years. No children; we married late, liked books, and liked each other and that was all. His heart was dodgy—anatomically speaking, I mean—and it killed him. I was all undone. That man. The first time we met, he called me *cookie*. I said 'I beg your pardon?' and he said 'You heard. When are we having dinner?' so I said 'We might as well have it now.' Then a week later he agreed to marry me—"

"You asked him?"

"I don't mess about."

"And he never brought you here while he was alive?"

"No. He told me he was a misfit in his home-town. But it wasn't true. I barged into people's homes and found him in their photo albums, being carried around on people's shoulders. Homecoming King! People here are nice to me just because I'm his wife—was his wife, I mean. When I opened this store, so many people came by and bought books. Not to read them, I don't think. Well, Joe Webster might read *The Canterbury Tales* one day . . . anyway, it was a gesture, to help me set up. I'd never seen anything like it."

"I didn't know you cared about being liked."

"It isn't a matter of like or dislike, and you know it. People are nice to me for his sake. They

109

remember him. It's a different Leonard they remember—he was becoming the man I ended up falling head over heels in love with. But that's fine. We've all got different pieces of him to put together. It means I'm closer to him here than I would be in Newton Abbot."

I squeezed her hand. From where I was sitting I could see the chess set on her window seat. It was always there; once I asked her if she liked chess and she just sort of hissed and left it at that. The black army faced the white army across their field of checkered squares; the kings and queens seemed resigned, companionable. There was never any change in their configuration. But no dust, either. No neglect.

"I'm only going to say this once, so don't fly off the handle," she said. "Flax Hill is home to me because I loved Leonard Fletcher. Not the other way around."

"Right, but I'm not trying to—Arturo's not—the air tastes of *palinka*, you see," I said, idiotically. "Here in Flax Hill, I mean."

Mrs. Fletcher took this in her stride. "Does it indeed? It tastes like lemon curd to me. Needless to say, I consider lemon curd to be an excellent comfort food. Now get back to work. Here are customers, and you're behind."

*that day i* walked Phoebe and Sidonie all the way home instead of just three-quarters of the way. As usual I walked on the outside of our trio, taking the position of a gentleman protecting ladies from roadside traffic. As usual Phoebe's siblings were waiting for us outside the elementary school, three rowdy little girls of indeterminate age and the shortest of short-term memories. Every school day they asked if they could play with my hair, and I let them. Every school day they squealed: "It's just like sunshine!" and I wished they'd find a new sensation. Ordinarily I stopped when we reached the corner of Tubman and Jefferson—less because there was a tangible change in the neighborhood and more because that was when we started seeing groups of colored boys leaning against walls with their arms folded, not talking or doing anything else but leaning. I figured they were the Neighborhood Watch, and left them to it. So did the white boys who followed us along Jefferson calling out Sidonie's name. We got to Tubman Street and the catcallers evaporated. But that day I kept going because I wanted Sidonie to come to dinner. Phoebe had already excused herself on account of having to watch her sisters while her mom was at work. But Sidonie was an only child, and hesitated. "Ma probably needs me to help her tonight," she said. "But maybe if you came and asked her yourself . . ."

I wavered, needing time to get everything on the menu wrong and then get it right. Sidonie said: "Hey, you've got a lot to do before dinnertime, right? Save me a slice of that chiffon cake; it's going to be in my dreams tonight."

Phoebe said, "Me too!" and her sisters said, "Me too, me too!" I told them it'd be Sidonie who brought them the cake, and passed the Tubman Street Neighborhood Watch without incident. Farther along Tubman, a mixed group was crammed into a motorcar; girls sat on boys' laps, waving transistor radios in time to the music that poured out of them. These kids looked a little older than Sidonie, and ignored us completely. The houses were smaller and newer and better cared for than in Arturo's part of town. Their doors were pastel painted, the front yards were meticulously well-swept, and their windows sparkled in the way that only the truly house-proud seem able to achieve. We passed other groups. Boys and girls, singing, wisecracking. Lone dutiful daughters and sons laden with groceries. One boy with a buzz cut was carrying what looked like a week's supplies for an old lady who called him "Tortoise" and "Useless." His friends pulled faces at him when the old lady wasn't looking, and he grinned good-humoredly. "That's Sam," Phoebe said. "He's my boyfriend. He just doesn't know it yet." And she and Sidonie giggled.

Then I saw Kazim. He was part of a bunch of boys gathered around an open window, trampling some poor gardener's petunias. There was a green parakeet in a cage inside the living room, and the boys were trying to teach it a new phrase. This is what they were trying to teach it to say: *Fuck whitey*. The parakeet stumbled backward along its perch. Sidonie put her hand on my arm to keep me walking, and I did keep walking, but I looked back. The group's main teaching method seemed to be intimidation. They crowded the square of grass beneath the window, repeating the phrase over and over, all voices together. I heard the parakeet pleading "Hey diddle diddle, he-ee-ee-y diddle diddle!" but the boys insisted: *Fuck whitey, fuck whitey*. I saw Kazim and he saw me. He looked away first. He had been laughing until he saw me.

"I guess Kazim's found better things to do than read books," I said to Sidonie, or to Phoebe, or maybe just to the air. Phoebe and Sidonie looked at each other, and Phoebe said: "I don't know what you mean, Miss Novak."

I jerked my thumb at the boys across the way. "Yes, you do. I saw him."

Phoebe said: "Saw . . . Kazim?"

A man about a quarter of a block down opened his window and issued a warning that he was on his way to end the lives of anyone responsible for creating "this racket," and the parakeet boys scattered.

Sidonie said: "That wasn't Kazim."

Phoebe said: "I guess we all look the same to

you." She smiled to show she wasn't saying it in a mean way, and ran in at her front door with her sisters hot on her heels.

My temples began to throb. It was Kazim; I knew it was him. What did Phoebe and Sidonie take me for, and why had they just closed ranks like that? Were they trying to tell me that I was on my own if I said anything about Kazim back at the bookstore?

Sidonie stopped at a peppermint-colored door and said: "Voilà—chez Fairfax." I didn't answer her, just looked all around me, picturing the walk back down to Jefferson without the girls. All the lines washed out of everything I tried to fix my eyes on. It was like a floodlight had been switched on just above my head. Sidonie said something I didn't hear, then: "Miss Novak? It wasn't him. Really. Kazim's not a round-the-way boy. He stays home drawing and doing his wizard stuff. Relax. We all make mistakes."

*i sat down on a* wicker bench in the hallway, next to a table stacked with *Ebony* and *Jet* magazines. Intriguing text hovered beside the faces of the colored models on the covers: *Are homosexuals becoming respectable? End of Negro race by 1980 predicted by top scientist.* An older, far less haughty-looking version of Sidonie approached; she was in a wheelchair, and spun the wheels with her arms. I stood, then sat down again, not wanting to stand over her. Elsewhere in the house a television set blared and women talked over it and each other.

"Welcome, welcome," Mrs. Fairfax said, shaking my hand. She said I should call her Merveille, or Merva if I couldn't manage to say Merveille. "In America I am Merva . . ."

Sidonie must have told her I was a teacher: "You are so kind to invite Sidonie to dinner. Some other time . . . let Sidonie bring you; you will dine with us, I will give you such a dinner. Does Sidonie behave herself? Is her schoolwork good? Does she read too much?"

Merveille made me drink something so sweet it made my teeth ache; she said it was called sorrel. She was a hairdresser; she worked from home and Sidonie helped her in the evenings. She must have seen that I was wondering how she managed to do people's hair—maybe everyone who met her for the first time wondered about that—she tapped my wrist and said: "I manage. People have to sit a lot lower than usual while I work, but they don't mind because they leave looking good. Not just good . . . very good." Her husband was a Pullman porter working the train route to Quebec and back. She showed me her appointment book. She had clients all the way up to midnight.

Imagine having a mother who worries that you read too much. The question is, what is it that's supposed to happen to people who read too

115

much? How can you tell when someone's crossed that line? I said Sidonie was top of my class and that everybody liked her.

It was getting dark when I left, and I thought about calling Arturo from a phone booth and getting him to come pick me up. But it would take too long. So I just walked fast, with my head down, and didn't raise it again until I got back to Jefferson Street.

*snow kept me* company as I embraced *The Joy of Cooking*. She sat up on the counter with an apron over her dungarees and tasted the cake batter and the cream sauce for the chicken. She looked extremely doubtful about the cream sauce, but how sophisticated could her six-year-old palate be anyway?

"Maybe you'll get a mother for your birthday," she said. I dabbed the end of her nose with a square of kitchen paper, even though there was nothing there.

"Who said I want a mother? Maybe I want a daughter."

"What kind of daughter?" Snow said, with the air of a department store attendant, invisible stock list in hand.

"I said maybe. It depends. I might forget to feed and water her."

"That would be very bad, because mothers have to give their daughters cookies all the time."

116

"Oh, like Grandma Olivia and Grandma Agnes give you cookies?"

"Yeah, but then they pat my stomach," she said, stabbing toothpicks through the anchovy ham rolls. She hit the dead center of each one. She parted her own hair in the mornings with that same extreme precision. I think she observed her father's work more closely than he might have guessed.

"Okay, so cookies yes, stomach pat no. What else?"

"You have to hide her."

"Hide her?"

"Not all the time. Only sometimes. Like if a monster comes looking for her, you have to hide her."

"Well, of course."

"Even if the monster comes with a real nice smile and says 'Excuse me, have you seen my friend Snow?' you have to say 'She's not here! She's gone to Russia.'"

"I'll do better than that. I'll say: 'Snow? Who's Snow?'"

She clapped her hands. "That's good!"

"Anything else?"

"You have to come find me if I get lost."

"Lost? Like in the woods?"

"Not just there. Anywhere."

"Hmmmm. Let me think about that one. It's a big job. Meanwhile, do you think you can get your daddy out of his workroom so he can help you dress?"

She threw her arms around my neck, gave me a kiss, and hopped down from the counter. What made her so trusting, so sure of people's good-will? If I was like her I wouldn't have shrunk back later when Olivia Whitman draped a gray fur stole around my shoulders and said: "Happy birthday!" It felt expensive, thick to the touch but a lighter weight on the skin than it looked. Mrs. Fletcher asked: "Is that chinchilla?" and gave me a stern look, as if I were at fault for accepting it.

(The only thing I felt guilty of was already knowing that it was chinchilla fur—Olivia had worn it the week before, when she took me to see *The Magic Flute* in Worcester. We'd smoked cigars outside the opera house and she asked me how I liked the show. "Isn't it marvelous?" she said. I said that as far as I could gather it was a tale about a woman who could be led out of captivity only by a man, and that the man could save her only by ignoring her.

"Correct," she'd said.

"Uh . . . I really like the costumes," I said.

Olivia switched my cigar from the left side of my mouth to the right side and looked approvingly at me through her opera glasses. "Yes, the tale is what you just said it is, but it's also about two people who walk through fire and water together, unscathed because they are together. You'll agree that that's not a sentimental interpretation, that that's literally what happens? The trials those two undergo are about being beyond words."

I shivered, and she'd offered me the stole. "Chinchilla. It keeps you warm." But I'd declined. Cuban cigars and chinchilla stoles; this was more Mia Cabrini's scene, and I was better off not developing a taste for it.)

Olivia stood back, admiring the effect. "Yes, it never looked quite right on me. But Boy, you were born to wear this."

Arturo whispered, "Poor Viv—" in my ear. Vivian said a stole like that wouldn't have lasted long in her wardrobe anyway, what with her talent for spilling things. But she minded; of course she minded, here was a fur stole she'd probably grown up coveting and I'd swiped it right from under her nose. Her fiancé didn't even have the good sense to say he'd get her one. Or maybe it was good sense and a healthy awareness of his salary level that kept him from saying it.

All through dinner Arturo and I held hands under the table, like a couple of kids, and that made the dinner quite wonderful, even though Mrs. Fletcher kept staring at Olivia as though committing her to memory. It got so bad that Olivia turned to her husband and said: "Has it happened at last, Gerald? Have I become a curiosity?"

Gerald clinked wineglasses with her and said:

"You were always a curiosity, darling." And Arturo proposed a toast to curiosities.

Webster and Agnes didn't eat much dinner, but that would have been the case even if we'd been at a restaurant. Webster was three weeks away from getting married and consequently she was on the diet to end all diets. Arturo thought it was rude of her to eat so little, and was ready to tell her so. I said, "Look . . . I wouldn't if I were you." I'd fasted before, so I knew how being hungry can make a girl get a little bit enigmatic. Webster's psychology was one short straw away from abnormal. She'd conceived a disgust for the moon, kept calling "her" fat. "Fat hog, fat hog . . . what does she eat, to bloat up like that? Nothing up there but air, right? So greedy she stuffs herself with air . . . or stars . . . ?" Ted and Arturo started talking shop during the first course, just making remarks about the new catalogue they were putting together and how hard it was to find professional hand-and-ankle models who didn't demand that a full makeup team be present at the shoot. Webster said, "Talking shop, Teddy?" and gave him such a ghoulish smile that he broke his sentence off there and started reminiscing about wedding speeches he'd heard and liked. I didn't care whether or not Webster ate what I cooked. She cared enough to show up, and that was great. The same went for Agnes, though Snow was probably the main attraction for her. She was sitting directly across from Snow, and her eyes lit up whenever Snow laughed, which was often, since the girl shared a private joke with every spoonful of potato salad on her plate.

There was a brass water pitcher set up in the center of the table, and a couple of times I found myself smiling at my reflection in the side of it, but stopped just before anyone caught me. The smile was a chinchilla fur kind of smile. *Look what I got you,* it seemed to say. *And I can get you more.* But I wasn't the only one smiling at myself that night. Snow was too, peeping out from under her eyelashes. She might have been copying me. I couldn't tell. When she got tired, she lay her head down beside her ice cream dish and just slept. It was Agnes who put her to bed, blushing at the way everybody at the table went slightly gooey eyed at the resemblance between them.

# 8

*i*'m sure I didn't mean to make anyone feel uncomfortable," Mrs. Fletcher said the next morning. She put on a pretty good show of being abashed, folded hands and glum head shakes, but I wasn't fooled. When I saw that I wasn't going to get an explanation out of her, I changed the subject and told her about meeting Sidonie's mother and very briefly masquerading as a teacher. She covered her eyes and groaned.

"I wish you hadn't told me that."

"Oh, so I should've told Sidonie's mom that her daughter doesn't go to school but comes here—"

"And drinks much more soda than is good for her and associates with disagreeable women and reads novels she's permitted to select without supervision or even orderly thought, yes. Then her mother would have made her stop coming here."

"Well, exactly."

"But since you failed to inform Mrs. Fairfax of those facts, now I've got to do the forbidding."

I licked an envelope flap. "I don't see how that follows, but sure. Let's see how long that lasts."

Mrs. Fletcher still hadn't uncovered her eyes. "No, really, Boy. This goes for all three of them. They've got to go to school."

She didn't seem to notice that those were more or less the same words I'd said to her on my first day at the bookstore.

I said: "Well, this joke has fallen flat. I never met Mrs. Fairfax; I don't care for that neighborhood. Everything's the same as it was this time yesterday, okay?"

She didn't answer.

"Those kids won't know what to do with themselves if you send them away."

"Oh, rubbish. I know them. They'll mope for

five minutes, then they'll go to school and grow up and make something of themselves, that's what they'll do. There are ladders they've got to get up. Ladders made of tests and examinations and certification papers that don't mean anything to us, but Phoebe and Sid and Kazim can't get where they want to go without them. I've been selfish. No more."

We were busy with customers from opening time onward, so when Phoebe and Sidonie came by at about two p.m., I was sure that Mrs. Fletcher had reconsidered. She couldn't ban them. She'd miss them too much. They both made a rush at the shelf that had *Les Misérables* on it—Sidonie to confiscate it and Phoebe to snatch it out of Sidonie's way. Kazim came in after them, calling out to the back room: "What, what, what, did you miss me?"

"Oh yes—very horribly awfully much," Mrs. Fletcher called back. "Wait there. I'm trying to make this man understand that it's a nineteenth-century first edition he's trying to buy. He seems to think it's an item of clothing, keeps talking about 'jackets'—"

Kazim sidled over to the cash register and handed me a piece of card he'd folded into quarters. "When you look at my comic strips, you're always saying—and what happened next? And after that? And after that? So I drew this." I set my elbows on the desk and looked at him, and the more I looked, the less sure I was that I'd seen him in the group gathered around the parakeet. I was afraid to be wrong. I was afraid not to be able to tell the difference between Kazim, who I'd seen nearly every day for the past six months or so, and any other fuzzy-headed colored boy with eyeglasses.

Mrs. Fletcher came out and sent me to the back room to wrap up her customer's purchases. I missed what she said to Sidonie and company because the man kept wanting to know things— whether I could recommend a good place to eat while he was here, and so on. The kids were gone by the time I got out front again, and I went after them with cake I'd saved from the night before. I'd only brought two slices, but it didn't matter because Kazim was the only one who accepted. Phoebe held out her hand, but Sidonie glared at her and she dropped her hand just as I tried to place the carton into it.

"Ever since we started going to the bookstore I wondered what it'd be that put a stop to it," Sidonie said. She and Phoebe had their arms around each other's waists, holding each other up. "I knew it wouldn't be anything we did. I thought maybe some customer would damage a book and it would look like we were to blame, or Mrs. Fletcher would get her sums mixed up one day and think one of us stole, or—any number of things. But no. You did it."

"We told you it wasn't him." Phoebe had tears in her eyes. "It *wasn't*."

Kazim just eyed his cartonful of cake as if willing it to provide answers. I cleared my throat. The truth wouldn't sound like the truth coming from me. It might even contradict whatever Mrs. Fletcher had told them, and Mrs. Fletcher was their friend. "Go to school," I said, and watched them leave.

*a week passed* before I could stand to look at the comic strip Kazim had drawn for me. It was about a king called Mizak and his queen, Sidie. Every December a little boy and a little girl approached the throne, the girl "from above" and the boy "from below." Their names were Mizak and Sidie too, and the boy Mizak struggled with King Mizak for the right to the name and the next twelve months of life. The girl Sidie fought Queen Sidie for the same rights. When King Mizak and Queen Sidie were dead, the boy and the girl were dressed in their robes and crowned with their crowns, aging with preternatural speed every month until December, when the children came again. "It does us good to fight for life," Queen Sidie said, and her lips were wrinkles that clung to her teeth. Her words were empty; she and King Mizak were too weak and weary to put up a real fight. It was slaughter, and the boy and the girl were merciless. They said: "Remember you did the same."

Kazim used to give me strange looks whenever I tapped a corner of one of his comic strips and asked what was next. He thought it was strange of me to ask. *What's next is what happened before.*

# 9

*a*rturo's birthday gift to me was a weekend trip to Florida. Snow came with us, and brought Julia with her—a framed photograph she held out of the hotel-room window so that they could admire the view together. We got sandy beach and weathered cliff all in one window frame: a double whammy, as the hotel manager called it.

Arturo piggybacked Snow all around the hotel grounds and she showed Julia the coconut trees and the tropical fish whose tanks lined the reception walls. I followed with my purse stuffed full of Snow's dolls, who wanted in on the hotel tour too. The other guests found us picturesque, and the maids and bellhops pretended to. Really we were in their way. But: "Isn't that nice," they said. "Isn't that nice . . ."

In the afternoon we got Snow settled by the pool with her seven dolls in a row beside her, watching muscular men in swimming trunks making showy dives into the water and oohing and aahing as if she were at the circus. The key thing about Florida was that almost everybody we saw was good-looking in exactly the same way. They were all tanned and excitable, closing their eyes in ecstasy as the breeze tousled their hair. I perched on the end of a sun bed and held my sun lotion out to Arturo.

"Okay, I get it, Boy." He laid his hand flat between my shoulder blades; I felt a print forming in the lotion. "You don't want to be alone with me."

"That isn't true, and you know it." I picked up the bottle, walked around him, and worked my hands down his back.

"Could have left Snow with either one of her grandmas . . ." he said.

"You do that too much. And I like having her around. I like having you around too." I nipped his earlobe, laughing when he looked around and asked me if I wanted to get us barred from poolside. Later that evening, when Snow was fast asleep, we went out to the beach with blankets and torches, and the sound of the waves swept around us, rising and falling. Water raked the sand we lay on and locked our bodies together, tugged us apart a little. But only a very little. Only as far as we let it.

As we walked back to the hotel, I said: "So we're never going to talk about Julia?" A straight question, just as Mrs. Fletcher would have asked it. (Why am I always imagining that I'm other people?)

Arturo asked what I wanted to know.

"What do you want me to know?"

He looked down at our feet. We were walking in step, which was taking some effort on my part.

"Our parents were good friends, double-dated all the time—it felt like they'd picked us out for each other. Whatever they did, it worked, because she's almost everything I remember about being a kid and being a young man—I got my first job so I could buy her an opera record she just had to have; still remember what it was—Offenbach's *The Tales of Hoffmann.* It was never 'Will you buy me candy?' with her; she always wanted stuff that . . . I don't know, stuff you always felt in danger of losing her to. Books, music. If you took her to one of those big art galleries, you wouldn't be able to find her again until closing time. I was in a running battle with the Phantom of the Opera. The Phantom won, but—"

"Arturo." I held him closer, walked with my head above his heart.

"I gave him a run for his money. I never had eyes for anyone but her, right up until she died. And even then, for a long time after . . . it just didn't seem true that she was gone. She had to have Snow by Caesarean, and when she came home, she got a fever. She said she was just tired, and she'd just sleep it off. I knew why she was saying that: She hated it at the hospital; didn't want to see any more white coats or nurses' uniforms. Two days, she kept saying, *I'll just sleep it off, Arturo—don't fuss.* Her mother and mine kept telling me I didn't know what it was like for a woman after she's got through childbirth, that I should just let her hold her baby and rest. She died in the night, Boy. It seemed impossible. She was laughing and singing to Snow in the afternoon, then in the middle of the night she woke me up saying *Call a doctor, call a doctor,* and I was downstairs for an hour or so trying to get hold of someone. I couldn't. It was Saturday. I went back upstairs and Julia was so quiet. It didn't feel final; it was more like she was thinking and was about to speak. It looked like she was breathing, but it was just air escaping. I remember I covered Snow's eyes. And . . . I don't want to say any more."

He sighed when I told him I was sorry. "I've still got Snow," he said. It sounded rehearsed, a phrase he'd assembled around his real feelings like a screen.

"Hey. Hey, you. I'm here too."

I thought that was that, but in the morning I woke up to find him kneeling beside my bed. His eyes were on me; I think they had been for a long time.

"Say you love me," he said. The sun hadn't been up for long, and Snow was snoring in the bed beside the window. She wriggled when he spoke, then tucked her head deeper into her pillow. I tried to fake a return to sleep myself, but Arturo said: "No. Say you love me." I sat up and he trapped my heel in his hand, so hard that my other foot, the free foot, drew up in a weak pirouette.

"I'll stay with you," I said. We both spoke lightly, we were both smiling, but I didn't know what Arturo was going to do if he found he couldn't make me say I loved him. Not much, surely. Snow was right there, after all. And she wasn't sleeping. She didn't give herself away even for a second, but that kid was keeping tabs. I knew and she knew.

He stood up and went over to his suitcase. "I made you something."

It was the first piece of jewelry he ever made me, and it was the equivalent of an engagement ring. I say "equivalent" because it was a bracelet, a white-gold snake that curled its tail around my wrist and pressed its tongue against the veins in the crook of my elbow. When I saw it lying on its bed of tissue paper, I didn't want to pick it up, let alone put it on. All I could think was: *I will fear no evil, I will fear no evil, I will fear no evil.* That snake was what he'd made for me, it was what he thought I wanted, was maybe even what he thought I was, deep down.

I'd said I'd stay, so I stayed. I put it on for him. I said I'd marry him. He said: "Are you sure?"

I ran my fingertips over the scales, dozens of colorless hexagons that warped even as they reflected. According to them, the room was a lilac-wallpapered blur, and my forehead was west of my nose. I didn't go inside Arturo's workroom, and he'd never invited me there, just came out when he was done for the day, sweating hard. He said it was because of the details, having to get them right. The switch from pliers to magnifying glass to the rubber mallet, back to magnifying glass, then the reach for the scoring knife. He said that most of the time he felt as if he were making a monstrosity right up until the last step. It's not work I could do, breaking something and then breaking it again and again until it looks the way I want it to. I'd falter, and try to go back to where I'd started. I'd just be there all day making solid gold blobs.

I said: "What do you mean, am I sure? What kind of question is that? Of course I'm sure." And I kissed him.

"It's just that sometimes you get this look . . . you know how in movies people come around after fainting or hitting their head and immediately start asking, 'Who am I? Where am I? Who are *you*?' I've seen you looking like that sometimes, and I can't tell if that's just how life strikes you or if you're only like that when you're around me. I kind of like that look. It's endearing. But what if one day you figure out who you are and where you are and who I am and realize it's all a big mistake?"

"Impossible. For the last time, I'm sure."

Magic words. As soon as I'd said them, Snow was halfway to the ceiling, waving her arms and yelling "Hurray!" Arturo climbed up onto his own bed, stating that it was the principle of the thing. I was the one he'd said yes to, so he had to bounce higher than Snow. Then of course I had to show them who the real bed-bouncing champ was. They surrendered pretty quickly.

I put the bracelet in the hotel-room safe, and checked on it once a day. We were almost carefree for the rest of the weekend, Snow, Arturo, and I; they were carefree, we built sandmen and taught Snow's dolls how to play beach volleyball with water balloons. The snake was always there each time I checked, and there was no way to go back to Flax Hill without it.

*when mia saw* the bracelet, she said: "Oh, Boy." She spun the jewelry box around on the tabletop, wouldn't even touch its contents.

I said: "I know."

"I mean, could that scream 'wicked stepmother' any louder?"

"I *know*."

Mia ruffled my hair. "It's okay, it's fine. It only looks like that. That's not how it really is."

# 10

*i* shouldn't have been surprised to discover that there was a man three blocks away from the boarding house who specialized in bespoke wedding-cake toppers. It was Flax Hill, town of specialists. He had a storefront full of ready-made cake toppers available for sale. Clay ballerinas and baseball players and owls, numbers shaped out of wax, all of which were far less unsettling than the wedding-cake toppers. Each tiny bride and groom had this beseeching smile painted onto their face. The kind of smile that suggested dark magic was afoot, a switch had been made, the couple leading the first dance were not who they claimed to be, and wouldn't someone please intervene? That's what I'd think if I saw a pair of smiles like that on top of a wedding cake, anyway. But Webster had set her heart on having a pair of cake toppers made by this particular specialist. Something about his father having made her parents' cake toppers, and his grandfather having made her grandparents' . . . so I sat with her while she went through photographs of her and Ted together. Mr. Cake Topper Specialist wanted the photographs to work from, and she dismissed every photo I suggested. "Maybe we'll have to take a new one," she said.

I'd collected my bridesmaid's dress from the seamstress's store the day before and run into a couple of Webster's other bridesmaids. We'd debated whether or not to tell her that if she didn't end her diet now she wouldn't look pretty on the day, just brittle. As her friend Jean put it: "She's got no business getting this thin for a December wedding. If there's snow, she'll catch pneumonia so quick she won't know what's hit her."

"Ted keeps saying, 'Let's just elope,'" Webster said, and gave me such a wicked grin that I didn't have the heart to say anything about brittleness.

Brenda, Webster's neighbor, knocked on the door. "You've got a gentleman caller, Novak. No, no, not Loverboy. Though it could be Loverboy Mark Two. He says it can't wait."

"Is he handsome?" Webster asked, following me to the staircase. Brenda shrugged. "I guess so. In a freckled kind of way. Some girls get all the luck."

Webster and I took a peek over the banister. We saw a mop of light brown hair, then Charlie Vacic looked up and gave us the full winsome-puppy-dog treatment. I was already on my way down the stairs, so the push Webster gave me was wholly unnecessary, as was her crowing that she was going to tell Arturo on me, which brought seven of our fellow tenants out onto the landing to see who I was two-timing my fiancé with.

"Hi," I said, pulling him into the front parlor and

closing the door behind us. "What are you doing here?"

"How are you, Charlie, long time no see, how's med school, was it a long bus ride, can I offer you something to drink?" Charlie said. He dropped into an armchair and closed his eyes. I sat down too, in the chair opposite his. My knees had turned to water.

"I'm well, thank you, Boy," he supplied. "Yes, it has been a while. Med school's fine, I'm not failing, and I've avoided hypochondria by deciding my time's up when it's up. The bus ride aged me by about ten years and a cold beverage would be the best thing that could happen to me right now."

What could I do or say, other than bring him a glass of someone else's root beer that I found in the icebox? He drained the glass without speaking, so I got him a refill. Then he was ready to talk.

"I got your letter. Are you really getting married?"

I looked into his eyes. He couldn't return the gaze steadily, kept focusing on my left eye, then on my right. I could guess what he was thinking: that there were two of me, that was the explanation, that was why I was acting like this. I had applied this rationale to the rat catcher the first time he'd punched me. First you try to find a reason, try to understand what you've done wrong so you can be sure not to do it anymore. After that you look for signs of a Jekyll and Hyde situation, the good and the bad in a person sifted into separate compartments by some weird accident. Then, gradually, you realize that there isn't a reason, and it isn't two people you're dealing with, just one. The same one every time. *Keep switching eyes all you want, Charlie. You're going to hate the conclusion you reach.*

I answered: "Yes, Charlie, it's true."

"When?"

"Soon."

He loosened his collar, swallowed air. "Why?"

He smiled when I didn't answer. Not an amused smile, a nervous one. The quirk at the left corner of his mouth when he smiled. For so long I'd wanted to kiss him just there. He was Charlie. Maybe I could tell him: Listen, there's this little girl who makes herself laugh. You hear her from the other room, and when you try to get her to explain, she just says: "Don't worry about it." And maybe it's the thief in me, but I think this girl is mine, and that when she and I are around each other, we're giving each other something we've never had, or taking back something we've lost. Maybe Charlie would say: Let's kidnap her, go to Europe, and raise her as our own. We're young. Starting over won't be so hard for us. But even if some madcap spirit did pick that moment to possess Charlie Vacic, what I felt for the girl wasn't all that distinct from what I felt for her father.

"I wish you'd written to let me know you were coming," I said. "Where are you staying?"

"I'll find someplace. Take it easy, I'll be out of your hair soon enough. Tomorrow, probably. Why are you doing this, Boy? Don't you understand that I just want to take care of you any way I can? Or do you think I don't know what I'm saying when I say things like that?"

"I love you," I said, then sat there, appalled at what had just come out of my mouth.

He moved forward in his chair, rested his forehead against mine. "I know. So, please, Boy. I'm asking you, please. Don't marry him."

"I don't want to be taken care of, Charlie. That's not what I want."

"How dare you write me a letter like that? You wanted me to come here and say this. Don't marry him."

Just one kiss, I thought. But then I couldn't pull away.

Out in the hallway, Mia bawled: "Anyone seen Boy Novak? That girl owes me a pastrami sandwich." That might have been her way of making a tactful entrance. We'd let go of each other by the time she tried the door handle. I introduced them, praying Mia wouldn't say *"That* Charlie?" She didn't.

Instead she said: "Come to lunch with us," and

137

looked up at him with a smile that made me want to stick a *No Trespassing* sign on him. Charlie excused himself on the grounds of having to find a room, but once Mia and I found a quiet booth at the diner, I had words with her about that smile she'd given him. Not straightforward words; I just asked a few questions about her love life, whether she was seeing anyone she liked, etc.

"No, not really—I'm just snacking right now."

"*Snacking,* Mia?"

"That's the only way I can think of to put it to you, my dear, innocent Boy. But about that Charlie . . . why did he say 'Good-bye' when he left? I mean, 'Good-bye,' not 'See you later.' Isn't he in town to see you? Did you just break his heart? Don't you know how to let 'em down easy?"

*webster was all aglow* at her wedding, and Ted was in awe.

("I get to grow old with this woman? This woman right here?"

Arturo slung an arm around his neck and told him it was clearly a charity case.)

There was hardly a dry eye in the house. The miniature Ted and miniature Webster stood on top of the cake looking resigned, if not content. They realized that nobody was even going to think about rescuing them. We filled the reception room with paper flowers that each of us seven bridesmaids had spent a total of twenty-one hours folding—three hours a day for a week. It was gratifying that Webster sobbed over the flowers. She seemed to understand that we were trying to say good luck and trying to say that we were there just in case. Her official name might be Mrs. Ted Murray now, and she might have forsaken the Mamie Eisenhower haircut for long romantic waves that she flung to and fro like some kind of cape, but to me she was just the usual Veronica Webster.

Webster and Ted were on honeymoon when I married Arturo at Worcester City Hall. Olivia, Gerald, and Vivian were there. Mia too, and Snow. I hadn't asked Mrs. Fletcher because she'd made it clear that she disapproved. I hadn't asked Agnes because being Julia's mother would have made the ceremony difficult for her. Mia gave me away, and I think Olivia was scandalized by that, but managed not to comment. I wore a plain dress that was somewhere between white and gray; its skirt was long and straight, and Snow said that when I stood still, I looked like a statue. Arturo wore a red bow tie and his hair slicked back. And his power doubled, maybe even tripled—that power he had of making me feel certain. The black of his hair, the red of his tie, the gold band I slipped onto his finger. Outside it snowed lightly, lifelessly, thousands of white butterflies falling to earth. Becoming Mrs. Whitman was a quiet affair that I didn't have to diet for.

# 11

*i* remember Vivian Whitman said something a little odd at the wedding, as we were walking down the steps of city hall in the snow. She said: "You know, you've made my mother happy today. I think she only ever wanted one daughter, and nature never did give her the one that fit the bill." I said: "What? Last time I looked I wasn't a law student—" And she said: "Oh, come on. Look at you!" I'd thought she was just getting emotional because she thought Arturo and I should have made our wedding more of an occasion, but when the hothouse calla lily arrived, her remark was the first thing I thought of. The little card that came with the lily said: *Congrats, Boy, and welcome to the family! Sorry this is late; I only just heard. Always wanted a sister, and never did see eye to eye with my biological one—Clara.*

Snow wandered over, eyeing the purple blooms, assessing their potential for wearing in her hair. I told her to forget it.

"The calla lilies ah in bloom again," she announced, in a surprisingly decent imitation of Katharine Hepburn's voice.

"That's right."

"Where'd it come from?"

I watched her face as I said: "Your aunt Clara sent

it," but there was no flicker of recognition. She lost interest, said "Mmm hmmm," and wandered away. It's true that kids are inquisitive, but sometimes you forget that they pick and choose their projects.

I took the plant pot to Arturo's workroom and knocked. He didn't answer, so I kept knocking, switching hands when my knuckles got sore. Eventually he came to the door wearing goggles that covered half his face and asked: "What's the big idea?"

I held up the lily. "It's from Clara."

He removed his goggles, read the card she'd written, and laughed.

"Any particular reason why you've never said anything about her? Snow doesn't seem to know who she is, either."

"She's estranged from our parents. From our mother, really."

"What did she do?"

"Oh, God. A lot of stuff, Boy. Too much to talk about."

"So she's estranged from you too?"

"No. She's my big sis. It was her, then me, then Viv. Matter of fact it was Clara who put a roof over my head for a year. When Julia died. Snow was too young to remember. Don't mention the roof over my head part to my mother, she'd have a heart attack."

He kissed me and ducked back into his workroom.

• • •

*mia said she'd* never heard of a Clara Whitman, and Webster broke her Vow of Silence against me (punishment for getting married while she was away) to say the same thing. Mrs. Fletcher breathed out when I said Clara's name. She breathed out and held on to the nearest bookshelf and said: "So you know. All this time I've been thinking how wrong it was of Olivia Whitman to send that girl away and act as if she only had two children."

"What did she do?"

Mrs. Fletcher shook her head. "Nothing out of the way, Boy. Was just herself and fell in love. I must say, I'm glad you find it so humorous."

"I don't. I don't know what to think. You say she didn't do anything, Arturo says she did a lot of stuff he can't even talk about. I mean, which is it?"

Mrs. Fletcher peered at me for a long time. Her expression became grim. She said: "They didn't tell you about her."

"You tell me. Someone's got to. How did you meet?"

"She contacted me about a book she wanted to buy for her husband's birthday. It was the first I'd heard of her, and I didn't believe her when she said she'd been born in Flax Hill, and that Olivia Whitman was her mother. Then she came by to look at the book, and I saw she was a Whitman all right. She said the book was too expensive and went away, then came back the next day, said she guessed it was worth the price, paid up, and left town. That was four years ago. I haven't seen her since."

"Where does she live?"

"In Boston, I believe."

"With her husband . . ."

"Yes. Her married name is Baxter."

"Any kids?"

"I don't know."

"What was the book she bought from you?"

"It was an 1846 edition of *The Narrative of the Life of Frederick Douglass.*"

"She's a historian?"

"No."

I couldn't think of anything else to ask; a riddle ran all the way through the account I'd just heard. I questioned a detail and the answer didn't tell me anything. Finally I said: "Okay. Do you have her address or telephone number? I'd like to talk to her. Introduce myself. Thank her for the flowers, that sort of thing."

Mrs. Fletcher hesitated, and I said: "Nobody else needs to know about it. I guess I just want as much family as I can get. Surely you understand that?"

I tried the telephone number she gave me three times, but the phone on the other end just rang and rang, and no one picked it up.

# 12

C harlie sent a letter to the boarding house and Mrs. Lennox sent it on to me at Caldwell Lane.

This doesn't count as bothering you; it's just that there's something that's been on my mind and I can't do anything to get it off my mind but tell you. I've always liked the way you listen—you have what they call an impartial air, like the ideal judge. Then afterward you just say four or five words and the case is closed. This is about my aunt Jozsa, in the old country. You know, we read the papers, but it's hard to say what's really going on over there. We just know it's something. Aunt J was sent to an internment camp in Szeged, which is so crazy, I don't even know how to express the insanity of her having been interned—hand on my heart, she's red all the way through, risked her life for the party and the cause on too many occasions to talk about back when the fascists ran things. So we don't know . . . someone with some sort of grudge against her must have denounced her. The camp officials wanted her to confess disloyalty and collaboration with enemies of peace (enemies of the government, I guess) and she racked her brain for weeks and weeks but couldn't think of anything she'd said or done that could even be construed as disloyal or treacherous. So then she started putting some of her own statements of the past few weeks to herself, to see how they sounded. She remembered that once, at a party meeting, her mind had wandered, she'd looked out of the window at all the snow and whispered to her friend: "Will spring never come?" So maybe it was that. Aunt Jozsa told my dad she sat in her cell repeating those words until they became sinister . . . and incriminating. But when she confessed to having asked if spring would come, her interrogator just said: "Oh, I see we've got a joker here."

I don't know, Boy. I think she got close to going crazy. But when Stalin died last March, they let everybody out of the camps and Aunt J went home again. I wrote to her right away. She hasn't seen me since I was a boy, but she says I'm her favorite and stupidest nephew. I wrote: Hey, Aunt Jozsa, what can I do for you, what can I send you? A plane ticket

145

maybe? I mean, I could do it too, with a little help from my dad and my uncle in Milwaukee.

She answered: Send me candy, my boy. Send a lot of that great American candy. Send an amount that will shock me, send enough to make the neighbors say "That is a LOT of candy, the New World is certainly being kind to the Vacics."

So I did, Boy. I sent her a cardboard box by freight. A couple of feet wide, a couple of feet tall, and heavy. At the bottom of the box I put a note saying that there was more where that came from if she came to America. She's a skinny woman and I now know for sure that she doesn't really eat much candy, because she only found the note a couple of weeks ago—a year and a few months after I sent her the candy box. She wrote: You know very well I can't live in your shitty capitalist country, Charlie. I'm not even interested in visiting.

I got angry. Because who was it who locked her up—communists or capitalists? I asked her that question, and I asked her what had become of her communism now. And I've got her reply right here; I'm looking at it as I write to you—she says:

I don't know. I don't know anything. But it will not always be like this.

That's it. What am I supposed to do with that?

C

Charlie's Aunt Jozsa, who just couldn't walk away from certain principles. I thought of her, on and off, for days. I didn't reply to his letter, but if I had, I would've told him that his aunt probably called him her favorite because their hearts worked the same way. Charlie and I were still in love. How strange it is to wake up in the middle of the night with that feeling that someone has just left the room, that just moments before someone has been whispering: *Me and you, you and me,* soft music that stops playing the moment you really begin to listen. Who'd have thought that Charlie Vacic could be so tenacious? "People underestimate the freckled." He'd told me that more than once, with all seventy-two of his own freckles scrunched up together. I'd underestimated him too, and I had to face up to the reason why.

It's true that nothing really happened the night I ran away. It's a night two weeks before that I don't like to think about. It was a Saturday and Charlie Vacic was back in the city visiting his mom. He met me for a slice of pie at the diner where I worked, and then he walked me home. I told him and told him there was no need to walk me right to my door, but he insisted, and the rat catcher came out with a covered cage just as we reached the front doorstep. I bet he'd timed it that way. I bet he'd been watching us from the window. "Hello, Charlie," he said, friendly as could be. "I've seen the way you look at my daughter. You think she's pretty, don't you?"

Charlie said: "More than just pretty, sir. I think she's beautiful."

They both turned to me and went on a looking spree. I left them to it and wished I could sail over their heads and into the acid blue sky. They didn't look for long, it was more a practiced series of glances; they knew what they were looking for and seemed to find it. It was a wonder there was anything left by the time they were through looking.

"Say thank you, Boy. Didn't you hear what Charlie said? He thinks you're beautiful."

I told the sidewalk thank you, and the rat catcher took me by the arm, thanked Charlie for "bringing me home safe and sound," and closed the front door in his face. We walked side by side down the hallway to our apartment door, the rat catcher and I, and he scraped away at me a little more with his dull nickel gaze. "So you're a beauty, hey?" He slapped me. "Or are you not?"

"I'm not."

"So you're ugly?"

I nodded.

Another slap, harder. "You have to say it."

"I'm ugly."

I went to my room, switched on the radio, and lay down with a book. But I didn't read it. I left the door open and watched for the rat catcher's approach, feeling very bitter toward Charlie Vacic. He'd really done it this time. I heard the rat catcher moving around the apartment and waited for him to yell that it was time I made dinner, but he didn't. I smelled cooking. Good cooking. When my father called me to the table, there was chicken paprikash and dumplings and cold beer to cool the heat of the paprika. Foodwise it was the best dinner I'd had yet, and I ate a lot. We didn't talk, he watched foam swirling in his beer, but he kept biting his lip, and I stopped eating when I clocked that he'd bitten down so hard that blood came through. The rim of his beer glass was smeared with it. I muttered a compliment to the chef, went to bed, and lay on my swollen stomach in the hope that it'd be flat again by morning. Yeah, ideally in the morning my stomach would be flat again and the rat catcher would already have left for work and life would be as good as it could get.

I woke up in the basement with the rats. I tried to lift myself out of the chair I was in, but my arms were tied behind me and my ankles were so tightly bound to the chair legs that they already felt broken. There was no light, and the rats crunched on the newsprint that lined their cages. The rat catcher loomed over me and I smelled wet fur. The blinded creature he held paddled the air with its front paws. A paw thudded against my forehead, but if I hadn't seen it happen, I wouldn't have known. No part of my face would move. I looked up into the rat catcher's clear eyes.

"I'm glad you liked the paprikash, stupid. Do you think Charlie really means it when he calls you beautiful, Boy? Do you think he could be the one?"

I watched the rat lap hungrily at the corner of my mouth with its pink, delicate tongue; I saw it, but couldn't feel it. The numbness was total. It froze my fear. After a moment he hauled the rat back up into the air and it snapped its snout this way and that, seeking me.

"There is no exquisite beauty without strangeness in the proportion, is that not so? Let's fix it so that Charlie is truly mesmerized by you. Let's fix it so that he stares. Seven scars should do it."

There was a teardrop on my cheek; I know this because my father flicked it with a finger and thumb to make it fall faster. With effort I closed my eyes. *No way out. Get through this, then kill him. Figure out the rest later.*

"Why are you shaking like that?" my father asked, tenderly. "Do you think that if I scar you no one will love you? You've got the wrong idea, girl. This will help your true love find you. He'll really have to fight for you now."

There was a thickness to his voice; I cracked one eye open. He was crying. The rat hung limp and lay its head on my cheek in a confiding way, exhausted and childlike. Drool bubbled from its jaws, but it didn't bite me. Perhaps it had become too hungry to eat. I don't know if that happens to rats, I don't know . . . a second later the rat was dead, its head smashed against the basement floor, and my father was running up the stairs, cursing, still crying. A true thing I can still hardly believe of myself is this: I fell asleep again until he came back to untie me.

I was reluctant to look at myself for a couple of days after this happened—the anesthesia had worn off and my lips and right cheek were sore. I couldn't tell how much the rat had been able to do. I didn't touch the sore places, not wanting to worsen any infected bites. But there were no bites. I probed the skin with my fingers—there wasn't even a rash. The rat catcher stayed out of my way and I stayed out of his. The trouble is I can be such a slow thinker at times. But once I got the situation in focus it stayed clear. No matter what anybody else said or did my father saw something revolting in me, and sooner or later he meant to make everybody else agree with him. Worst and weirdest of all was his weeping—I think he'd really believed that he was doing something good for me. He'd faltered that time but the next time he wouldn't.

Mirrors see so much. They could help us if they wanted to. In those days I spoke to every mirror in the apartment. I questioned them, told them I didn't know what to do, but none of them answered me. The girl in the glass exaggerated my expression, her gaze zigzagging as though watching a waterfall. She was making fun of me for sure, but I decided not to take it personally.

**mirror: ['mɪrə]**
*noun*
1. A surface capable of reflecting sufficient diffused light to form an image of an object placed in front of it.
2. Such a reflecting surface set in a frame. In a household setting this surface adopts an inscrutable personality (possibly impish and/or amoral), presenting convincing and yet conflicting images of the same object, thereby leading onlookers astray.

*Beautiful Boy, ugly Boy, rat, rat, food for the rats, sick and sickening . . .* it took two weeks for my thoughts to twist themselves into a membrane that I could break only by leaving, or by murdering the rat catcher. I'm not sure Charlie could have rescued me from that. And I think I decided not to love Charlie because I thought I had to be rescued. For practical reasons but also as a proof of love. It's better that Charlie and I didn't make an automatic transaction, love exchanged for rescue. All you can do after that is put the love and the rescue up on the shelf, moving them farther and farther back as you make room for all the other items you acquire over the years. This way a ragged stem still grows between us, almost pretty. Though really we should crush it now, before the buds bloom skeletal.

I didn't say his name aloud to anyone. If Mia asked how he was, I pretended not to hear. But Charlie Vacic just wouldn't let up. I'd think he was done, but a week or so later he came back ten times as strong.

Every now and again I'd look at Arturo, just look at him until he said "What gives?" He was a little surprised at me for not wanting to make my mark on the house, but I wasn't interested in undoing what Julia had done. Across the years we accepted each other, Julia and I, neither of us exactly thrilled by the other's existence, but there was enough difference between her and me to suggest that her Arturo wasn't exactly the same as mine anyway. My puzzlement regarding him was greater: I didn't understand how he could do the things he did. He took Snow cherry picking, he took me hiking around the lake, he swam at the pool with his father every Thursday afternoon, took Agnes Miller all the way to Baden-Baden because her chest wasn't as strong as it used to be and he thought a spa week might help. He behaved as if he belonged with us, belonged to us. But he was crazy if he thought Julia was finished with him. I mean, it was bad enough with Charlie, and he was still alive.

Did I talk in my sleep? Was it the flag in my side of our closet? Somehow a corner of it always emerged whenever I reached for something to wear. Arturo and I never spoke about it, but somehow he knew that there was someone else. He must have, because it was around that time that Arturo began to make chains.

Ankle chains, wrist chains, necklaces made of heavy brass links. He laid the collection on a bed of red velvet, piece by piece, as he completed them.

"What do you think of these?" he said. And I told him they were ugly. I was angry with him for making such threats; I thought he should know better than to do that.

"Why don't you try them on?" I said. I didn't yell. If anything, I made my tone pleasant, modeled it on the way the rat catcher had spoken once, half a second before he grabbed my head and tried to smash it against a wall as if it weren't even connected to my neck.

I think I unnerved him, because he did what I said. He put all the chains on, four bracelets on each wrist, anklets on over his socks, necklace upon necklace upon necklace. He held his hands out to me, and I tried hard not to grin, but it didn't work. "Come on, Boy. I'm sorry."

I undid the bracelets first. "Something to think about in future: Hinting that you think you can hold me against my will only makes me mad."

"Got it." He looked as if he was going to add something else, some excuse or explanation, then decided against it.

"You've got around eight months to become a new man," I told him, dropping chains onto the floor. "I mean . . . is this the kind of father my child's got to look forward to?"

"Eight months . . . ?"

"That's what Dr. Lee says."

He yelled "Gee whiz" so loud and for so long that Snow came running from Olivia's house screaming, "What? What?"

We told her she was going to have a little brother or sister and she said: "Oh, good. Make it a sister, okay?" and ran straight back to her court of dolls.

*i made my list* of names in secret. Partly so that no one would know I was copying Julia's idea, and partly so that no one would know how wild my hopes were. Olivia suggested Scarlett for a girl and Alexander for a boy, and I thought: *Not bad.* Gerald suggested Artemis for a girl, which made me suspicious that he'd somehow gotten hold of my list. I'll never get into the habit of calling him "Pop" like he wants me to—I can't make myself say it casually or kindly. The word comes out sounding like a deliberate insult, and I don't want to apply that word to someone like him, someone who gets enthusiastic over English marmalade and Swiss fountain pens. The way his hair sits on his scalp makes me smile too—it's all his, since nature can't seem to do without its jokes. That luxurious mop is wasted on a bank manager. It ought to be grown a tad longer and then employed at a ritzy Parisian music hall, helping some show-girl hit the big time. From certain angles Gerald's hair assumes the personality of a disarmingly earnest counterfeit, a Brylcreemed wig that would feel so happy and honored and gratified if you'd only say it had fooled you for a second.

"And for a boy?" I asked.

"Why, Girl, of course," he deadpanned.

My reflection changed as I got bigger. Well, obviously it changed, but what I mean to say is that when I looked into the mirror, I couldn't see myself. That's not quite it, either. I'd look into the mirror and she was there, the icy blonde with the rounded stomach, the thickened thighs and arms—just as I'd become accustomed to wearing it, the snake bracelet wouldn't fit anymore. I also went up half a shoe size, which pleased me because it was another bridge burned between me and the rat catcher. Come into town, rat catcher, come looking for your daughter, come holding a pair of the shoes she left. Say to everyone who'll listen: "If the shoes fit, she's mine." Gather witnesses . . . the more the merrier. They'd see me wedge my feet into the narrow shoes, see how far my heels spill over the back of them. Then they'd hear me tell him: "I'm so sorry. Keep searching. Good luck."

When I stood in front of the mirror, the icy blonde was there, but I couldn't swear to the fact of her being me. She was no clearer to me than my shadow was. I came to prefer my shadow. She came into the shower cubicle with me and stood stark against the bathroom tiles, so much taller than I was that when I began to get backaches, I could find shelter crouched under her.

Snow was the one who came up with the right name. We were lying on the couch together, her chin on my shoulder, Arturo's arm around us both as he read poetry to my stomach. He said he'd read poetry to Snow before she was born, and hey, if it ain't broke, etc.

"Maybe Margaret for a girl?" Arturo said. "This Maggie sounds okay, doesn't she?

> Gentle as falcon
> Or hawk of the tower.
> With solace and gladness,
> Much mirth and no madness,
> All good and no badness."

Snow yawned. "What's a falcon?"

"It's a bird," I told her.

"And the other thing in the tower?"

"A hawk. It's another kind of bird."

"Bird for a boy and Bird for a girl," Snow said. "Birds sing and fly."

She was right. I put her to bed, and when I went next door to spin Julia's lullaby around on the gramophone, she said: "No, you sing it to me."

"Snow, you know I can't carry a tune. And your mother has the loveliest voice, let her—"

"She's tired of singing the same song every night," Snow said, firmly. "And you're my mother too. Aren't you?"

I drew a chair up beside her bed and sang. *All I do is dream of you the whole night through . . .* It was a horrible rendition, and I quite enjoyed attempting it, setting the notes free from the song as each one went farther and farther astray. Snow was nice about it. I think she pretended to fall asleep faster than she usually did just so I'd stop. I switched off all the lights except her nightlight, then went downstairs and threw my list of names into the trash.

*when i got too big* and too distracted to meet the demands of being Mrs. Fletcher's assistant, I stayed home, ate my way through the fruit baskets Mia and Webster sent over, and listened to Julia Whitman's voice. *You're every thought, you're everything, you're every song I ever sing . . .*

I hoped Bird would sing like that, would have a voice as strong and rich as the one I listened to, with all those teasing little trips and breaks in it. It was a voice Snow didn't seem interested in hearing anymore—"I'm almost eight years old now," she said, as if that had anything to do with it—but maybe in time Bird could make her listen again.

A simple solution, maybe. Just like running away from home, just like staying away from Ivorydown because of the woman I'd seen there. But the thing about these simple solutions is that they work.

# 13

*b*ird was born in the spring. I say "was born" because the pain was so tremendous that I just let it come. It was like quicksand. The only way to make it out alive was to stop struggling against it, to submit. I'm told I was in labor for thirteen hours, but I really wouldn't know. There was the quicksand, then there was Bird in my arms, safe and well, and dark. No. It wasn't just her shade of gold (the closest skin could get to the color of my husband's eyes. I think I made some dumb joke: "Look at this kid, born with a suntan—"), it was

159

her facial features too. As the nurse said when she thought I was too wiped out to hear: "That little girl is a Negro."

I didn't want to show her to anybody. Not to her father, not to her sister. No one. The doctor told me that Arturo seemed like a reasonable man, that he could talk to Arturo for me if I wanted, that everything could still be okay, and I realized that he thought he was talking to an unfaithful wife. I laughed and laughed, high-pitched laughter that roused Bird to try to outdo me with her crying. The doctor thought I'd gone to bed with a colored man, and I had. He was my husband.

What did I think Arturo would do when he saw Bird at last? Whatever it was I'd prepared for, he didn't do it. He held her, gave her Eskimo kisses, and said she was a smash hit. Snow climbed up onto the bed, did a triple take, then said: "Let's keep her!" Arturo didn't even try to touch me; he knew I wouldn't let him. I looked at him over the top of Snow's head and I mouthed: "Who are you? Who are you?"

He came back later in the afternoon, without Snow. He brought a hip flask full of apricot *palinka* with him (he refused to reveal its source) and we passed it back and forth, drinking in silence, not quite looking at each other. When the flask was three-quarters empty, he asked: "You drunk yet?"

Everything had become polka dots, especially

him. I found this endearing . . . I may even have smiled. "A little."

"Me too," he said. "We'd better talk."

In his mind he was no more colored than I was; he'd never even met his grandparents or cousins, his parents were the only ones from their families who'd decided to move north from Louisiana and see if anyone called them out on their ancestry. His father had stood in line behind a colored man at the front desk of the Flax Hill Country Club and eavesdropped as the colored man tried and failed to gain membership. "We're fully subscribed," the colored man was told. But Gerald Whitman was offered a membership form to fill out without further ado. It was too bad for the other guy, but Gerald liked golf and didn't see why he shouldn't play it in those surroundings if he could get away with it. Gerald had thought: *Well, what if I just don't say . . . what if I never say?* He'd passed that down to Arturo, the idea that there was no need to ever say, that if you knew who you were then that was enough, that not saying was not the same as lying. He asked me a question that threw me into confusion because I couldn't honestly answer yes or no. He asked if I'd have married him if I'd seen him as colored.

"And Julia?"

"Mom says as soon as she saw Joe and Agnes Miller she knew they were the same as her and Dad. You should have seen how long their faces were at the wedding—Mom's face, Dad's face, Agnes's face, Joe's. But Snow turned out to be . . . Snow, and we got to go on not saying."

Snow was blameless. And Arturo was forgivable; maybe because he said that he felt that Bird was his, ours, in a way that he hadn't felt with Snow. He said that for a long time he'd looked at Snow and seen her as Julia's child. Snow's beauty had seemed so strange to him for a while, so blank, like a brand-new slate. But Bird looked up at him confidingly, in a way that made him grin. "This kid is pretty sure we're old friends."

It was Olivia Whitman I could not forgive. When Bird and I came home, she was our first visitor, and she took one look at Bird, a cold, thorough look, then turned her gaze away. "Well, she's healthy, thank God." She then began to insinuate that I'd two-timed Arturo and gave me to understand I had another thing coming if I expected Arturo to raise another man's child. I said: "You think I won't slap you, Olivia, but I will. Keep going and you'll see."

Next she implied that my background was questionable. She didn't know where I was really from, she hadn't met my father, she'd taken everything I said on trust.

"Nice try, but I'm not going to stand here while a colored woman tries to tell me that maybe I'm the one who's colored."

I sat down with Bird, who wailed because she

preferred me to stand. Olivia sat down too, on the same couch, but leaving a large space between us. Now that I knew about her it was incredible that I hadn't seen it before. Or had I? Tea with her and Agnes and Vivian had made me think of Sidonie; it hadn't just been my mind wandering.

"The last person who threatened to slap me was a white woman. Blonde, like you. No Southern belle, either. Just trash."

"I guess that's how we operate."

I told myself, *Stop it. Whatever else she says, don't rise to it.* I wanted a grandmother for Bird. Olivia wasn't the one I would have chosen, but she was a generous grandmother to Snow and if she put her mind to it, she could do it again. Bird was beautiful too, with her close curls and her bottomless eyes, and she was only just getting started.

"I was working at a grocery store," Olivia said. "And I didn't fetch a box of soap flakes down fast enough for that woman's liking, so she said: 'I'll slap you, girl.' 'I'll slap you, girl' to a grown woman. And I knew I'd lose my job if I went at her, so I just said: 'I'm sure you've got a lot of things to do, ma'am, and I'm as stupid as they come. Please be patient with me.' That was standard, that kind of cringing and crawling. I didn't want it to be. She was not my better, I don't care what anyone says, she wasn't. None of them were. I thought: *If I have a daughter, I don't want anyone talking to her like that. I don't ever want to hear my daughter wheedling at anyone the way I do every working day.* I thought: *If I do, if I ever hear that in the voice of a child of mine, I'll make her sorry all right. I'll wring her damn neck.* Couldn't very well wring my own neck, could I?"

Olivia's voice was very calm, but her hands trembled. I backed up, moved farther away so that Bird and I were pressed against the arm of the sofa. I didn't think she was going to lash out. No, I wanted to keep us from catching what was in her, what was there in her voice and her eyes. But babies have some unfathomable criteria for what they consider attractive. Bird was wriggling like crazy. Her intuition should've told her that Olivia was terrible, just the worst, but I was having trouble keeping the kid from stretching her hands out in Olivia's direction. I don't know, maybe she already had expensive tastes and liked the scent Olivia was wearing.

"What you don't understand is that we're being kept down out there. All the way down. In my town you couldn't vote unless you passed a literacy test. How does that stop colored folks from voting, you ask? You didn't see what the colored school was like, how big the classes were. The teachers did what they could, but half my male cousins could hardly read. They lost patience before the girls did. No matter how literate a colored man was, there was always some excuse

164

to whip him. There were other things too. Little things. You'd save up and go out for a nice night at a nice place, all right, fine. All the high-class places we were allowed to go to, they were imitations of the places we were kept out of—not mawkish copies, most of it was done with perfect taste, but sitting at the bar or at the candlelit table you'd try to imagine what dinnertime remarks the real people were making . . . yes, the real people at the restaurant two blocks away, the white folks we were shadows of, and you'd try to talk about whatever you imagined they were talking about, and your food turned to sawdust in your mouth. What was it like in those other establishments? What was it that was so sacred about them, what was it that our being there would destroy? I had to know. I broke the law because I had to know. Oh, only in the most minor way. Gas station restrooms when Gerald would drive me cross-state on vacation—one day I used the White Only rest-room and nobody noticed me. Gerald begged me not to, but I just got my compact out, repowdered my face, and walked in. I felt like laughing in all their faces. The rest room experience is more or less the same, in case you were wondering."

"Olivia," I said. "Look at Bird. Look at her." I drew the baby blanket down a little so that Olivia could really see her. But the woman just wouldn't look, and it broke my heart.

"Every now and then there'd be a colored

cleaning lady in there, in the White Only restroom, I mean, scrubbing a washbasin that nobody
was using right then. And she'd look at me and
know, and I'd look at her. They didn't do anything
or say anything, those cleaning ladies, but for
hours and hours afterward I'd just want to pull all
my skin right off my body. So I said to Gerald:
We've got to go north, let people take us how they
take us, then we won't feel like we're betraying
anybody. But it's the same thing over here. Same
thing, only no signs. The places you go to, do you
see colored people there? Let me answer that for
you. You see them rarely, if at all. You're trying to
remember, but the truth is they don't exist for
you. You go to the opera house and the only
colored person you see is the stagehand, scattering
sawdust or rice powder or whatever it is that stops
the dancers slipping . . . folks would look at him
pretty hard if he was sitting in the audience,
they'd wonder what he was up to, what he was
trying to be, but being there to keep the dancers
from slipping is a better reason for him to be there,
he's working, so nobody notices him but me.
Listen, I love that Grand Theater down in
Worcester and I love all that dancing I see there,
been there at least once a year for the past . . . oh,
how old is that son of mine . . . for the past thirty-
seven years or so. Almost forty years! But
sometimes right in the middle of the second act
my vision darkens just like a lantern shade's been

thrown over it, and the dancers are colored, every shade, from bronze to tar, and every hand touching strings in the orchestra is colored too, and the tops of their heads are woollier than sheep, and the roses in my lap, the ones I throw to the prima ballerina at the end, even the petals of those roses are black, burnt black. And then I think, Well, it's out, the truth is out . . .'"

She glanced at Bird. "This one's dark like my eldest, Clara. See if Clara will take her."

*i said i didn't care* that Bird was colored. I said that to Mia, and to Webster, and to Mrs. Fletcher, who replied: "That's the spirit. Keep saying it until it's true."

Nothing got past Mrs. Fletcher. It's true that it was hard. Olivia and Gerald attended Bird's christening, and Gerald kissed her, but Olivia didn't. And it was hard to take Bird for walks, pushing her stroller around town, and watch people's faces when they saw her. I saw them deciding that if Arturo meant to claim her as his daughter then they weren't going to contradict him. Once I passed Sidonie and Merveille, deep in conversation, the daughter pushing her mother's wheelchair, and I almost escaped them, but Merveille instructed Sidonie to bring her up to the stroller so she could bless the baby. Merveille invited me to coffee when she found out I'd lied about being Sidonie's teacher, and it was excruciatingly awkward for the first half hour or so. I felt sick about having lied to her; there are people it's a bad idea to tell the truth to, but never Merveille. She didn't have to set me at ease—not by any means—but she did, by telling me about her grudging respect for Olivia Whitman. She said Olivia's "masquerade" had been ugly, but that she couldn't help but appreciate a woman with sangfroid. "Let us say that means 'cold blood.' No—nerve is what she has. Nerve." It turns out Olivia respects Merveille Fairfax too, because of the stink she raised over a decade ago about Flax Hill's colored children having to go to a separate school when it was their right by law to be educated alongside their white peers. Apparently Merva got up a letter-writing campaign, *The Boston Globe* ran an editorial piece about the situation, and the school board gave in under the pressure. Olivia said most people weren't overtly against joining the schools, more people than she expected were in favor of it, but a few called Merva bad names in the street and asked her if she thought her daughter was too smart for the colored school. And Merva smiled and said: "Every single child in this town is too smart for the colored school." That put her on Olivia's list of people not to trifle with.

I looked at the sky while Sidonie and Merveille gasped and cooed over Bird, so I didn't see their expressions. But when they finally let me go on my way, Sidonie put her hand on my shoulder, and that hurt me all the way home.

Yes, it was hard. Snow would place a finger on each of Bird's palms and raise her little hands up when they closed into fists. She'd say: "I'm your best friend, Bird." Bird seemed to understand and believe this, and her eyes searched for her sister when she was away. Bird adored Snow; everybody adored Snow and her daintiness. Snow's beauty is all the more precious to Olivia and Agnes because it's a trick. When whites look at her, they don't get whatever fleeting, ugly impressions so many of us get when we see a colored girl—we don't see a colored girl standing there. The joke's on us. Olivia just laps up the reactions Snow gets: From this I can only make inferences about Olivia's childhood and begin to measure the difference between being seen as colored and being seen as Snow. What can I do for my daughter? One day soon a wall will come up between us, and I won't be able to follow her behind it.

Every word Snow said, every little gesture of hers made me want to shake her. Arturo told her I was just tired. It was true that I was up at whatever hour Bird chose. I rarely let him go to her instead. He got good at changing her diaper really fast, before I really noticed what he was doing. "You think I'm gonna let you tell her I never helped out?" he said. Our daughter suckled so slowly,

169

with the sucked-in cheeks of a wine-tasting expert. I'd nod over her while she fed, slipping in and out of sleep.

"Snow is not as wonderful as everybody thinks she is," I said to Mia on the telephone, and my reflection smiled bitterly at me.

"What did she do?"

"Nothing yet. But I'm wise to her."

Bird was napping in her crib, and I had to whisper so as not to wake her.

After a tense silence, Mia said: "I think you just need to rest, Boy."

When I was pregnant and Olivia and I were still friendly, she told me that this would be the part of my life that brought me closer to my mother than ever, that this would be the time I felt what my mother had felt for me. Was this it? I'm learning that loving that kid as much as I do means that in some way we're still not separate. I'm hungry when she's hungry, and the cold hits me the same way it hits her, it makes me that much clumsier in scrambling to get us what we need.

I began to have dreams that made the ones I'd had about the rat catcher look like tea at the Ritz. I'd fall asleep and discover that I was Bird, my own little Bird. Snow being my big sister, that's the bad dream. I'm the smaller girl and Snow has her arm around me, and she's like a rose with a touch of dusk, so abundantly beautiful that it feels contagious—we're touching, so . . .

"I'm your best friend, Bird," Snow keeps saying, and it's a hall of mirrors we're walking down, and I don't look the way I feel, I hate the mirrors but it's okay as long as I just keep looking at her. She's laughing. She's my best friend. There her arm is, around me, but the mirrors say I'm alone, that I haven't got a sister, and Snow thinks it's hilarious. I have to get away from her, there's this terrible emptiness in the way she smiles and the words she keeps saying, I have to get away from her.

I don't set too much store by dreams, but it's probably unwise to ignore this kind. These are the kind of dreams that show you you're not doing so well, that you haven't accepted what you thought you'd accepted, that you're a mess, lying there like you've been hit by a bus, your heart and mind standing over you tutting and trying to figure out what even happened, never mind fixing it. *This doesn't feel like my life, it feels like somebody else's. I'm standing here holding somebody else's life for them, trying to keep it steady while it bobs up and down like a ferocious balloon. Make this little girl let me go—I don't know if I want her. Can't I start over?*

The snake bracelet Arturo gave me lies in its box for now, but soon I'll be ready to wear it again. I've missed the feel of cold scales around my wrist. I can't discount the possibility that the bracelet's been molding me into the wearer it wants. There was an afternoon that I raised my hand to Snow, fully intending to swat her like a fly. She'd asked me if she could lift Bird out of her crib and walk around with her. She'd asked this a few times, and I'd told her no. She was too small and too clumsy to walk around with a baby. I didn't tell her this; I just said no. Snow said she'd be very careful. She said please please please please. She leaned over Bird's crib and pressed the side of her face against the side of her sister's face as if showcasing the contrast between their features, and she gave me a look of radiant, innocent virtue that made my skin crawl. Somehow it was spontaneous and calculated at exactly the same time. My hand came up to knock that look off her face, and I think if she'd looked fearful or piteous or anything like that I'd probably have hit her. I was gray-skinned with exhaustion, fat around the middle, my eyes were smaller than the bags beneath them, and Snow's daintiness grew day by day, to menacing proportions. I would've hit her and decided it was self-defense. I wouldn't have seen the rat catcher (or the snake bracelet) in my actions until much later. But Snow noted that split-second jerk of my arm with an expression that mixed incomprehension and curiosity—she had no idea what I was about to do, but she had a feeling it was going to be new to her and therefore interesting—I settled my hand on the nearest crib post and spoke to her gently: *Your sister's sleepy,*

*Snow. Go play outside.* She left, looking back at me, still curious. Maybe there is no Snow, but only the work of smoke and mirrors. The Whitmans need someone to love, and have found too much to hate in each other, and so this lifelike little projection walks around and around a reel, untouchable.

In the middle of another night of mirror dreams I got up and checked on Bird, who seemed to be having herself a highly satisfactory sleep; she was smacking her lips. Next I went into the bathroom, where I turned on both taps and held on to the edge of the sink with a feeling of terror. I didn't switch on any lights. It didn't seem impossible for the rat catcher to be right behind me, ready to dunk my head into the water and hold it down until I drowned this time.

I heard myself saying *I don't know what to do. I don't know what to do.* But I was saying that only to divert my attention from what I was about to do.

I washed my face, then went into the parlor, picked up the phone, and tried Clara Baxter's number. This time she answered immediately, which threw me a little bit. I mean, I gave the operator her number, and the next thing I knew Clara said, "Hello?"

"Hello, Clara. This is Boy—you sent me some flowers a while ago, and—"

"Hello, Boy. How are you?" Her voice was clear

and gentle, and it sounded to me as if she was smiling.

"I'm fine, Clara. Thank you for the flowers," I said. Then I held my hand over the receiver and tried to finish crying without making any noise.

"How's the little girl? Arturo told me her name's Bird. It's a pretty name."

She waited for me to answer, then she said: "Don't you worry 'bout a thing, Boy. When Bird starts eating solid food, you bring her over here. She can stay with me. I won't blame you. No one will blame you, and you can come visit her whenever you want."

"Clara."

"Yes?"

"Your mother sent you away?"

"Yes, she sent me to Mississippi, to live with my aunt Effie."

"And you're not . . . you're not mad at her?"

"No, Boy. I don't like her much, but I'm not mad at her. Aunt Effie did right by me. And now I'm living how I want to live. Wouldn't have been able to do that under Ma's thumb, don't you know. You didn't have a mother yourself, did you?"

"No, I didn't."

"And you're all right, aren't you? We turn out all right."

(Do we?)

"Let Bird start on solid food before you come see me," Clara said. "And don't be too hard on

Arturo. He doesn't mean any harm, couldn't do any if he tried."

"I want you to take Snow," I said. "Just for a little while. Please."

*just for a little while.* Just for a little while. It was Arturo who took her to Boston. She was wearing a straw boater and had her pockets stuffed full of cookies, just as she had the first time I ever saw her. She gave Bird three hundred kisses and said: "That oughta hold ya 'til I'm home again." Agnes Miller took ill; I knew it was because Snow was going away from her. She waved her handkerchief from her bedroom window by way of saying farewell. Up until then I hadn't realized she lived in Olivia and Gerald's house, that a room in that house was all she had to call home.

I was the last one she hugged before she jumped into the car with her father.

"See you next week," she said.

"Yeah," I said. "Next week."

Snow is not the fairest of them all. And the sooner she and Olivia and all the rest of them understand that, the better. Still, I'd snuck Julia's records into the kid's luggage because I didn't want to leave her with nothing.

*one*
*two*
*three*

# 1

*l* ately I've become the kind of girl who likes to think on paper, settle down with a notepad and a decent pen and an aniseed jawbreaker so big that my back teeth clasp around it as if it were a long-lost part of my skull they're welcoming home. When I'm older, I'll be a reporter like Aunt Mia, who isn't really my aunt in any biological sense, but is much closer to my idea of an aunt than my dad's sister is. I can usually get Aunt Mia to splash a little wine into my orange juice when Mom's not around. And she's not exactly a chore to look at. I've observed reactions to her on the street. Women look at her and get this happy "What a waste" expression on their faces, like the sight of her is making them feel good about themselves but also they think someone ought to give her some beauty tips. Aunt Mia wears flat shoes and really practical tortoiseshell hair slides and slacks and blouses in clashing colors; it can get pretty extreme. You think hmmm, could be a story there. *She was an ordinary librarian, innocent of any crime, but one day she fell into a giant paint box and has been on the run from the fashion police ever since . . .*

So the women who pass Aunt Mia get a little extra pep to their step, but the men look at her the way I might look at a hot fudge sundae in the hours between lunch and dinner. You know, when you're not sure if it's a good idea to go ahead—you're interested beyond a shadow of a doubt, but you wonder if it might turn out to be a little too much for you. Men seem to realize that Aunt Mia's already making the most of herself. She and Aunt Viv are probably just as smart as each other, but Aunt Mia's a lot more educational to be around than Aunt Viv, or she's more my kind of educational.

Something about Aunt Viv is all curled up at the edges, like—I'll die if she ever sees this, but she won't, she won't—like a piece of old bread. I'm mean. Dad's warned me about it; I know the risk I run when I find fault with people more often than I look for something to appreciate. It's like having grit in your eye; you see less and less of the real person standing right in front of you and more and more of the grit in your eye. I get the message. I've noticed that she doesn't keep trying to test *his* vocabulary, though, so I feel like it's easy for him not to get cranky with her. Also *The Ed Sullivan Show* isn't one of Dad's favorite TV shows, so when Aunt Viv drops by on a Sunday to watch it with us, it's not Dad's parade she's raining on. Her face whenever the Supremes come on . . . she'll try to be girlish and sing along but her eyes say *SOS SOS it's an alien invasion.* Aunt Viv with her fingers patting away at her super-straight hair, like she's trying to wake it up or calm it down or show it off or hide it or who knows . . . I guess she tries her best to look out for me, but I've got better things to do than be precious about my complexion. Aunt Viv says it's not so much a matter of making improvements, it's more to do with stopping things from getting worse. But I can't sit in the shade on a fine day, not when the sun wants me. It's too much like playing hard to get, which I've heard all about and don't believe in at all.

Aunt Viv lives alone and is always saying how much it suits her, even when no one was even talking about that. She had a fiancé but he abandoned her; she doesn't know that I know a man ever fell in love with her. Gee-Ma Agnes says he broke the engagement off because of me. Apparently Aunt Viv's fiancé had no idea she was colored until I was born, then he saw me and said: "Wait a minute . . ."

I don't buy it. Aunt Viv wouldn't speak to me at all if that was true; she'd be the way Grammy Olivia is with me. Grammy Olivia sometimes smiles at me by accident, like when she's just turned away from somebody else who's made her laugh and her eyes fall on me before she's done smiling. Otherwise I get nothing from her. I remember being very small, or her being tall enough for me to expect to see a crown of clouds on her head when I looked up at her—and I made her a daisy-chain bracelet. I put it in her hand and she said "Thank you" and left it on the coffee table, but I picked it up and presented it to her all over again. The second time she held the bracelet over her wrist without letting it touch her skin, as if it looked cheap to her and she didn't want to put it on in case it gave her a rash. Then she said something to my mother. That's Grammy Olivia, a voice above my head, not even speaking to me, saying: "She gets darker and darker every day." Mom didn't answer, but she pushed me a little behind her, somehow managing to hug me at the same time. A backward hug is the only way I can think of it, Mom putting herself between me and Grammy Olivia. I'm reconsidering. Aunt Viv may have had a lily-livered fiancé after all. If so, then Dad's right about her, and Aunt Viv's strength is in not blaming me. Another thing that happened a little while after I was born was that Mr. Clarke at the butcher's started giving Grammy Olivia extra little bits of cheap meat she hadn't ordered. Ham hocks and chitterlings. "I guess he figures Livia knows how to cook 'em up real good," Gee-Ma says, cackling so much she can hardly speak. "Not our Livia." Mr. Clarke's just trying to be nice, but Aunt Olivia separates the little bag from the rest of her order and gives it to the housemaid who comes in twice a week, makes her take it home with her, ignoring Gee-Pa Gerald's "Been too long since I tasted chitlins . . ."

Grammy Olivia gets extra meat but Aunt Viv

lost her fiancé. Do I feel bad for blowing Aunt Viv's cover? Not really. I accidentally brought truth to light, and bringing truth to light is the right thing to do.

Aunt Mia had a stomachache last week. It wasn't your usual type of stomachache. You don't normally call someone to come hold your hand through a stomachache, and that's what Aunt Mia did. She called Mom at three in the morning, maybe because she knows that Mom never just lets the telephone ring. If it rings when she's in the shower, she yells: "Don't just stand there, get the phone! Get the phone!" Aunt Mia called at three in the morning and it woke me up, and I stared at the silvery-blue moons painted on my ceiling, heard Mom talking to Dad. *Something-something-something-gotta-look-in-on-Mia.* By the time she was downstairs putting her shoes on, I was down there too, pulling on Dad's old velvet blazer, the one he bought years ago and immediately wished he hadn't. Mom said: "So it's like that, huh," and I said: "You know there's no school tomorrow." Mrs. Chen, Louis's mom, drove us over to Worcester in her taxi. I think Mom tried to pay her extra for her trouble, but Mrs. Chen kept saying: "Not necessary. I don't sleep much anyway." Aunt Mia didn't come to the door, so Mom let herself in with the key she has, and Aunt Mia was in her bed, on top of her sheets, not underneath them, looking greenish with nausea.

Mom sat on the bed and tried to get Aunt Mia's head on her lap but Aunt Mia said: "What, do you want me to puke?" So we just took a hand each and held on. I asked if I could get her anything and she pulled a smile out from somewhere and said what a well-brought-up child I was and, no, she couldn't ask for anything more. After a while Mom jerked her head to bid me be gone, and I went into the kitchen, poured myself some chocolate milk, and wandered into the parlor to look at Aunt Mia's wall of heroes. Most of her heroes are colored . . . like I am. Aunt Mia says she didn't go out looking for colored heroes. She says that's just the way it worked out. Mom and Aunt Mia murmured to each other and I studied the faces of journalists who spoke out against inequalities and wouldn't shut up even when people threatened to kill them. If someone threatens to kill you for speaking up about something they've done, they must be feeling their guilt. So maybe that's how you know you're on the right track.

There was Ida B. Wells of the Washington *Evening Star* ("gutsy as hell"), her hair gathered up into a gorgeous pompadour that I'm going to try to copy as soon as my chin will agree to tilt up in just as dignified a way as hers. There was Charlotta Bass, publisher of the *California Eagle* . . . she's still very much alive, that one— Aunt Mia got her autograph and tucked it into the frame along with the picture. There was Robert S. Abbott of *The Chicago Defender* with his bowler hat on, his eyes stern and kind—when I fell asleep, he was the one who stuck up for me. "It is possible to *develop* a nose for a good story," he told Charlotta Bass and Ida B. Wells, when they pointed out that I didn't have one. He borrowed Dad's voice to say that, and I liked him all the more for it.

I knew that there was more to be discovered about Aunt Mia's stomachache, and I followed my nose a little, or tried to, anyway, not wanting to disappoint Robert S. Abbott. On the bus home the next afternoon I asked just one question and Mom looked at me with that quick flash in her eyes, the knife look. "Try to remember that it's none of your business, Bird."

Something happened, that much is clear, something bigger than indigestion. But I don't know if I'm ready to cross Mom in order to get this particular scoop. It looks like Aunt Mia's feeling better now, anyway. I can return to this matter once my skills are honed. I'll call that choosing my battles.

In the meantime I'll be finding out who my enemy is, and what exactly it is he or she has got against me. Proof or deduction, I'm not fussy about how I get there. I don't know what it's like to wish someone ill. Sure, I've occasionally told Louis Chen that I hope a monster eats him, and he's told me to go boil my head a few times, but that tends to be in the heat of the moment, and anyway we're getting married once we get old enough, so we don't have to make nice all of the time.

Gee-Ma Agnes (not my grandmother in any biological sense, but . . . it's similar to the way things are with Aunt Mia) says I've definitely got one. An enemy, that is. I told her what happens to me sometimes, with mirrors, and she said: "Watch out; that's your enemy at work, trying to get rid of you."

I don't think she was trying to be spooky. She was shelling pistachio nuts and she made her words sound as if they were a comment on the color of the nut meat. People assume Gee-Ma doesn't have anything to say because she's small and shaky and doesn't seem to follow conversations very well. But Gee-Ma can get interested in conversation when she wants to. The stories that make everyone else say "Get outta here" are the stories Gee-Ma takes an interest in. We used to watch reruns of *The Twilight Zone* together, and she'd slap her knee and crow: "He's right! Rod Serling is *right.*" She doesn't like *Bewitched* and *I Dream of Jeannie* because "Magic is not a joke, Bird."

Phoebe the housemaid acts like Gee-Ma is too old to move—"You stay right where you are," she tells her, and dusts carefully around her. She asks

Gee-Ma real simple questions, real slowly: "Enjoying that soup, Mrs. Miller?" Phoebe should maybe stop and think of Mrs. Fletcher, my mom's boss. She's the same age as Gee-Ma Agnes. Just last year Mrs. Fletcher began living in sin with a bookbinder called Mr. Murphy. I have reason to believe that Mom and Dad interfere with each other pretty regularly; there are those mornings when I find Mom making breakfast and she's wearing the shirt Dad was wearing just the night before and she hasn't even buttoned it up, she just uses one of his neckties as a belt. The first moment of seeing Mom like that is always really, really gross, and now it seems that grown-ups just never stop interfering with each other. Me and Mom and probably half of Flax Hill saw Mr. Murphy and Mrs. Fletcher getting all cozy together on a picnic blanket on Farmer's Green, feeding each other cherries, yet. Their combined age is around one hundred and thirty years, but Mr. Murphy isn't shy about kissing Mrs. Fletcher's hand in public. More than once Mrs. Fletcher has laid her head on Mr. Murphy's shoulder and giggled like she's never seen a shoulder before. Imagine what those two are like when there's no one else there. Mrs. Fletcher isn't even one of the quiet ones, so if that's the kind of thing she gets up to, then there's no telling what Gee-Ma's got up her sleeve.

Gee-Ma's husband moved back to Mississippi

when their only daughter died. "He did invite me along," Gee-Ma says. "He did invite me along, I'll give him that." But she liked Flax Hill better and anyway they hadn't married for love. She won't explain what they married for; another thing on my list to find out. She says the main thing is that they didn't marry for love and neither of them really tried to make it grow, they sort of just expected to love each other after a certain number of years but it didn't work out that way. All that happened was that she'd be having a nice day until she suddenly realized he'd be back from work in ten minutes, or he'd look at her during a gospel service and the sight of her seemed to get him all upset even though she was wearing a nice dress, and spotless gloves, and a smile.

I've seen Gee-Ma's wedding photos and the "Well, here goes" look her and her husband both had on their faces, but in my head Gee-Ma's husband is a colored man, not a sort of Italian-looking one. There was a man in Worcester last month . . . Aunt Mia was walking Mom and me to the bus stop and the man was huddled up in the doorway of a store that had closed up for the night. He drew even farther back into his corner when Aunt Mia tried to put some change into his hand. Words wobbled out from deep inside his beard: "Don't want no trouble, don't want no trouble, don't want no trouble." There was a glass

188

bottle in his pocket and he folded his hands around it as it bumped against the wall.

Mom tapped my shoulder to make sure I kept walking and she called out: "Just put the money beside him, Mia," but Aunt Mia didn't listen until the man pushed her hand away. Then she dropped the coins at his feet and came running after us. "Gin and pride," she said. Mom said it was most likely misery that was getting to him, not just gin or pride. Some ways of behaving seem distantly related to others. Now when I think of Gee-Ma's husband getting all upset just because she smiled at him, he looks like the man in Worcester who badly needed the money in Aunt Mia's hand and pushed it away.

Grammy Olivia says Gee-Ma Agnes's husband is weak and Gee-Ma's much better off without him. But Gee-Ma says that at heart her husband is still a boy from Itta Bena who couldn't get used to not having to take his hat off whenever he speaks to a white person. "You can't even say 'the poor fella'—not really," Gee-Ma says. "He's probably really glad to be back to Mississippi, relieved that the world's the right way up again and there are fountains specially marked out for him to drink from. I guess it's not so different from those prisoners who get to feeling at home behind bars. I forgive him." Gee-Ma Agnes talking about forgiving people tends to make Grammy Olivia say: "Indeed!" Especially when Gee-Ma tells people she forgives them before they even realize there's anything they were supposed to apologize for. But Gee-Ma probably means well when it comes to her husband, the evidence of this being that they're still married, and she remembers him in her prayers.

What I told her about me and mirrors is this:

Sometimes mirrors can't find me. I'll go into a room with a mirror in it and look around, and I'm not there. Not all the time, not even most of the time, but often enough. Sometimes when other people are there, but nobody ever notices that my reflection's a no-show. Or maybe they decide not to notice because it's too weird. I can make it happen when I move quickly and quietly, dart into a room behind the swinging of the door so it covers me the way a fan covers a face. Maybe I catch the mirror off guard somehow. It starts to look for me—"look for me" isn't quite right—I know mirrors can't see. But the image in the glass shifts just a little bit off center, left, then right, then back again, like it's wondering why it isn't reflecting all that stands in front of it. *I know a girl just came in; now where's she at?*

I swear this is true.

I'm a hide-and-seek champion. I always win. It's gotten so my friends don't want to play anymore. "Don't you think we're a little old for that now, Bird," they'll say. Or they say I cheat. Maybe I do. I don't know. Does catching the mirror off guard count as cheating? But if they had the option, there's not a one of them who wouldn't use it. Connie, Susan, Ruth, even Paula, who breaks out into a sweat every time we make her cross the road before the lights say go.

The first time it happened—this is the time I told Gee-Ma Agnes about—I got scared and I gave the mirror a whack with my shoe, trying to fix it, I guess.

It was just like any other Saturday afternoon except that I walked past my bedroom mirror and something was missing, some tiny, tiny element. I stood still, chuckling; it didn't seem serious at first. The gap grew and grew. It was me. I wasn't there. I saw the dusty blue wallpaper behind me, my hot-pink hula hoop hung on its special peg to the left of me. But I shouldn't have been able to see the whole hoop from where I stood. My head and shoulders should've been in the way, but they weren't, so I broke the mirror, and kept right on hitting it long after it broke, a cartoon mouse squeak coming out of my mouth, loud, loud. And the oval glass, that dear old glass that used to stand on my dresser, it tried to give me what I wanted, tried to give me my face, but it kept showing me bits of faces that weren't mine. There were slivers of Mom's face, and Dad's, and Aunt Mia's, and Grammy Olivia's, and others, some shreds no wider than my index finger. I don't know who they were, there was even a man or two, faces chasing each other like photographic slides when someone's trying to show you their vacation in a hurry—in the end I had to knock the frame flat and run for Mom, who vanished all the broken glass with no questions asked.

It's rare for Mom to ask me questions. Maybe she's the enemy. Seems unlikely, though. We get along, in a big-brother-little-sister kind of way. Mom plays big brother. We can sit together for hours in almost complete silence, her smoking and sharing a magazine with me, reading the other side of the page I'm on. Occasionally she'll remember where she is and make a comment: "You don't say much, do you, kid?"

"Must've learned that from you."

"Ha! Got a few ideas of your own, though, haven't you?"

"Just a few, Mom."

Mrs. Fletcher tells Mom over and over that she should be making more conversation with me, because apparently I'm at a "dangerous age." (She's got to be talking about menstruation. I haven't started yet, but there's probably some risk of bleeding to death if you're taken unawares the first time. I won't be caught unawares, though. That's not how I'm going out.) When I was too young to walk home alone, Mom would pick me up from the Chens' house, and once as we were walking through the woods she put her hand on my head. I looked up and said: "What are you touching my head for?" She said: "You know, all I expect is the unexpected. It's been like that since the day you were born, and I wouldn't have it any other way. Is there anything you need, kid? What do you need?"

It felt good when she said that. It felt like she really would do anything. Mom looks foreign, like a Russian ice skater; her backdrop ought to be one of those cities that has a skyline topped with onion-shaped domes. I can just see Mom whizzing around with her hands tucked up inside a huge white muff, bloody sparks flying up behind her as the blades on her boots dig up all the hearts she broke before Dad got to her. Customers at the bookstore tend to look surprised when Mom opens her mouth and this New York City voice comes out. Her white hair sways down in tendrils, and her skirts brush the floor—she's so graceful, swan-necked; when she's getting all dressed up, she finishes by putting on a simple necklace Dad made, and it's as good as if he took out a billboard and advertised. There's that bracelet that winds around her arm too. Even when she wears long sleeves, a platinum snake lies there beneath the cloth, draining its favorite vein drop by drop, or resting until she has instructions for it. If she ever told that snake to come after me, who could stop it? The way snakes swallow small, live creatures, the terrible way they cram their food down with their sticky fangs and their yellow eyes rejoicing—I've seen pictures.

For the longest time I thought Mom had bought the bracelet for herself, or that it was something she'd inherited, but then Dad mentioned that he'd made it for her. It isn't like anything else of his I've seen; he works a lot with wood grains and the web patterns you get on the undersides of leaves. A lot of people want to feel natural and connected to the earth right now, that's how Dad sees it, and folks don't get as excited about showy pieces as they used to. He said he made Mom's bracelet out of a misunderstanding, and Mom laughed and said: "Don't be so sure." She's tall too, tall in a way that you only really notice at certain moments. The statues of Greek gods were built two and a half times the size of the average human being; I read that in a book Miss Fairfax lent me. The book describes the magnification as being small enough for the figure to remain familiar, but large enough to make you feel mighty strange standing near it. You sense some imminent threat, but common sense tells you there's no danger, so you don't run away. You keep a distance that appears to be a respectful one, and you don't run away, just keep hovering on the point of doing so. Mom and I have the same eyes. I'm all mixed up about seeing my eyes in a face like hers, her eyes in a face like mine.

Mom told me she would get me whatever I

needed, but I didn't need anything right then. "You tell me when you do," she said. When I wanted those blue moons painted on my ceiling, she got it done without wanting to know why. We went down to the general store and got the paint right away. When we came back, she fetched out the stepladder and got the moons done in about an hour and a half including a cigarette break. She got the shape of the moons exactly right too. One thing to keep in mind with Mom is that I'd better be sure I really need something before I ask her for it, because she doesn't give advice. For example, stucco moons might have been better. But you tell Mom "Blue moons, please," and bam, there they are, enjoy! We're not close the way Louis and his mom are close, but . . . while she dabbed away at the ceiling I danced in and out of the room with her ashtray, singing along to the radio: *La la means I love you,* words I was too shy to say to her without the music, words I don't remember her ever saying to me. Mom was the only one who immediately saw that I'd dressed up as Alice in Wonderland for fancy-dress day at school. The costume made it glaringly obvious— the white ankle socks, the black Mary Janes, the fat ribbon tied in a bow around my head, the blue dress with the blue and white apron over it—it's in all the picture books. But when I came downstairs, Dad said: "What a pretty little house-keeper!"

Mom laughed. "Is that what Alice grew up to be?" Then Dad said: "Alice . . . ?" and looked at me again with his head to one side, and we realized he seriously thought I'd dressed up as a housekeeper. He began: "But Alice . . ." and Mom said: "Yes? What? What's that about Alice?" and he mumbled something about Alice's hair being long and suddenly became fascinated with the newspaper. But everyone was like that, all day. "Who are you supposed to be?" they'd say, giving up after guessing "housekeeper" or "washer-woman." Then the next thing would be: "But Alice . . ." the beginning of a sentence nobody seemed to know how to finish. Louis Chen's sailor "costume" went over well, maybe because it was real—his grandfather had worn it when he'd been a crew member on a fishing boat off the West Coast about a million years ago. He tried to give his award for best costume to me; he said mine was much better (once I'd explained it to him) but I couldn't let him do that. He'd won fair and square. After school Mom and I went into the photo booth at the Mitchell Street diner and pulled terrible faces to scare away people who don't know Alice when they see her, but in the last box of the photo strip we're having a laughing fit. It turns out that the average annoyed American only needs to pull three terrible faces before she feels better.

Who says Gee-Ma knows all there is to know

about the reasons why a person might not show up in a mirror, anyway?

Possibilities:

a. It's an optical illusion or a symptom of eye disease. (Eye disease doubtful: The optician has my vision down as 20/15 in both eyes and says that if I keep eating my greens and don't try to read by flashlight I can be an airplane pilot if I want, fly for real like every Bird should.)

b. I'm not human. (Pretty sure that I'm physically and emotionally similar to all the other kids I know. There's maybe even just a little more emotion than there's supposed to be, like on school mornings when Louis jumps into the seat I've been saving for him and I get a little dizzy because he's so close and I want to tell him I missed him even though it's been less than sixteen hours since we last said good-bye, even though he just burped me "Good morning" in a grossly immature way. One day I couldn't bite back the "I missed you," and he nudged me with his elbow and said: "Uh . . . I guess I missed you too, weirdo." As for vampirism, a love of sunny days and garlic bread makes *that* very improbable.)

c. The enemy thing. Someone wishing and willing me out of sight. (Me: *That's kind of an exciting thought, being that big of a deal to someone.* Gee-Ma Agnes: *Sometimes I think you're almost grown up, then all of a sudden it looks like you've got a long way to go.* I'd love to get her back for that one day, just clap a hand to my forehead and say: "Oh! Sometimes I think you're a member of the teenaged set, then it hits me that you're ancient." Of course that's only a fantasy—Gee-Ma knows exactly when to get tears in her eyes and make you feel like a criminal. I asked her to teach me how to do it once and she welled up right there and then said: "I don't understand what you're asking me, child.")

d. "Enchantments be not always ill." (An unknown friend with good intentions?)

e. This is something that happens to everybody but they deny it.

f. I'm a nut job. (No comment.)

Maybe I need to try to look at this from the outside, get some facts down.

What is known about this Bird Whitman?

She's thirteen years old, and still looking for a way to put an extra two years on somehow, so she can catch up to Louis Chen. He says it can't be done and he'll always be older, but given the way mirrors have been behaving lately, anything's possible.

She tells everyone her middle name is Novak. All her friends have middle names and she'll be damned if she has to go without one.

Her dad prefers the waffles she makes to the ones her mom makes. The secret is buttermilk.

She's five feet and four inches tall, already quite a lot taller than her girlfriends, and she hasn't finished growing yet; where will it end? Gee-Ma Agnes says Bird is getting to be "as tall as Annie Christmas," and Annie Christmas was an actual giant (if she existed at all), and while Bird has got nothing against giants, she refuses to stand taller than five feet and six inches without shoes. This is simply a matter of personal taste. All right, fine— Louis Chen just happens to be exactly five feet, six and three-quarter inches tall and reckons he'll go up another couple of inches and then call it a day.

Her best friend's family makes her realize that her own family isn't as happy as it could be. The Whitmans aren't *un*happy. But the Chens are so much more . . . together, always have about a million things to tell each other, keep trying to make each other laugh. Louis rushes his dinner on

the evenings his mom's around to give him
driving lessons, and his father takes him by the
wrist and recites *Climb Mount Fuji, / O Snail, /
but slowly, slowly.* That makes Louis slow down,
as well as making him smile. He looks up to his
dad. Mr. Chen works at the piano bar on Tubman
Street; the crowd's more mixed than it used to
be, but it's still mostly only colored people.
According to Mrs. Chen, some of the regulars,
especially the old ones, still stare at Mr. Chen as if
they never saw an Asian man before. Some of
them ask him how he learned to play ragtime so
good when he wasn't born with it in his soul, and
Mr. Chen just looks at them all through a pair of
opera glasses and says: "Ha ha." Even if there
hadn't been Chens in New Orleans since 1900,
Mr. Chen would still have jazz in his soul, I think.
Mrs. Chen picks him up in her taxi and when they
get home, they count up the day's tips. Mrs. Chen
claims never to get nervous about driving her
taxi. She says she's got an instinct about who to
let into the car and who not to.

Mr. and Mrs. Chen are raising Louis to believe
that he can be good at anything he wants to be, if
only he keeps at it. Louis is the only kid the Chens
have, and they act like he's all the kid they want.
Louis likes to tease Bird that the two of them are
going to live in Flax Hill forever, him driving a
taxi just like his mom, her making her way up to
chief editor of the *Flax Hill Record*, both of them

getting a little restless during butterfly season. But Bird won't even let him joke about it. They're getting out. Manhattan looks good, loud, and busy. If not there, then LA, where he'll set up a management agency and turn starlets into big names and she'll start out writing gossipy pieces until she gets the chance to do in-depth profiles.

Bird has an older sister. Snow. They've met, but that was when Bird was a baby, so it doesn't really count. It isn't clear why Snow doesn't live with Bird and her parents, but she comes up in conversation a lot, as if she's expected to walk in the door at any moment.

Gee-Ma Agnes: *Snow's getting to be so green-fingered; that mint she grows freshens up iced tea just like a charm.*

Gee-Pa Gerald: *Did I tell you about the crossword Snow and I did together over the phone? That girl persuaded me it's better for our brains if we just put in any old letters and call it a word afterward. Then we talked definitions. "Hujus," for instance—what do you reckon one of those is? Go ahead and guess; you'll never get it.*

Grammy Olivia: *Gerald, do you think this so-called bebop Snow listens to might be real music after all? I almost hear it but I'm not sure. I thought we'd heard the last of that noise ten, fifteen years ago.*

Snow, Snow, Snow, blah blah blah. Bird's mom

doesn't talk about Snow; she just listens to the others talking about Snow and she gets that look people get when they feel like they're being bored to death and there's nothing they can do about it. Two weekends a month, three times on Snow's birthday month, Bird's father goes to Boston and comes back with bright eyes, a sprig of fresh flowers in his buttonhole, and photographs to show Bird and the grandparents down at number eleven. Bird never knows what to say when she looks at the photographs of her father with another daughter who was there first, had him first. Snow looks like a friend to woodland creatures; a unicorn would lay its head down on her lap, and everybody knows how picky unicorns are. Or, in the here and now, Snow could easily be one of those girls who've been in the news for going around singing "Peace, peace" and offering soldiers flowers to hold along with their guns, making the soldiers choose between bad manners and looking ridiculous. Bird has heard a story (she doesn't think it's the whole story) about her dad and her mom setting out to visit Snow one weekend. Apparently they took Bird along with them, but just as they arrived in Boston, Bird's mom made Bird's dad turn the car around and drive all the way back home again. Bird's dad is big on finishing what he's started—"It's all about the follow-through, it's all about the follow-through," so Bird's mom must have said or done something pretty spectacular to make him turn around like that.

Bird played a little fact-finding prank one day (and was surprised that it began to work) but was foiled by circumstance. The prank Bird pulled was voice imitation. Bird's been talked at by Gee-Ma Agnes for so many hours of her life that she knows exactly how Gee-Ma Agnes sounds. Not just her accent, the crystal-clear elocution wrapped around the raw Mississippi molasses, but also the way she breathes between some words and mashes others together and stresses half of a word and lets the other half slip away. When Gee-Ma Agnes says "I do declare!" it has an entirely different effect than when Grammy Olivia says it. It was Grammy Olivia whom Bird fooled that afternoon; Bird was in Gee-Ma Agnes's bedroom and Grammy Olivia was busy folding clothes next door. Phoebe the maid had just brought the week's wash back from the laundromat. "Agnes, come get your good pajamas and this bed jacket before I steal them," Grammy Olivia called out, and Bird realized Grammy Olivia had forgotten that Gee-Ma Agnes had gone to hear an afternoon lecture on mystic poetry that Kazim Bey was giving in the church hall. Grammy Olivia considered Kazim Bey to be of questionable character because he inked comics for Marvel and any day now there'd be scientific proof that superhero comics and 3-D movie theater glasses were leading causes of insanity. Also Mr. Bey was from a Nation of Islam family and all Grammy Olivia knew about the Nation of Islam was that they wore black suits all the time and they were "too polite . . . like undertakers, or Englishmen."

"Agnes," Grammy Olivia said. "Agnes!" Then she remembered Gee-Ma Agnes had left half an hour before and muttered to herself that if the maid had heard, she was going to start thinking she could slack off whenever she pleased. Up until that moment Bird had been reading a copy of Gee-Ma Agnes's Last Will and Testament. Gee-Ma had given her permission—well, she'd said it didn't matter whether Bird read it or not because she didn't suppose Bird would be able to understand much of it. Bird understood enough. She understood that Gee-Ma was leaving all her earthly possessions, stocks and bonds and whatnot, to Snow Whitman. One exception was a houseboat currently moored in a residential harbor in Biloxi, Mississippi, and another was a lapis lazuli anklet "fit for a harem girl," both of which Gee-Ma was leaving to Bird so she could have the wild times Gee-Ma never got around to having. Bird found the thought of dancing around a houseboat with a precious anklet on pretty satisfactory, but was ready to swap the houseboat and anklet in exchange for Gee-Ma having the wild times herself and just keeping on living. Gee-Ma reckons death isn't anything to run toward, but it certainly isn't anything to run from, either. She reckons it must be just like sleeping, and sleeping is something she's always looked forward to at the end of a long day. Both Gee-Ma Agnes and Grammy Olivia have their funerals and coffins and burial plots all paid for, only Grammy Olivia also has a guest list for her funeral and strict instructions that anybody who isn't on the list can't come in. This makes Bird's dad laugh and sigh at the same time and intrigues Bird, because it suggests Grammy Olivia is worried about unsavory characters from her past showing up to damage her reputation. There must be something about having your hands on someone's signed and dated Last Will and Testament that gives you the nerve to impersonate her. Bird decided to try one tiny little sentence that she could laugh off if Grammy Olivia wasn't fooled: "No, I'm here, Livia . . . I'm here."

"So do I bring you your night things, Agnes? Is that how it is now, you just sleeping all the time and me waiting on you hand and foot?" Grammy Olivia wanted to know.

"I'll come get it in a while, Livia . . . you always were in a hurry," Bird said, and covered her mouth with her hand afterward, laughing silently. "I was thinking, you know, about that time our son went out to visit Snow and Boy made him turn the car around . . . just as they were almost there. Really seems kinda *flighty* of Boy, doesn't it?"

Grammy Olivia sniffed. "Don't think on it too long," she said. "She knows what she's doing to that child, that's why she can't face her. And you know what I've told the woman. You know I told her she better beware the Gullah in me. I told her 'If Agnes dies or I die, if either one of us dies before you let our baby come home, you'll find there's a curse on your head.' She said fighting talk only makes her stubborn. Well, I warned her."

Bird was thinking up her next question when Gee-Ma Agnes returned and called up the stairs: "Well, the whole thing would probably have left you stone cold, Livia, but I like what those mystics say. How 'bout this: *Gamble everything for love—if you are a true human being—if not, leave this gathering!*" Grammy Olivia said: *"Agnes?"* and came to see who was in Gee-Ma's bedroom, but by then Bird had already stepped into Gee-Ma's wardrobe and was holding bunches of clothes hangers still with both hands behind the closed wooden door. You may be sure that since then Bird has been practicing her voice imitations, with future opportunities in mind. She can't do her mom, but any other woman who's spoken to Bird more than a couple of times is a snap to imitate. This is a secret skill, and nothing that would make a grandmother proud.

Grammy Olivia looks at the pictures of Bird's father laughing with his other daughter and she shakes her head and sighs. Snow's studying history at college, just like Bird's father did, and Bird's grades . . . well, Bird's grades are below average. "Who's the better daughter?" Bird asks her father. "Me or Snow?"

He kisses her forehead and says: "Snow in winter, you in spring, Snow in summer, you in the fall."

Bird sleeps in the same room Snow used to sleep in. Wait . . . there might be something in that. The mirror stuff only tends to happen in a handful of places. A couple of rooms in Bird's house and a couple of rooms over at her grandma's—if Bird takes a seat in the chair beside Gee-Ma Agnes's bed, there's almost guaranteed invisibility there, for example—maybe it happens when she steps into spots that belong to this other girl named Snow? There's a photograph of Snow's mother in Bird's bottom drawer—no one's had the nerve to take it out of the room. There's a piano in the house that nobody plays—it doesn't pick fights with anybody and it doesn't draw any particular attention to itself. Visitors can talk about it if they like, they can ask, "Hey, is that piano in tune?" but instead of an answer they get: "Well, it's Julia's piano." That piano is staying where it is, and Julia Whitman is calm inside her photo frame. She'll see her daughter again, she has no doubts about that. Could Snow be the enemy (or the friend)?

If Snow came back and asked for her room, that would certainly not be okay with Bird. Bird really likes her bedroom. There are quite a few cobwebs in it and Bird has no intention of tampering with a single one of them, no matter how many times her mom says her room is a disgrace. At the very most Bird might dust a cobweb off with the tip of a feather, but only to keep it looking spick-and-span. A lot of the time there are tiny memorials on the walls, in the corner behind the wardrobe, little specks only Bird and the spiders understand the importance of. Flies and other weaker insects have fought epic battles against the spiders and they've lost, leaving behind them a layer of a wing, or a thin black leg joint that holds to the wallpaper for as long as it can before drying out and peeling away. Bird enjoys the stealthy company of the spiders, and in all other respects her room is tidy. Her mom has asked her if she thinks she'll continue to enjoy the stealthy company of the spiders after one of them has taken a bite out of her, and Bird answers: "We'll see." In the evening, when the street lamp just outside Bird's window switches on, the gray cobwebs quiver and glow around the blue moons. It's the kind of view that Bird doesn't mind risking a spider bite for. Back when she used to say bedtime prayers, right after she'd prayed for her mom and her dad and her grandparents and the Chens and Aunt Mia and Snow and anybody who was sick or in trouble or all alone, Bird would throw in seven words for herself: *Let spiders spin webs in my hair.* It'd be great if they could be persuaded to spin little hats for her, dusty towers of thread that lean and whisper. Sometimes she gets tired of hearing nonsense from people who think they're talking sense; it makes her want people to be scared of her, or at least to hesitate the way they sometimes do around Louis because "I don't know . . . maybe he knows kung fu or something." If she were Louis, she'd take advantage of that, though on the other hand she supposes allowing people to believe that you were born knowing how to destroy a man with a simple kick could backfire. No, a spiderweb hat is a better warning to beware. Bird would look out from under this hat with the watchful eyes of a girl from long ago, each pupil an unlit lamp, waiting for the magic ring to be rubbed, for the right words to be said. She'd give a lot to know why she and her mom have those eyes—the eyes of people who come from someplace strange they can never go back to. Bird and her mom and that servant-of-the-lamp look they go around giving people. Bird can't think of a single excuse for it. She's just as much her dad as she is her mom, and her dad's all darting flashes of warmth; he laughs, he holds both your hands, and his eyes tell you that here is here and now is now. That must be how he manages to go back and forth between those two daughters of his without getting all torn up. Snow goes to the back of his mind when Bird's at the front of it, and vice versa. How could he ever have taught history?

Looking at this from the outside makes me afraid, as if I'm not Bird at all, and never was. Gee-Ma makes no allowance for me being a middle school kid when she talks to me, but then again I think she's getting less and less able or willing to fix her mind on exactly who it is she's talking to. When she calls me "child," it feels as if she were trying to turn me into a different girl, the one she'd rather have there with her. There. It's said.

Dad always comes back from Boston with something Snow wants me to have. The stuff she sends isn't quite right for me—pairs of pink hair ribbons, meant for pigtails, for instance. I wear my hair short. I mean short-short. It looks like a cap of curls clinging to my head and I like that better than braids or bushiness. (Bushiness looks so good, but hurts so bad under the comb. I used to have to go to Tubman Street to get my hair braided. Maybe Merva Fairfax wove blessings or ill wishes into my hair with her nimble fingers . . .) Snow might think this is just a phase I'm going through and that I'll want to grow my hair out soon. Pink, though? No.

Other things Snow has sent me: papier-mâché wings to wear on my shoulders . . . those looked great, but didn't fit. The straps were too small, or my arms too big. There was also an unusual music box that I found cute in the daytime. My idea of a music box used to be that it was a nice version of a jack-in-the-box—all you had to do was open the lid and the music twinkled out at you and maybe there was a ballerina twirling around in there too. This music box didn't have a lid. The display case was a wolf, stood on all four paws, and made of cloudy gray glass that looked as if it were full of breath. His head was lowered to the ground and his tongue was sticking out a little bit—you could almost hear him panting. He had a hole right in the middle of him, bigger than his stomach could ever be, really it was heart space, lung space, and stomach space combined. The hole was filled by a little tin doll, painted peach, smiling and wearing a red felt cape. She had a lot of joints to her and you could take her out of the wolf's stomach and stuff her in again. To hear the music wound up inside her you had to turn a key. I couldn't do it without wincing. Having to turn that key in her back just to hear thirty seconds of *Peter and the Wolf* . . . her smile was so hopeful: *Ya having fun? Are ya, are ya?*

When it got dark, I didn't like to turn my back on the music box. It never made any moves. I think it was me who changed. At night I tend to wonder where things come from. I'd look at the wolf and at Red Riding Hood with her knees up, not even playing dead, openly living there, and I'd try to think who could've made them and what that person meant by it. It wasn't like the things people make around here, which are just so pretty they make you smile and feel lucky and rich just to be looking at them. The music box was closer to the snake on Mom's arm. That was another gift that had to be given away in the end, like the wings were. It isn't Snow's fault; it's just that we don't know each other.

# 2

*d* ad says newspapers don't hire reporters with bad grades. Aunt Mia says grades aren't as important as being able to learn on the job. I know whom I'd rather believe. It'd be nice to get an A for once, but that would mean getting organized and doing all my homework at home instead of scribbling a few half-witted sentences about *The Adventures of Tom Sawyer* or whatever it is at lunch break an hour before the report is due. I'm not completely hardened. I do still die a little bit inside when Miss Fairfax holds an essay of mine up to the light and asks: "Bird Whitman, do I see mayonnaise? Again?" That leads to me doing more homework in detention, where I work with an eye on the clock and often don't finish a sentence if it means staying a second longer than I have to. Louis waits for me, and every time he waits he says it's the last time. He only talks like that to show his independence; the boys in his class see him waiting and say I've got him well trained. I just look at him and say: "You're a pal, Louis." I tell him I don't take him for granted. I tell him I honestly don't know why he bothers with me. And he actually *blushes*—it's the cutest thing in the world—and grabs my schoolbag and carries it to our next destination. Class work in class, and homework at home, I'd be a better student and a better daughter if I stuck to that, but I went and had a bad Monday at school and I brought it home with me.

It started at recess. I was lying on a bench listening to Connie Ross going over her half of the poem we'd had to learn for Spanish class: *Caminante, son tus huellas / el camino, y nada más; / caminante, no hay camino . . .* it was a poem I was falling in love with, I think. I must've been, because I'd whisper a couple of lines from it to myself or to the cobwebs: *Wanderer, there is no road, the road is made by walking.* The poem tells me it's no big deal that I'm not like Snow. I can be another thing; I'm meant to be another thing.

Connie practiced and then I practiced, and we were excited, we were word perfect, maybe I was going to get my first A grade for this. Louis was a few yards away, playing at being a boxer; he and Jerry Fallon were mainly just sidestepping and jabbing their fists at each other, occasionally taking a dive as one or the other of them got hit by a fake knockout punch. Louis was commentating as well as fighting: "I'm Ah Wing Lee, Oregon State's Chinese Lullaby, you're Hubert 'Kid' Dennis of Montana, the year is 1933, we're in Portland and this is our grudge match—yeah, you defeated me once, but once is all you get—you spring left, I spring left—"

A girl in Louis's class named Barbara Thomas stepped up, beckoned to Louis, and whispered in his ear. It's not that I'm the jealous type—I noticed that he'd stopped commentating before I noticed the girl Barbara whispering away into his ear. When she'd finished, he laughed, shrugged, said he wasn't going to waste any steam on a dumb prank, and went back to his boxing match. I knew that fight and commentary inside out from reenactments in Louis's front yard. "I swing . . . you duck right . . . you think maybe you stand a chance, you come up and find yourself in the middle of a storm, there's nowhere to turn, fists coming at you from every which way, you guard your head on one side and there's already another knock incoming on the other side—you're about to drop, oh, you're down!"

When it's just he and I, Louis lets me be Ah Wing Lee. Each time he switches to the role of referee at the end and lifts my arm and declares me the winner, I go weak at the knees for real. How corny is that?

I'd been minding the boy's jacket, and when he

came over to the bench for it, I asked him what Barbara had been whispering about. He didn't want to tell me, said I didn't own him and he could have a private conversation with any girl he pleased, but I broke him down in the end. Someone had written LOUIS CHEN IS A VIETCONG in yellow chalk down at the other end of the school yard. Barbara wanted him to hear it from a friend first.

"That's not actually the dumbest thing I ever heard, but it's in the top ten," was all I said, and we went back to class and forgot about it until the head teacher's voice came over the PA system, instructing the "person or persons responsible for the yellow-chalk graffiti" to report to his office immediately.

So then everyone started asking each other, "What graffiti?" Some people had already seen it, and they told what they'd seen while others looked at me as if they expected to hear my opinion. There was no opinion for me to give. I said to Connie: "Dumb, right?" Connie said: "We're above and beyond this," and we went up and began to say the poem we'd learned, but the headmaster got back onto the PA system and cut my part of the recital in half. No one had turned themselves in, so he'd selected two members of the tenth grade at random—they were to go and scrub the wall immediately, remaining in the yard for as long as it took to remove the graffiti. He stressed that he didn't think the two boys he was about to name were the culprits, but one of the boys was Louis's friend Jerry Fallon. That sucked. It also got the whole class talking again—some people coughed out "Vietcong" into their hands while my Spanish dried up, and I wondered how big the letters chalked onto that wall were, that two people were needed to scrub them away.

By the end of the next lesson, word had got around that Louis was inviting whoever it was who had made the Vietcong jibe to meet him on the corner of Ivorydown and Pierce Road at three forty-five p.m. sharp, where he'd school them in geography the hard way. That's a lonely turning off Ivorydown, a spot eleventh graders choose for robbing ninth and tenth graders of their lunch money. I met Louis by his locker and said: "Tell me it's a rumor. You're not really going to fight over this?"

He said: "Stay out of it."

"What's changed since recess?"

Louis sighed. "It's getting out of hand. People are saying stuff. Gotta shut 'em up. You've got detention anyway. Call me at six and I'll tell you what happened."

There was no time to get any more out of him, but in my math class I heard so much idiocy I could hardly stand it.

"I'll bet Chen wrote that himself, just 'cause he felt like getting talked about today."

"He probably *is* a Vietcong."

"Vietcong just love coloreds. And coloreds love them right back."

I forced a laugh. Sometimes all the other kids want is for you to show you're a good sport. If you stand out, you can't expect people not to mention it.

"Yeah, like that boxer . . ." That was Larry Saunders, pretending he couldn't remember Muhammad Ali's name when it was practically written on his heart. "Didn't he say he's on their side? He won't fight in Vietnam 'cause he's an American Vietcong."

"He didn't say that," I pointed out, on the brink of flipping my table over and my neighbor's too. "He just said he didn't have any quarrel with them. It's not the same thing."

"Words, words. If you're not fighting 'em, you're on their side," Kenneth Young said. Kenneth and Larry both have fathers who served in Korea, and they talk about their big brothers who are serving the country right now—Larry's big brother is an air force officer and fits the muscle-bound action man profile pretty well, but Kenneth's brother works at a naval base. Kenneth calls it "security" and makes out that his brother is important—I asked Dad and apparently "security" means checking passes and pushing buttons to open doors. Big deal. But Dad says that both Kenneth and Larry are afraid that their brothers will get badly injured or die. "Their brothers are their heroes, and if anything happens to William Saunders or Robert Young, Kenneth and Larry might blame everyone around them, because we're the citizens those men will have died for, and maybe they won't believe we were worth it. Are we? Have we ever been worth it, any of the times before?" Dad was having a Gee-Ma moment when he said that; he was talking to somebody who wasn't me, somebody who answered silently and made him hang his head. (I have a letter to Snow that I never sent. *Dear Snow, Have you really got to be everywhere?*) I was supposed to be in bed, and Dad was just talking. Late at night in the parlor, with a drink in his hand, telling his thoughts to Julia's piano. If Mom had been there, she'd have said "Oh Lord" and made him eat something to soak up the drink.

Okay, so Kenneth Young was bound to feel some type of way about people who deny that there's any duty for them to do. And "Shut up, Fat Kenneth" wasn't the most mature or persuasive response I could've made to him, but I had a feeling that Connie, Ruth, and Paula would've studied their fingernails and failed to back me up no matter what I'd said. The others went on and on. They sounded like they were kidding around, but the things they said—*Colored folks are so angry these days, lose their rag over nothing at all, rawwwrrrr, like wild animals. My dad says those Black Panthers are Vietcongs just waiting to happen. Give 'em an inch and they'll take a mile, gun us all down in broad daylight.*

I skipped detention. I was first out of my history class and met Louis at the school gates; it was easy to spot him because he was on his own, exposed, down on one knee tying his shoelace. I put my foot down next to his.

"Hi."

He didn't look up, took his time getting the bow to droop just right. "Hi."

"Let's go."

"You're not involved."

"The hell I'm not. You need me. If it turns out to be a girl we're up against, I'll punch her for you. Hurry, before Miss Fairfax comes."

The other kids went quiet when we walked past them, but we didn't look behind us to see if we were being followed. He said he'd told his other friends not to come. That shouldn't have stopped them, but there was no point in saying so. He didn't seem worried at all, but I was shaking. I don't like real fights because people get so caught up in them, even watching them you get all caught up in them, and if that's what it's like watching them, how do the people who are right in the middle of the fight know how to find their way to the end of it alive? A few years ago one boxer killed another in the ring, just kept hitting him and hitting him, didn't realize the other guy was dead, didn't mean to kill him, just wanted to win. I won't let Louis take up that sport professionally. He's going to have to find something else to do. Louis's arm brushed mine and for a moment I thought he was going to try to hold my hand. "Don't even think about it," I said. We'd never have lived it down if anyone saw.

"You're really pretty, Bird," he said, looking straight ahead of us. We were walking up Ivorydown, and the wind was blowing leaf scraps into our eyes.

"You don't have to say that."

I'd have liked for him to say my name again, though. You know how it is when someone says your name really well, like it means something that makes the world a better place. In Louis Chen's case, he sometimes says my name as if it were a lesser-known word for bacon.

"I wanted to say it," he said. "Don't get big-headed, but I think you're the prettiest girl in school."

I pretended not to hear. We reached the corner of Pierce Road and Ivorydown and waited with our backs up against the rough bark of a tree trunk. After ten minutes we decided, with a mixture of disgust and relief, that Yellow Chalk Guy (or Girl) wasn't going to show, and we were ready to leave when three hefty boys from the eleventh grade turned up. These three didn't take lunch money; they were less predictable than that. They might stop you and give you a stash of comic books, or they might rip up your homework. We knew their names, but never said them in case it made them appear. One of them was directly descended from Nathaniel Hawthorne who wrote *The Scarlet Letter*; that one's mother had mentioned it at one of Grammy Olivia's coffee hours. Mom says everybody immediately began to feel oppressed by their humble backgrounds because they'd forgotten (or didn't know) that anyone who's descended from Nathaniel Hawthorne is also a descendant of John Hathorne, the Salem judge who put just about as many innocent people to death as he could, so was it any wonder that Hawthorne was so good at describing what it felt like to be racked with guilt day and night.

"Did we miss it? Did he show up yet?" one of the eleventh graders asked.

"Who?" I asked, since Louis was taking too long to reply.

"The guy who called your friend here a Vietcong."

"Do you think we'd still be standing here if he had shown up? What do you think we'd be doing here?" I asked. I got away with it because I put the question as if I were curious rather than just giving sass. But one of the boys told Louis: "I guess your girlfriend likes to talk."

More kids showed up, in threes and fours and fives. They stood at a distance from us, filling the newcomers in on what was happening. "They're waiting for the guy who called that boy there a Vietcong. Boy got sore about it, says he's going to bust this other guy's head." Within half an hour we were surrounded, Louis and me, caught in a circle of snickering kids, without a single one of our lousy so-called friends in sight. Louis checked his watch and took a couple of steps forward, trying to look purposeful, I guess, trying to look like a boy who didn't know about everybody else but he was going home. Nobody said we couldn't leave, but the circle got tighter and people stood shoulder to shoulder.

"He'll be here soon enough," someone said. It sounded like Fat Kenneth Young.

"Yeah, he probably just had detention."

"Patience, my friends, patience," said the eleventh grader with the witch-hunter's blood.

It was around then that I began to be sure that the person who'd started the whole thing was right there in the circle, hidden like a worm in an apple, and I hated him or her like I hate all sneaks.

"Just come on out," I said. "Come out right now."

"Who are you talking to?" said a long-faced boy with red-rimmed eyes. "Hey, is she talking to me?"

Louis gave me a nod. Somebody was going to get their head busted no matter what, and it looked like he'd just picked that somebody at random. He put his fists up, the circle around us broke, poked apart with the steel tip of a parasol, and Grammy Olivia looked through the gap and said: "What in the world is all this? Louis Chen, I hope you don't intend to hit a girl for the entertainment of these feral beasts gathered here."

They let us pass. They muttered, but they let us pass. It put me in awe of Grammy Olivia's Saturday morning coffee hour, because that was part of the reason we went in peace—everyone's mother, aunt, grandmother, or great-aunt goes to Grammy Olivia's coffee hour. Also Gee-Pa Gerald regularly plays golf with Worcester's chief of police, et cetera. Also Grammy Olivia's tone of voice offers you ten seconds to do as she says or the rest of your life to be sincerely sorry that you didn't.

She walked ahead of us without turning around, Louis nudged me good-bye and peeled off in the direction of his house, and I went up to her as she was letting herself in at her front door. "Thanks, Grammy Olivia." She frowned, picked a leaf out of my hair, and said: "You're welcome, Bird."

I'd have liked to ask her about what had happened over on Ivorydown; she seemed to understand it. But I didn't because I thought I might cry while asking her and then she'd wash her hands of me altogether. Grammy Olivia's got no time for weeping willows; I've heard her say so.

Dad was in the parlor, reading the paper and tugging at the collar of his shirt. Dad in a suit is a persecuted man. I asked him what the state of the nation was, and he said the president had taken it into his head to raise taxes and so everybody was probably going to move to Canada out of spite. On a more local level, good old Flax Hill would probably last just about another day. A new restaurant had opened on Colby Street, and Mom and Dad wanted to see about the food there, so they'd booked a table and were going to share it with their friends the Murrays. "Can you see if your mom's ready to leave?"

"Oh . . . is she doing that 'every question you ask me adds half an hour to your waiting time' thing again?"

"She's a hard woman, Bird."

Upstairs Mom checked her lipstick while I stood behind her holding two pairs of earrings, a pair in each hand. She'd picked them out and couldn't decide which to wear. In the mirror I looked like her maid, and that made me want to throw the earrings at her head and run.

For reasons of my own I take note of the way people act when they're around mirrors. Grammy Olivia avoids her own gaze and looks at her hair. Gee-Ma Agnes peeps reluctantly and then looks glad, like her reflection's so much better than she could have hoped for. Aunt Mia shakes her head a little, *Oh, so it's you again, is it?* Louis tenses and then relaxes—*Who's that? Oh, all right, I guess I can live with him.* Dad looks quietly irritated by his reflection, like it just said something he strongly disagrees with. Mom locks eyes with hers. She's one of the few people I've observed who seems to be trying to catch her reflection out, willing it to make one false move. She waved away the earrings I held and reached for a third pair. Gold pendulums. They swung hypnotically, and we looked at each other with those eyes of ours that are so similar.

I asked her what Snow was like. "She's okay if you like that sort of thing," Mom said. Denise Arnold had said that about the gold-plated fountain pen Gee-Pa Gerald gave me last birthday. I guess it's a thing you say when you're jealous and don't have the guts to come right out and be sincerely nasty.

"I don't get it; do you like that sort of thing or not?" I muttered under my breath. Mom kept letters from Snow. She opened them and must have read them, and she kept them in her jewelry box. There weren't very many, maybe about ten. I'd seen them, but I'd been biding my time. You can't bide your time forever. I gave Mom a chance to say whatever she wanted to say about Snow, and that was all she wanted to say. So once she and Dad had left for their dinner date I took the letters and I read them. Afterward I felt less sure that Mom wasn't the enemy. Of course her replies weren't there, so I wasn't getting her side of the story. But it looked bad. There'd been months and sometimes years between each letter, so the handwriting changed. It started off big and wonky and basic.

Dear Boy,
How are you? I hope you're feeling better. How's Bird? Aunt Clara and Uncle John are nice but I don't like it here.
All my love,
Snow

Dear Boy,
Don't you miss me? I miss you and Bird and everybody. Uncle John is like a big ~~black~~ dark mountain and he laughs so loud it makes me jump. Remember you said I could come home thirty days ago.
All my love,
Snow

After a few more letters, Snow learned cursive.

Uncle John and Aunt Clara are perfect treasures. I'm afraid that the way I laugh might be too loud for you now. Dad tells me I make quite a racket. I figured that if I couldn't beat Uncle J, I'd better join him.

In the later letters she shortened "All my love" to AML, then she dropped it.

> You were like some sort of glorious princess who swept into my life and I just wanted to sit at your feet all day and amuse you. Did that get on your nerves? It's really stupid of me, but I can't see what it was that came between us. Will you try to explain it to me?

That one got me. According to my calculations, Snow would have written that when she was fifteen. She stopped asking how I was and started asking what I was like. She stopped asking to come home and started asking just to visit.

The last letter was a year old, and addressed to me. Mom had opened it and read it and then slipped it into the jewelry box along with the others.

> Hi, Bird,
>
> It's your sister here. Can you read yet? I hope so. I've seen pictures of you and you've grown so much I don't recognize you. You look like a super stylish tomboy. The kind of girl who wouldn't have spoken to me when I was your age and probably still wouldn't speak to me now. I'm sorry we haven't been able to spend

time together, but what do you say we catch up? I'm afraid I've been forgetting you. I used to think I knew all these things about you, but now I can't remember what they were, and anyway, how much can you know about a baby that's a few months old? I'd love it if you wrote to me with some information about your personality.

Yours affectionately,
Snow

I put all the letters back where I found them, all except the one that was mine. That one I wrote a reply to. Well, ten replies. Fifteen. Each one contained too much of something. One reply was too chatty, another too dry, yet another too blunt. Mom was on my mind. My writing to Snow was me apologizing for Mom, in a way, even if I didn't mention her. That was the problem. Mom, the glorious princess who swept into Snow's life and then kicked her out without a word of explanation. I got overwhelmed and climbed into my bed, pulled the covers over my head. A weight gathered on my forehead and another one landed bang in the middle of my chest. There was something false about the pain—it wasn't even anatomically correct. I was ashamed that I couldn't switch it off even though I knew it wasn't a truthful pain.

*Don't you let this get the better of you, Bird,* I said to myself. *You write to Snow and let her know she's got a sister if she still wants one.* I wonder if Snow knows that story; I don't remember all of it, but at one point a woman takes two toads, the ugliest she can find, and she whispers spells to them and sends them to her stepdaughter's bath, where they're supposed to lie on the girl's head and her heart and make the girl ugly inside and out. And the toads do as they're told, they find the girl and one jumps up onto her head and the other onto her heart, but in the blink of an eye they turn to roses, because that girl's the real deal and there's no harming her.

The phone rang. I knew it was Louis, and I patted the phone apologetically as I walked past it. Dad has a photograph of Snow in a heart-shaped frame, beside the one of me and him and Mom wearing cotton-candy beards. I unlocked Dad's studio and sat there looking at Snow and her soft, open smile and the pink bow in her long wavy hair. I looked at her until I began to feel as if she could see me and was smiling specifically at me, and then I started my reply all over again.

Dear Snow,

Yes, I can read now. I don't recall ever having met you, but I'm sure that even as a baby I must have been very proud to be associated with a girl like you whom I've only ever heard good things about. I'm your usual kind of thirteen year old with the usual kind of personality—usual kind of usual kind of, good grief, oh well—except that I don't always show up in mirrors. I'm hoping that might help me in my future career someday, though I'm not yet sure exactly how. I don't know what's deceived you into thinking I'm cool, but if it's the way I turn up the cuffs of my pants, I only do that because Hannah Philby came back from her French vacation wearing her pants that way and everyone said "ooh la la" and copied her. So you see I do what I can to be just like everybody else.

Please tell me more about yourself (you're almost twenty-one now, is that right?) and about Uncle John and Aunt Clara, and I hope it won't be too much trouble for you to address your reply to me care of Louis Chen at 17 Duke Street. To tell you the truth I'm getting shy, Snow, so I'll have to give you the info about Louis Chen next time and end this letter here.

Just your usual kind of sister,
Bird Whitman

PS—Can I ask you something? Do you understand how beautiful you are? Does anyone ever tell you, or does everyone assume that you already know? And does it ever bother you, or do you mostly just enjoy it? I haven't put the question very well and I'm sorry about that. I may have made it sound like I'm jealous, and naturally I am. But I also want to know what it's like.

PPS—I'd really appreciate it if you could skip any false modesty in your reply. If you reply. Hope you do. Thanks.

# 3

*a* week later Dad made another trip to Boston and brought me back a gift from Snow—a small, square, white birdcage with a broken door. I hung the cage from the ceiling and watched it swing, and I was happy. I can't explain, maybe it isn't something that needs explaining, how the sight of a broken cage just puts you up on stilts. The promise that the cage will always be empty, that its days as a jailhouse are done. So this was how it was going to be between Snow and me. No more words, it was too late for them, I'd asked her the wrong questions. She must have wished for an easier sister, one who asked her what to do about boys or how to turn the tables on the latest girl to snub me in the school cafeteria. I couldn't grant that wish. But I wanted to send something back to her, something more than just two words Dad said to her on my behalf. I didn't have anything she was likely to want. I had some handsome seashells, but everybody who's ever been to the beach probably has seashells. You don't even realize you've been collecting them like crazy until you try to sit down and they stab you through your shorts. My scrapbook filled with headlines from the *Flax Hill Record* was too much of an inside joke to send, and might only remind Snow of all the things she'd missed out on. Not that she'd missed out on much. Marriages, christenings, funerals, an asbestos scare, a spate of prank calls made to the mayor, a small fortune in Mexican pesos discovered in one of the drawers of an old pie safe. I'd also kept a record of the time a strong wind blew over Mr. Andrew Luckett's barn and all the bats that had been living there hid out in the woods and then flew around town for three nights, looking for somewhere else to live. In the "famous people I have met" section there were the news clippings that covered a dispute between the Hammonds and the Websters over the origins of a meatloaf recipe that had been published in *Good Housekeeping* under Veronica (née Webster) Murray's name. Both sides hired lawyers and the matter almost went to court, but Suky Hammond discovered that she'd misread a word in her great-grandma's recipe, a word that changed everything, and everyone agreed that the only person to blame was Suky Hammond's great-grandma, since her handwriting was barely readable, and even she would've been mortified to learn that she'd been the cause of such a falling-out between friends and neighbors.

Mom sells invisible ink pens at Mrs. Fletcher's store, and I decided to buy one for Snow. Sometimes you write down barefaced lies, or words you don't really mean, just to see how they look, and it's comforting to think that after six hours the words will just disappear. No need to show them the door, they'll just be seeing themselves out. I found it comforting anyway, and hoped Snow agreed. I'd probably get a discount because I was the manager's daughter and also because a little handwritten sign in the store window said SPECIAL PRICES FOR MALADJUSTED INDIVIDUALS. INQUIRE WITHIN, but I'd still need money. Preferably money I'd earned. Ruth Cohen was giving up her paper route because she wanted more sleep on Saturdays, and I talked to her about taking her place.

A couple of days after that Mom and I had to shop for the week's food. I go to the grocery store with her as often as I can because it's better if I have final approval of the things she buys. Her combinations can be a little Martian otherwise. She made us lobster thermidor once, because someone in a novel she was reading had gone on a crazy lunchtime rampage and lobster thermidor was what she'd had. The flavors were really interesting (Dad's words, not mine) but for a whole day afterward my stomach felt as if it had been kidnapped, boiled, and then deep-fried. I bet she put huckleberries in the sauce, or some other ingredient that isn't supposed to go into lobster thermidor.

For a moment at the grocery store I thought Mom was going to say something about Snow. She knew I'd kept my letter, the one Snow had written to me, asking if I could read yet. What Mom did was leave her jewelry box on her dressing table, wide open so I could see that all the other letters had been taken out. And she'd started blushing whenever I caught her eye. She'd be talking and I'd tilt my head at her and her face would flood dark red. At the grocery store she said: "Bird . . . Bird, you listen to me," and she was blushing again, my red and white mother. I said: "Yes, Mom?" and there was a nasty spike in my voice, but I didn't care. She ought to know that if you want to set yourself up as queen and have everything the way you want it and keep sisters apart then you're not going to have a big fan club. She ought to know that where there's a queen there's often a plot to overthrow her. She ended up just looking down at the shopping list and reading it aloud, and I picked the items up and put them in our cart, except for the stuff that sounded like it'd come out of one of her books. I've never known a grocery store to stock larks' tongues or quince preserves anyhow.

Mom came and sat on the end of my bed that night, took a long, deep pull on her cigarette, and sent a jet of smoke up toward the birdcage. "You value objectivity, right?"

I decided not to give her an answer, but she wouldn't leave without one. A skin-crackling silence rose up between us. It was new and truly awful and nothing like our other silences.

To put a stop to it I said: "What's 'objectivity' mean?"

"Don't give me that, Miss Reading-Age-of-Sixteen-Plus. Miss Fairfax has started saying the only reason your schoolwork's sloppy is because you're bored; it doesn't challenge you."

"No . . . I'm just lazy, Mom. And I try to be objective, but I keep forgetting."

"I'm asking you a favor. I want you to concentrate on being as objective as you can about your sister." (Whoever heard of anyone being objective about their sister?) "She's a pretty convincing replica of an all-around sweetie pie, but . . . I think being objective may be the only way you'll see that there's something about her that doesn't quite add up. Something almost like a smell, like milk that's spoiled. Maybe it's just as simple as her being an overpetted show pony; I don't know. I'd be happy never to find out. You want to play investigator, so investigate. I'm here on standby. But . . . Bird, what could you have to say to a replica? You're so much yourself. Whatever else happens, don't let her mess that up. Okay?"

If that was Mom's attempt to make me believe that my sister was bad news, it was a flop.

"Look—I've got to get up early tomorrow," I said.

I wasn't being mean—Aunt Mia was taking me to a conference for teen journalists. It was being held in Rhode Island, and I had special permission to take the day off school.

"Right," Mom said. "Right. Hey, sweet dreams."

I closed my eyes but she stayed in my room. She walked over to the window, drew the curtains around her, and stood there, smoking. It had been a foggy day and she'd done this before, on other foggy days—I knew she liked the view from my window, liked to trace the blurry shape of the hill with one finger. I was mad at her but glad that she was watching over me. I don't know exactly when she left. I woke up a couple of times and she hadn't left my room—an owl said *tyick tyick* outside my window, and the curtains rustled and Mom muttered: "*Tyick tyick* yourself, owl." In the morning she was gone. She'd killed four spiders. There were no bodies, but their webs gaped at me.

*the conference wasn't* too bad. I was there to eavesdrop for Aunt Mia. She was writing an article about what to expect from the journalists of the future, and she figured they'd clam right up if there was a grown-up around. I didn't get very many quotes for her—the journalists of the future were introverts. They listened to the speakers up on stage, took notes, and occasionally asked each other how to spell a word. Some of them looked suspiciously like jocks and cheerleaders who'd put on eyeglasses and intelligent expressions just for the chance to be around kids from other schools, but apart from that I enjoyed being part of a silent, highly observant crowd that stored its opinions up until they were good and ready. I befriended a girl named Yasmin Khoury—she was sixteen, and looked like the princess of a faraway land, but claimed that her father was a janitor. We called ourselves the Brown People's Alliance, though she said I was only just brown enough to qualify, so she'd have to be the spokesperson until we got a few more members. We sat together at lunch break, drinking ice-cold milk out of wineglasses.

Yasmin said: "So . . . have you got a boyfriend?"
I nodded.
"Really?"
"Ouch."
Yasmin patted the long braid that ran down her back. "Oh, I didn't mean it that way. You should break up with him, though. Before it's too late."
"Too late for what?"

"How do I put this . . . boys take up a lot of thinking time."

"They do?" (I'd never considered Louis to be a time-tabled activity before. I love, and I mean love the way his hair falls across his forehead in a wave, and come to think of it, the time I spend thinking about pushing that wave of black hair out of his eyes could definitely be put to better use. His friends say: "Cut that hair, Chen," but he reminds them that it was a haircut that drained the mighty Samson of his strength. Yes, the boy I'm sweet on can be such a nerd sometimes.)

Yasmin Khoury had another question: "Do you know what a lobotomy is?"

"I think so. It's when they operate and remove parts of your brain, right?"

"Right. Boyfriends are the same thing. They shrink your brain. Any female who really wants to be able to think for herself shouldn't be wasting her time on boys."

"Oh."

"So are you going to break up with your boy-friend?"

"Uh . . . maybe. If we stop liking each other or something."

She was beginning to look around for somebody older and more revolutionary to talk to, so I asked a question to distract her. "What do you spend your thinking time on, anyway?"

She set her glass down on the table between

us. "I think about things that are gone from the world."

"What things?"

"Well . . . the ancient wonders. The libraries at Antioch and Timbuktu, the hanging gardens at Babylon, the ringing porcelain of Samarkand. The saddest thing isn't so much that all that stuff is gone . . . in a way it's kind of enough that it was all here once . . . but now it's all just garbled rumors a brown girl's father tells her until he thinks she's gotten too big for bedtime stories. None of the stuff that's gone has been replaced in any substantial way, and that depresses the hell out of me. Oh, never mind. Sorry. Forget it."

"Well, I won't. We're the replacement."

"The Brown People's Alliance?"

"Do you see anybody else volunteering?"

She laughed. "No pressure, huh . . ."

"So. Do you still think boyfriends and, uh, lobotomies are the same thing?"

"Yup. Nothing's going to change *that*."

I didn't tell Aunt Mia about the Brown People's Alliance because I know how she is. Nothing's off-limits with her; she would've put it in the newspaper and tried to pass it off as cute. She used to mention dumb convictions of mine in her articles, though Mom banned her from using my name: *A six-year-old girl of my acquaintance won't touch canned tuna fish because she believes it to be the flesh of mermaids. Words cannot*

239

*adequately describe her solemn, speechless anger as tuna salad is served and consumed. It's the anger of one who knows that this barbarism will go down in history and the sole duty of the powerless is to bear witness. "Reason with the kid," I hear you cry. "Set the record straight." Don't you think we've tried? Nothing can be done to convince her that canned tuna really is fish. Were Chicken of the Sea to remove all mermaids from their packaging and advertising overnight, she'd only call it a cover-up.* She quit making those little mentions when she realized that most of her readers thought I was her daughter. In their letters to the editor people kept writing things like "as the mother of a young child, Mia Cabrini ought to know . . ."

"So that's all you've got for me?" Aunt Mia asked, after I told her what little I'd managed to overhear. We were driving home in her little pink car. When she slowed down, I thought she was going to fling open my door and tell me to get out and walk, but actually it was because there was a stoplight ahead.

"That's all I've got. Sorry."

Aunt Mia said: "Somehow I doubt that, but have it your way. You're a deep one, Bird. Just like your mother."

*Don't say I'm like her. Don't say I'm like her.* That's what I was yelling inside.

"Hey, Bird—"

"Yeah?"

"Do I look forty?"

"Forty years old?" I asked, trying to buy time.

"Yes, forty years old."

Her eyes flicked up toward the rearview mirror. I was sitting in the backseat because she doesn't like to have anyone sitting next to her while she is driving. She says it makes her feel crowded in. I hadn't shown up in her mirror at all that car ride. I begged that missing slice of me—hair, cheek, chin, and the top of my arm—to appear behind her before she started to feel funny about not seeing it there, but the mirror didn't care whether Aunt Mia felt funny or not, or it was my reflection that didn't care. Thanks a lot, rearview mirror. Between talking and watching the road and trying not to crash her car, Aunt Mia's attention was fully booked anyway. Dad drives and Mrs. Chen drives but Aunt Mia just gets behind the wheel and hopes it's another one of her lucky days. For a split second she lifted her hand to adjust the mirror—I could tell she was starting to feel funny, starting to feel that something didn't fit, but couldn't figure out exactly what—then she said, "Ha," more to herself than to me, and looked ahead of her again.

"Well? Do I look forty?"

"Yeah."

She muttered something in Italian. I think she was cursing.

"But aren't you older than forty anyway?"

"*Cara* . . . this ice you're skating on is very thin."

I told her that she was obviously also gorgeous, but she said she didn't want to hear about gorgeous. She'd heard me calling a grilled cheese sandwich gorgeous just last week.

Neither of us said anything for a while, then I asked if she was okay.

"Sure I am."

"But your stomachache . . ."

"Stomachache? Oh. Stomachs. Sometimes they ache. That's life."

She kept her eyes on the road and got her smile right on the second try. I sat back and told myself that I was letting her keep her secret, that I could find out whenever I wanted. If I was able to mimic Mom's voice, that might even have been true. I could have called Aunt Mia up and got her talking. But Mom is impossible to copy. I try and try, and each try sounds less like her. I'm not able to play Mom's voice back in my head the way I can other people's. I'm beginning to think that it's my ear. Maybe I don't hear Mom properly in the first place.

*louis chen slipped* me a flower-scented envelope when he came over that dinnertime. *Bird Whitman, c/o Louis Chen* . . . Snow had perfected her handwriting to a copperplate script. I stuck the letter into the pocket of my overalls, where it rustled impatiently as we watched *Batman* and Louis tried to get me to say "Sorry, toots . . . I'm antisocial" just the way Catwoman said it. Everyone at school had moved on from Louis's being a Vietcong, and he said there were no hard feelings. (I had some, but he didn't ask me.) The new thing was a note someone had pinned to Carl Green's locker. The note read BARBARA THOMAS IS FAST and inquiring minds wanted to know whether this was true, and what Barbara Thomas was going to do to try to prove her innocence. Louis looked as if he was feeling sorry for her, especially when I pointed out that the only way she could prove she wasn't fast was by never kissing another boy until the day she died. But I couldn't think of a better person for such a thing to happen to, so I laughed. Going to middle school in the same building as the high school students makes you see the reality. School is one long illness with symptoms that switch every five minutes so you think it's getting better or worse. But really it's the same thing for years and years.

———◆———

Dear Bird,

Your letter was such a wonderful surprise; really it was. I'm still thinking about how to answer the question in your postscript. I wasn't expecting you to insist on honesty. Don't you find that most people try to make each other say things that aren't true? Maybe because it's easier, and because it saves time, and . . . now it sounds like I'm trying to sell you dinner that comes in a can. ("So they got us eatin' dog food now," Uncle J says.)

I haven't met very many people who seem to want me to say what I really think. So I'm out of practice. Wait for the next letter. I've got a question for you, though—what do you mean when you say that you "don't always show up in mirrors"?

> Best love from
> Your sister,
> Snow

———◆———

Hi, Snow,

It's great that you wrote back. Thanks for the birdcage! Please find enclosed an extra-special pen. Wait'll you find out what it does; you'll flip.

I'm writing this to you from detention; I'd better tell you right off that I'm not a delinquent or anything, but I'm frequently in detention. I've got this piece of paper underneath an essay about Flax Hill back in 1600, and every couple of minutes I turn the page of my notepad and write to you a little more. I don't know how much more I can say about Flax Hill back in 1600. According to the textbooks, this town was just a big grassy field and some primitive peoples, but Miss Fairfax says finding out more about the plants and what they could be used for is a way of finding out more about the people. So I'm listing plants that grew here back then. Clammy ground-cherry, starved panic grass, jack-in-the-pulpit, scaldweed, nimblewill—don't they sound like the ingredients of some terrifying potion? I don't think those are the real names for those plants. I mean, the people who saw those kinds of plants every day wouldn't have given them names like that. I'm guessing somewhere along the line it was decided that the Native American names weren't important because they were too difficult to spell, and then, abracadabra, scaldweed and panic grass. The other day I met a girl who said a lot of things are gone from the world and seemed to feel kind of cheated, and I guess this is just another thing she'd get disgusted about.

About being honest: so far I haven't noticed anybody picking out lies for other people to tell. Please give an example. Dad may have already told you that nothing ever happens around here.

When I say I don't always show up in mirrors, that is exactly what I mean, i.e., it is a statement of fact.

Your detained sister,
Bird

———◆———

Dear Snow,

It was nice of you to reply to me using the pen I sent you, but as you may have realized by now, the ink goes invisible after a few hours, and all I can say is it's a good thing you used a different pen for the address or the letter wouldn't have reached me at all. I tried to retrieve your words by tracing over the marks the pen made on the paper, but the result leaves me hopelessly confused, so be a pal and send it again—

Bird

———◆———

Dearest Bird,

The incident of the disappearing letter is only one tenth of the mischief that gift of yours caused in my life, but thanks anyway. I wanted my kid sister back and I got her back with a vengeance. Sisters come with a lot of benefits—let me know if you're ever in the mood for reading a really long poem and I'll send you "Goblin Market."

> For there is no friend like a sister
> In calm or stormy weather;
> To cheer one on the tedious way,
> To fetch one if one goes astray,
> To lift one if one totters down,
> To strengthen whilst one stands.

I used to think that was stuff a mom should do for you—I guess I felt I needed someone in my life to do those things and decided it should be a mom. But a sister or a friend, or a combination of both, that works too. Let's be those kinds of sisters if we can.

In my other letter I asked if you're aware of what happens to girls who say that they don't always appear in mirrors. Doctors get involved, Bird. Sometimes girls like that end up in clinics out in the middle of nowhere, being forced into ice baths and other terrible things I won't write about here. I just want you to be really sure you mean what you said. Are you sure?

AML,
Snow

Dear Snow,

Was that supposed to scare me? I'm already in the middle of nowhere. And, yes, I'm sure. It obviously bothers you, so let's just talk about something else.

Bird

---

Bird,

I was only asking like that because I don't always show up in mirrors, either. For years I wondered whether it's all right or not, but there's been no one to ask, so I've decided that I feel all right about it. It's a relief to be able to forget about what I might or might not be mistaken for. My reflection can't be counted on, she's not always there but I am, so maybe she's not really me . . .

. . . Well, what is she then? I guess we'll find out someday, but I'm not holding my breath. I think that maybe mirrors behave differently depending on how you treat them. Treating them like clocks (as almost everybody seems to) makes them behave like clocks, but treating them as doors— does any of this make sense to you? Yes, no?

My heart used to stop dead whenever I thought someone else had noticed. But I've found that other people usually overlook it, or if they notice, they think it's something the matter with them, not me. Four times in my life so far someone's started to ask me about it . . . "You know, for a second I thought . . ." and I've looked at them all mystified, as if they were talking gibberish. Then they start worrying about clinics and ice baths and soon after that they dry up. So, yes, when you say that it also happens to you, and you refuse to take it back—well. That unsettles me. Of course it does.

Either you're lying or you're the other thing—I don't even want to write it down. But if you're the other thing then I am too. And why would you lie? I've decided to believe you. Maybe it means we're not supposed to be apart. Or . . . there'll be some kind of mayhem next time we're together.

Aunt Clara and Uncle John send you greetings. And I send you love

as always,
Snow

Dear Snow,

Yes, you're grown up and I'm not. You've made that very clear. Have you forgotten how it felt when you were thirteen and people tried to humor you?

I guess you'd really like for us to have something in common, and that's why you're pretending you know what I mean about mirrors. But we have a father in common. That's more than enough. I strongly recommend that you talk about something else in your next letter.

Yours respectfully,
Bird N. Whitman

# 4

Hi, Sis,

Here I am, talking about something else: our Aunt Clara. She's a marvel. There's a photo of her enclosed but she doesn't photograph well. She won't mind me saying that. She's so lively in person, she's got these bright eyes and her hair floats out every which way around her face and often looks as if it's moving of its own accord. She thinks quick, talks slow, works porcupine hours—that's what she calls her night shifts at the hospital because she sees porcupines along the road on her way to work. She taught me nice handwriting and how to cook. I want to make her happy and proud of me. I made her cry when I was young, Bird, and I wish so much that I hadn't, or that either of us could simply forget it happened. It was during our first week together, one night just before she put me to bed and just before she left for work. She had a map of America on her lap and she was trying to explain to me that in some states colored people were equal to white people in the eyes of the law, and in some states they weren't. We had to stand with the people who were still struggling until everybody had the same rights everywhere, that's what she said. I was only eight years old (this is something I'm always telling myself in my own defense. I was only eight years old, only eight years old, Your Honor) and nobody had ever told me to my face that I'm colored, so I knew it and didn't know it at the same time. I thought that if I accepted what Aunt Clara was saying, then that map would apply to me, that map with the hideous borders she'd drawn onto it in red and blue. So I grabbed both her hands and

251

smiled at her, to try to get her to go along with me, and I said: "No, no, don't say that about me. That's awful. It can't be true." She wasn't surprised, just sad. She let out this one quick breath, like she'd just been hit really hard in the stomach, and she rubbed her eyes and said she must have gotten dirt in one of them. I crept back to her in the morning with questions—what about Dad, what about my grandma, and my other grandma? Yup, them too. I remember it was very early, and she was eating her breakfast standing up, with her uniform hung up over the door behind her—when she's not wearing it or washing it or pressing it or mending it, she keeps it in a plastic cover with a cake of lavender soap in each pocket—she was patient with me. It was Uncle John who said things like "Don't know how I'll go another day without boxin' this child's ears for her." He used to run a home school; eight of us sat cross-legged on the carpet in Uncle J and Aunt C's front parlor, learning Brer Anansi stories to begin with and years later reading our way through Othello and then a very interesting half-book called Peter the Great's Blackamoor . . . (Russia's another planet, Bird. Not only that, but the author stopped writing the book all of a sudden—nobody knows why. He lived in the nineteenth century. Maybe it just wasn't the right time for him to tell the story. Or maybe it doesn't matter what century it was, maybe he just didn't like the way the story was headed and it screamed and laughed and spoke in tongues when he tried to turn it around. We'll never know how it ends. He put it away and moved on to the next thing.) When Uncle John introduced me to the others, to my dear friends Ephraim and Laura and Abdul and Peter and Rukeih and Anita and Mouse, he told them they weren't going to have any problems with me as long as they understood it was going to take me a while to get to know anything about anything. Uncle John was a sharecropper somewhere in North Carolina but he wound up in jail at one time—he says he was guilty, but he won't say what it is he was guilty of, but he's not a violent man, so I doubt he hurt anybody. Aunt Clara was dating his cousin, who let Uncle John sleep on his sofa when he got out of jail and was looking for some work to do. But Uncle John stole Aunt Clara away from his cousin. He'd had a lot of time to read while he was in jail. "Did you know England had a queen whose father had her mother executed?" he'd say. "She never married." Aunt Clara would tell him he was making it up and he'd tell her more and more and they'd sit there talking themselves hoarse in Uncle John's cousin's kitchen until Uncle John's cousin would say, "Well, I'm going to bed, y'all," and leave them to it. He took his loss of Aunt Clara like a man and at the wedding he said he knew he could never be the encyclopedia that Aunt Clara needed. Our grandma told Aunt Clara that if she married Uncle John, she'd be disowned. Aunt Clara said: "Well, you found the excuse you were looking for, Mother."

Got to run, Bird—working this evening. Not porcupine hours, but I'll finish this letter to you tomorrow.

———◆———

All right, I'm back. Back with you and Aunt Clara. She grew up in Biloxi; Great-aunt Effie was a live-in cook for a white family called the Adairs, and Aunt Clara laundered their sheets and scrubbed floors for bed and board. Great-aunt Effie would tell her stories about the Whitmans as she worked. All stories about pulling off confidence tricks and getting in with the right people and lording it over other colored folks and getting the last laugh. Aunt Clara had to ask and ask before Great-aunt Effie admitted the unhappy endings—there was Addie Whitman, who spent her life playing servant in various cousins' houses because she was too dark and "ugly" to be allowed to marry, Addie Whitman who got herself a black tomcat for company. But even that cat, Minnaloushe, kept scratching her and hissing at her. Since Minnaloushe wouldn't love her, Addie Whitman thought she'd better teach him to fear her, so she forced the cat into a sack and swung the sack over Perdido Pass. She was only going to give him one good dip in the mouth of the river but she lost her balance, fell in, and drowned. Minnaloushe got away and was quietly eating dinner out of a silver dish— don't ask me why Effie remembers the color of the dish—at a neighbor's house later on that evening. Or there's Cass Whitman, who hung herself to show her parents and her brothers exactly what she thought of their having run her "unsuitable" fiancé out of town, or Vince Whitman, who fell in love with a white woman and proposed to her in front of a handful of his closest friends, who were shocked and terrified. She said yes, and she also said she would've loved him if he were purple or green or purple striped with green, and he said: "I'm so happy. That's all I wanted to hear." Then he led the party in a rendition of "The Star-Spangled Banner," half singing it, half saying it. Try it for yourself, not quite singing "The Star-Spangled Banner"—it changes the words, doesn't it? At sunset Vince and his new fiancée went for a walk in the park and he shot her dead, then himself. One clean, accurate shot each, like he'd been practicing. Aunt Clara says he must have been out of his mind, but Effie says he was a realist. According to Effie, our dad's the only Whitman she knows of who's dared to actually just go ahead and marry a white person. Aunt Clara and I reminded her that it's legal where we are, and therefore not so daring, but she's still pretty amazed by our dad, Bird.

I've met Great-aunt Effie enough times to go beyond first impressions, and there isn't a bad bone in that woman's body. But . . . that girl you mentioned, the one who feels cheated, Great-aunt Effie is like that. She thinks there are treasures that were within her reach, but her skin stole them from her. She thinks she could've been somebody. But she is somebody.

Somebody who's chased bullies away with broomsticks, somebody who saved for years so Aunt Clara could go to nursing school without having to ask her mother for the money. She's somebody who's reached out to hold Aunt Clara whenever Aunt C felt the world was about to end. She's somebody Aunt Clara loves, somebody she couldn't have done without. A woman like Effie Whitman thinking she could've been somebody . . . that pushes icicles all the way down my spine.

Great-aunt Effie knows how to make that cobbler that no one can resist, that gratin that pursues people into their dreams and has them sneaking downstairs in the middle of the night for another bite or ten, that cake that can cause a family rift over the last slice. The Adairs were paying her wages lower than any white cook of her standard would accept, but they were pretty good wages for a colored cook. But Great-aunt Effie didn't get too bitter about that. She says that sometimes she'd stand there watching the Adairs eat and she'd think how lucky this type of white family was that they employed cooks with a proper sense of right and wrong, conscience almost heavy enough to replace a slave collar. Without that proper sense of right and wrong, a colored cook might go astray. Such a cook—ever smiling, ever respectful, ever ready to go the extra mile—such a cook might fatten her employers up . . . not in a hurry, just little by little, fatten them and fatten them, add more and yet more cream to their coffee, add butter even (they'd say the coffee tasted too rich at first, but then they'd grow to like it), vile creatures that they were, accepting the ceaseless toil of others as their birthright. And when the family was too fat to run, this cook run astray might just take a brisk, ten-minute trip around the house, shooting every member of the family dead with the firearms they kept for their own protection. Aunt Clara and I said the exact same thing when Great-aunt Effie told us this little fantasy of hers: Jesus! And Great-aunt Effie told us in a very shocked tone of voice not to take the Lord's name in vain.

Hey—at least you've got the Novaks to fall back on (as you reminded me with that "N" you threw into your last letter), but the Whitmans and the Millers are the product of generations of calculated breeding, whether they'll admit it or not. The Whitmans have married to refine a look, they keep a close eye on skin tone and hair texture. They draw strict distinctions between degrees of color—quadroon, octoroon—darkest to lightest. But they can't stop a face like Clara's or Effie's rising up every now and again to confront them. And who can speak for the Millers? My other grandma, the one I don't share with you, sometimes says a little something about the Millers being "sensible people" who've made certain choices in order to remain comfortable just as any other "sensible" people would and what does any of it matter now that the world's changing? Agnes is a silly old woman, Bird, and it's hard for me to have any respect for her or for Olivia, it's hard for me to even stand the sound of their voices on the telephone. I've grown up around people whose families have lived their lives without trying to invent advantages—some of them have marched and staged sit-ins, others have just lived with their heads held high. And what about my mom? If she was alive, would she have a cabinet full of "treatments" for her hair and skin? Would she have very delicately led me to believe that there's something about us Whitmans that isn't quite nice, something we've got to keep under control? Aunt Clara's never said anything about how my mother might have felt about me. She's been careful not to go down the "If only your mother could see you now" path. She doesn't need to, anyway. It just so happens that I carry my mother around in three LP records. She sings and tells me she loves me, she's proud of me, she's right by my side. The records are wearing out and I'm not rushing the process or trying to delay it, I'm just letting it happen. Her voice skips and squeaks; she's started to sound unsure of what she's saying. All I can tell from those recordings is that my mom wanted me to remember the sound of her voice. I may or may not have hated my own face sometimes. I may or may not have spent time thinking of ways to spoil it somehow. (Maybe that answers your question about being "beautiful.") But I'm slowly coming around to the view that you can't feel nauseated by the Whitmans and the Millers without feeling nauseated by the kind of world that's rewarded them for adapting to it like this. In the meantime I'm letting Agnes and Olivia think I don't visit them because I'm scared of your mom. Are they good to you? Tell me. You can tell me.

I thought I'd finish writing to you today,

but I've got to go to work again. I can't be late. More tomorrow.

---

We live in a little suburb called Twelve Bridges. Everything's a little broken-down, especially the bridges. People don't make too much money around here, but what comes with that is a different definition of what it means to be well-off. You're chairman of the board if you need twelve dollars a week and you make twelve dollars a week. If you've also got someone within ten minutes' walk who can make you laugh and someone else within a five-minute walk who can help you mourn, you're a millionaire. If on top of all that you've got a buddy or three who'll feed you delicious things and paint you pictures and dance with you, and another friend who'll watch your kids so you can go out dancing . . . that's the billionaire lifestyle. We're friendly toward strangers because of a general belief (I don't know where it comes from) that we're born strangers and that the memory of how that feels never really leaves us. If I'm ever in any other part of the world and I pass a house that has white fairy lights strung across its porch, I'll think it's likely that I'd get along with the people who live there. If it's summer and the strangers out on the porch offer me a drink of water, an apple, the time of day, anything, then I'll have to stop and find out if they've ever heard of a place called Twelve Bridges.

Bird, Bird. What a long letter this has been. But that's what you get for wanting to be written to as if you were grown up. But also . . . I have plenty of people around me to talk to, and no one to be honest with. Write back just as soon as you can, will you, please?

Snow

⬥

Dear Snow,

First of all I don't think you should continue to feel bad about making Aunt Clara cry that time. You learned something from it and it sounds like she's completely forgiven you. Also . . . you know when something is so incredibly depressing that it's actually kind of funny? I laughed when I read what you said to her.

So you were left alone with Uncle John while Aunt Clara was working her porcupine hours? That's a Flax Hill kind of question, I'm afraid. If that had happened around here, people would talk. And having all your classes at home . . . I wish I was allowed to do that. I've been thinking a lot about those other Whitmans you wrote me about. There's that blood tie, and it's troublesome, and we don't know what we would have done if we'd been in their place. They're family and I still love them . . . can't think of any other way to turn a chain into flowers . . . but I maybe wouldn't ask Addie, Cass, or Vince Whitman for advice about anything.

There was more about them and Clara and Effie in that letter than there was about you. I'd like to know one thing about you—you choose which thing it is.

I wish I could tell you stuff about the Novaks, but they're a mystery. What I do know is that they most probably came to Ellis Island from Hungary, which is another world (along with Russia, as you said).

I'm glad you know Brer Anansi stories. I know some too. There are quite a few spiders in my room, possibly most of the spiders in the house. Here's something that happened a few months ago: I got curious about what the spiders in my room thought of Brer Anansi, or whether they'd even heard of him. I just wanted to know if he was a real spider to them. So one night when the house was as dark and as silent as could be, I sat up in my bed and whispered: Who speaks for the spiders?

And the president of the spiders came forward: I do.

(She didn't speak aloud, she sort of mimed. That's the only way I can explain it.)

I asked her if she'd heard of Anansi the Spider and she got cagey. She said: Have you yourself heard of Anansi the Spider?

I answered: Sure, sure. I can tell you a story about him if you want.

She said: Please do.

Halfway through the story about Anansi and the magic cooking pot, I got this feeling that the spiders didn't like what I was saying. Their expressions aren't easy to read, but they just didn't seem very happy with me. I said: Hey, should I stop?

No, said the president of the spiders. Don't stop now, we're all very interested.

But have you heard this story?

Yes we have. Anansi is very dear to us.

I finished telling that story and the president of the spiders asked me how many more Anansi stories I knew. I said I knew at least fifteen, and she got openly upset.

Do a lot of people know these stories?

Uh . . . yeah. Sorry.

How? How did this happen? The president of the spiders started gliding around the walls of my room, glaring suspiciously at the poor spiders she found in the corners of each web.

This is deep treachery, she said. Since when do spiders tell tales? Since when do we talk to outsiders?

Only one spider answered her—he was gray and hairy and an elder, I think—he said: Don't even worry about it, Chief! Let them think they know, but they don't know! They don't know!

Be that as it may, the president of the spiders said, someone must pay for this.

Her citizens began to beg. They swore on the lives of their mothers and grandmothers and children that the Anansi leak was nothing to do with them. I could see I'd stirred up some real trouble, and it was up to me to distract the president of the spiders while I still could.

Wait, WAIT, I said. I have another story—there are no spiders in it, but if you like it, can we forget the other one I told?

The president of the spiders folded her many arms. Very well. IF I like it, she said.

I told the spiders the story of La Belle Capuchine. The woman who told me this story was a maid employed by Grammy Olivia, and soon after she told me this story Grammy Olivia fired her. The official reason for this was that Leah wasn't doing her job properly, but I think the real reason is because Grammy Olivia overheard parts of this story. I really liked it when Leah told me stories. She wanted to be an actress. She did voices pretty well. I hope she's onstage somewhere right now. I've forgotten her exact words, but here it is as I remember it, except for the parts I've added because she told me that each time a story like this one gets retold the new teller should add a little something of their own:

If you wish to be truly free, you must love no one. But of course if you take that path you may also find that in the end you're unloved. La Belle Capuchine loved no one; she was a house slave, an unusually dark one, but unusually comely. All the house Negroes were good-looking and talked nicely and some of them played the violin and could chart the movements of the planets because the master and the mistress of the house got more fun out of their hobbies when they taught them to others. But La Belle Capuchine had seen other house Negroes come and go. Some of them made the mistake of getting too good at astronomy or musicianship. It didn't do to outstrip the master or the mistress. You weren't supposed to take an interest in the subject for its own sake, you had to remember you were learning it to keep someone else company. You had to remember to ask anxiously whether your attempt was correct, and you had to make mistakes, but not jarring ones. Other house Negroes had been taken ill—not always physically ill, but often by sorrows of the spirit. Very few people can feel well having to make marionettes of themselves, prancing and preening and accepting affection and abuse alike as the mood of their masters and mistresses take them. Very few people can watch others endure humiliation without recognizing the part they play in increasing it. But La Belle Capuchine was a practical person. She knew that the best way to get by was to be amusing and to flatter through imitation. Save her coloring and her overabundant head of hair, she looked just like her mistress, Miss Margaux, and that worked very much in La Belle Capuchine's favor. A visitor to the plantation caught sight of La Belle Capuchine, exclaimed that she looked exactly as Miss Margaux would if she were dipped in cocoa, and from then on everybody said it. La Belle Capuchine and Miss Margaux had the same dainty wrists and ankles, the same dazzling eyes; they even smiled in the same carefree way, though admittedly the smiling was something that La Belle Capuchine had taught herself to do. The two women had the same father, which explains some of the uncanny resemblance between them. The rest was down to La Belle Capuchine's hard work. Miss Margaux's tastes were La Belle Capuchine's tastes, Miss Margaux's opinions were La Belle Capuchine's opinions, every now and again Miss Margaux found it entertaining to ask La Belle Capuchine, "What am I thinking right now?" and have La Belle Capuchine give her the correct answer without hesitation.

The other house Negroes had learned not to bother speaking to La Belle Capuchine. She didn't consider herself one of them and addressed them as if she owned them—this was another way in which she amused her master and mistress and their family. But there was a footman named Michael who was pining away because of her beauty and, like dozens before him, he couldn't stop himself from trying to win La Belle Capuchine's heart. His words and serenades did nothing; she returned his gifts and letters unopened, or she showed them to Miss Margaux and together the two women laughed at the inexpensive trinkets and the spelling mistakes he'd made. The man ran out of hope and confronted La Belle Capuchine. He said that he could never blame anybody for trying their best to survive, but that she was the kind of traitor he'd never known before and hoped never to see again. La Belle Capuchine simply looked over her shoulder and asked, "Is someone speaking? For a moment I thought I heard somebody speak."

Now something had been happening on the plantation. The other house Negroes had been keeping track of what happened among the field Negroes as best they could. So far six of the field hands had killed a white man each. The punishment for this was very heavy for everybody who was even associated with any Negro who killed a white man; the master was trying to make sure everybody was too scared to try it again. But the field hands on that plantation continued to take the lives of their overseers even as the harshness of the punishments increased. There was a woman there who was a skilled fortune-teller. She'd asked her cowrie shells, "Who will set us free?" And the cowrie shells told her: "High John the Conqueror."

"When will he come?"

"The price of his passage is high. The highest: blood. First seven white men must die. Then High John the Conqueror will come."

When the men of the plantation heard what the woman's cowrie shells had told her, most of them said they didn't believe it. "The prince you're speaking of left these lands long ago, and there's no calling him back," they said. But there were seven whose hearts were heavy because they did believe what the cowrie shells had said, and they knew that their belief meant they wouldn't live to see freedom. Even so those seven drew straws to decide which of them would attack first. And so six overseers were killed, and there was such punishment for these killings that the plantation got the reputation of being a place of horror.

The morning after Michael called La Belle Capuchine a traitor, the blood of the seventh white man was spilled, and High John the Conqueror strode through the plantation gates, shining with a terrifying splendor; he did no harm to anybody (though some cried out that he should take revenge); he healed the broken bodies of those who had awaited him and those who'd said he was dead and gone. He wept to see what had been done in that place, and where he walked, he ruined the earth so that nothing that could bring profit would ever grow there again. Then High John the Conqueror came to the Big House, where La Belle Capuchine and the other house Negroes lived with Miss Margaux and Master and Mistress. Master and Mistress had tried to flee when they saw what was happening, but the house Negroes had locked them into a bathroom, along with their daughter and La Belle Capuchine. Miss Margaux was screaming and La Belle Capuchine was screaming louder. Master was yelling, "Shut up or I'll kill you both myself!" and Mistress had fainted dead away in the bathtub.

High John the Conqueror opened the bathroom door and stretched out a hand. "I go now," he said, "and all my people go with me."

Weeping tears of gratitude, La Belle Capuchine stepped forward, but much to everyone's surprise, High John the Conqueror pushed La Belle Capuchine away and took Miss Margaux by the hand.

"La Belle Capuchine," he said to her. "Your beauty is famous, and will become yet more so by my side."

Miss Margaux batted her eyelashes and didn't argue with him.

Miss Margaux's father and mother had fled as soon as the door opened, so La Belle Capuchine was the one who had to protest: "She is not me! She's Miss Margaux! I am La Belle Capuchine! Don't you see that she's white?"

High John the Conqueror looked at La Belle Capuchine and he looked at Miss Margaux. He looked each one of them over very carefully, from head to toe. "I think it's only fair to tell you that I see with more than just my eyes, and I cannot tell the difference between you," he said, finally. Miss Margaux wasn't about to give up her chance to go adventuring with a Negro prince, so she loudly dismissed La Belle Capuchine's desperate cries. "No, no. I am La Belle Capuchine. This is just a game we play sometimes, with chalk and boot polish."

"No chalk can have that effect," La Belle Capuchine argued, and, seeing Michael in the doorway behind High John the Conqueror, she called out: "Michael—you know! Tell him!" Michael turned away.

And so High John the Conqueror took his people away with him. Miss Margaux too, though that one didn't stay with him for long. What about La Belle Capuchine? Well, she was truly free. She loved no one and she was unloved. She lived out the rest of her brief days on the deserted plantation, and in the end her beauty was worth nothing, since there wasn't a soul around to see it and there was no comfort she could buy with it, not even a scrap of food, not even an extra half second of life.

The End.

I'm pleased to report that the president of the spiders is back on friendly terms with her citizens.

And yes, Gee-Ma Agnes and Gee-Pa Gerald are good to me and always came to my elementary school Nativity play when I had a part in it.

No fairy lights or riddles here, but I like Flax Hill best when the sky's stormy gray and the clouds get little bits of sun and lightning tangled up in them. There's a church up on the second hill, the less popular hill, and when you look through the tinted windowpanes, everyone in town looks like stained-glass angels, walking and cycling, moving in and out of small brick palaces, eating glittering rolls of sapphire bread.

What's this job you've got? I've got a paper route and dogs are always barking at me.

Your little sis,
Bird

———◆———

Dear Bird,

I can't tell if you want me to believe everything you say or only some of it. You talk to spiders and they answer you. All right, fine. Suppose I wish to converse with spiders too—how do I do it?

La Belle Capuchine: I don't know how much of it you forgot/added yourself, but Leah must have told you that story because she wanted to be fired. I mean, even I got paranoid reading it. I kept wondering if La Belle Capuchine was a code version of me. Take my paranoia and multiply it by a million and that's how Olivia must have felt about La Belle Capuchine. Also—believe it or not (and this may remind you of another matter you've banned me from mentioning)—I have a story about someone named La Belle Capuchine too. I thought Aunt Clara told it to me, but when I retold it to her yesterday, she said she hadn't heard it before.

La Belle Capuchine has a wonderful garden filled with sweet-smelling flowers of every color. She plants all the flowers herself, and she tends them herself, and every single one of those flowers is poisonous enough to kill anyone who comes close to them, let alone picks one. La Belle Capuchine is beautiful like her flowers, but she's a poison damsel. She eats and drinks poison all day long and she can rot a person's insides just by looking them in the eye. I don't think Mother Nature likes us much. If she did, she wouldn't make the things that are deadliest so beautiful. For instance, why does fire dance so bright and so wild? It isn't fair.

So far La Belle Capuchine has ended the world seventeen times. She does it by making her poison garden bigger and bigger until it's the only thing in the world. After that she takes a nap. But the world starts again from the beginning. And every time a few days after the new beginning somebody comes across a beautiful flower and picks it. That wakes La Belle Capuchine up, and then there's hell to pay. I think we'd better get used to

La Belle Capuchine, since she'll never be defeated.

The End.

Writing it down like that makes me see that there's no way this could have come from Aunt Clara. Of course this came from me. Of course it does. I felt abandoned for a while. By "a while" I mean years, not months or weeks. I'd be able to push Flax Hill and you and Dad and your mom to the back of my mind for a few days, but then there'd be nights when that turned me over and lay me on my side like a doll that had been dropped on the floor. I began to know what dolls know. It felt like I'd been discarded for another toy that was better, more lifelike (you). People sometimes said, "What a beautiful little girl," but I thought that beautiful was bad. I must have come up with my Belle Capuchine around that time.

I sprained my arm out here in Twelve Bridges when I was about twelve; we were ice-skating and I tried to break my fall with my hand, which is what Uncle John might call "unintelligent" . . . one hand against the weight of an entire body. The arm hurt for so long I began to be afraid that it would never get done hurting. Until the day Aunt Clara came and hugged me and I put both my arms up and around her without even thinking about it. The arm had healed. More important, it hadn't come off. So I reasoned I couldn't be a doll, and neither could you.

The one thing I'd tell you about me is that I'm a deceiver. In another draft of this letter I wrote that I wasn't always like this, but let's try the truth and see what it does. It's probably been official since the night Ephraim, Laura, and I were waiting in line for drinks at a bar over in the next town. We had brand-new fake IDs in our wallets; they'd been expensive and they were convincing and we were excited. Ephraim thought the line was moving faster than it really was and he ended up stomping on someone's heel. The guy Ephraim had bumped into was a nice guy, I think. He accepted Ephraim's apology at first. But everybody was a little drunk and a little tired of standing in line, so maybe, just maybe, it was to pass the time that one of the guy's friends started wondering aloud who "that nigger" thought he was, and the guy began to feel like he had to act a certain way in front of his friends—I could see him begin to feel it, saw the feeling growing on him, like a fur, only faster than anything natural can grow. He said:

"Yeah . . ." and he called Ephraim the same name his friend had, only I think he was ashamed to say it, because he stuttered.

Ephraim said: "Cool out, man. Nothing really happened. So why use that kind of language?" He's got a way about him, my friend Ephraim. Another guy might have sounded like a weakling, another guy might have sounded like he was backing down. But Ephraim was stepping up and giving the other guy a chance for everything to be okay. The other guy got braver once he'd called Ephraim a name, though, and he looked right at me and said that classy-looking girls should choose better friends. I was confused that he felt he could speak to me like that—I used to assume that when I'm with colored people the similarities become obvious, but I guess it's something people don't see unless they're looking to see it. I felt as if I'd left my body, felt as if I were standing over on the other side of a room, watching as a big lie was being told about me. I should have told that guy that when he called anybody that name in my hearing he was saying it directly to me. I should have told him never to dare call anybody that name again. All I did was turn to Ephraim and whisper: "Ephraim, let's go."

Laura shook her head and called me "un-bee-leeve-able." I was afraid that those boys would follow us out onto the street, maybe with broken bottles in their hands. I've heard how one thing leads to another, it's not only in the South that an evening gets that way . . . but they preferred to keep their place in the line. We looked for another bar to go to, but Ephraim and Laura kept rejecting each one we came across, kept saying it'd be just like the bar we'd left. Then they said they were tired and wanted to go home. I went with them. I'm wondering if that's all I can do for them. I can't seem to speak up, but I can go with them, silently. That was a little more than three years ago, so I don't think I can honestly say that it was only this year I became deceptive.

Aunt Clara thinks I transcribe interviews at a newsroom in the city. Uncle John thinks the same, and so does almost everybody else except Mouse. Mouse knows I didn't even make it past the first day of secretarial college and so efficiently transcribing a series of interviews would actually be a little beyond me. I told Mouse because I had to tell somebody, and also because I know a couple of things about her that she doesn't want me to tell anybody, so that makes her less likely to spill.

Bird, here's what happened on the first day of secretarial college:

I got there half an hour early. Near the entrance I was given a clipboard and a square tag with MISS S. WHITMAN printed on it. I went up a staircase and into a sky-lighted auditorium—it was as big as an auditorium, anyhow—filled with row after row of desk-and-chair sets, each chair attached to each desk with a gray bar. There was a black typewriter set on each desktop; more typewriters and desks than I could count. Seven or eight other girls had already taken their seats, looking straight ahead of them as if they'd already begun the march into infinity. I remember feeling doubtful about the bun I'd twisted my hair into just an hour before. I patted it, and it was more or less the same as theirs, not too high, not too low. The desks at the back were designated for Adamses and Allens, so I walked and walked until I found the Walkers and Williamses. There was a blackboard at the front of the room, hung on the wall like a picture frame. I found MISS A. WHITMAN and thought, Almost there. It felt as if my legs would buckle under me from all the walking I'd done.

MISS B. WHITMAN was next. Then MISS C. WHITMAN and MISS D. WHITMAN. Immediately followed by Misses E., F., G., and H. Whitman. None of them had taken their seats yet. "Who are all these girls?" I asked aloud. "Who the hell are they?"

MISS K. WHITMAN was the last straw, she was the moment I realized the secretarial college had an alphabet's worth of us. Mouse says I was surely hallucinating, but I know what I saw. I removed my name tag, left my clipboard on K. Whitman's seat, and went shopping with the money I'd saved to pay for the next month's classes. I bought lipstick and peaches and cigarettes and a ticket to a theater matinee. After the matinee I went home and was asked how college had been and I said: "It was fine."

I left the peaches in a bowl on my bedside table, and spent the next day filling out forms at an employment agency. There was an additional cover sheet that asked you to declare your race. The woman at the front desk said that it was just for the agency records, that it wasn't information they passed on to employers, but the girl next to me said to her: "You people need to think about what you're doing to us. You're bad people . . . you're making us paranoid. You're driving us crazy. Every time I don't make it through to interviews I'll be wondering whether it's because there are better candidates or because of color. Color, color, color; what you're doing is illegal and you know it. I should find myself a lawyer who's ready to make an example of you."

The woman at the front desk had heard it all before and she recited something about it being impossible to obtain any proof that employers were shown the information agency clients provided on the additional cover sheet. The girl who'd talked about suing the agency couldn't make up her mind. First she crumpled the cover sheet up in her hand, then she smoothed it out again and ticked her box. I left mine blank; I knew that I was within my legal rights not to say. Ms. Front Desk pushed my forms back across the table to me and said I had to fulfill all of the requirements. I told her, "None of these options say what I am," and she rolled her eyes. "Every day. Every day a philosopher walks in off the street and makes my job that little bit harder to do."

Then she said: "Why won't you say? Hmmm?" and I had to tick "colored" to show Aunt Clara I wasn't ashamed, even though Aunt Clara wasn't there and would never know what box I ticked. When I got home, I said college had been fine, and I counted up the remainder of my money and wolfed down the peaches. If I hid them and saved them for later, they'd only have rotted away. They were already getting too soft and my fingers sank through their flesh and closed around their stony hearts. The agency couldn't seem to find anything for me to do and I kept back from the brink of paranoia by reminding myself that I had no experience. I sort of happened upon my real job about a week later. The details of it don't matter, but it involves a hell of a lot more deceiving, with and without words.

You just hang on to that paper route.

Snow

———◆———

Snow,

You don't have to tell me anything about your job if you don't want to, but can you please just answer me this—is it dangerous? I mean, is there a chance you could get hurt? Yes or no?

I've been trying to see things from your point of view. Maybe it looks to you as if a whole bunch of things are expected of you. Maybe you're trying to live up to what you think people expect. But people really don't expect all that much. You should see how happy it makes Gee-Ma Agnes to get a note from you, just a little sign that you've been thinking of her. I'm guessing you'd go pretty far to make sure you don't disappoint anyone. But look . . . you don't have to prove anything.

I'm also guessing you might not like to be hearing all this from your younger sister. Well, I read about fifty pages of advice columns before sitting down to write to you, so really this is the wisdom of Dear Abby.

Bird

PS—Speaking with spiders and other things you call unusual . . . there's no special trick to it. When something catches your attention just keep your attention on it, stick with it 'til the end, and somewhere along the line there'll be weirdness. I've never tried to explain it to anyone before, but what I mean to say is that a whole lot of technically impossible things are always trying to happen to us, appear to us, talk to us, show us pictures, or just say hi, and you can't pay attention to all of it, so I just pick the nearest technically impossible thing and I let it happen. Let me know how it goes if you try it. And if you're thinking I'm going to grow out of this, you're wrong.

———◆———

Hi, Snow,

I'm in detention again. It's been five weeks since I last heard from you. According to Dad, you're not only alive but getting prettier and more gracious every day, et cetera, but what I want is an answer to the question in my previous letter. One word: yes or no?

A thing you should understand about me is that I won't keep a secret just because it's a secret. I've been told that this makes me a bad friend, but I actually think it makes me a better friend than the secret-keepers. (Time will tell.)

If you don't answer within the week, I'll show your previous letter to Dad.

I'm sorry to have to threaten you like this. Really, I am.

Bird

Stop fretting, Bird. I'm in no more danger than you are. And right now I'm feeling embarrassed for both of us. I was a fool to write that other letter. It was too much for you—don't try to tell me it wasn't—and I'm sorry. Get ready for Thanksgiving . . . I'm coming with Aunt Clara and Uncle John and an assortment of baked goods and trinkets, and the first thing I'm going to do when I arrive is give you the biggest squeeze you ever had in your life.

Snow

*over at the bookstore* I asked Mom if she was really going to let Snow come home for Thanksgiving. That's exactly how I asked it: "Are you gonna let her?"

Mom was deciding on prices for some books that had just come in the day before. Mrs. Fletcher had taught her to do this by smelling the paper and rubbing the corners of the pages between her fingertips.

Her hair was in her face, her eyes were closed, her nose was pressed to a coffee-brown page. "It's been discussed," she said.

"And you said yes?"

She wrote a number down on her notepad. Three figures, a pause, then she added another ninety-nine cents. "If you're saying yes, then I'm saying yes."

"Really? Well . . . I am saying yes, Mom."

"That's what I figured. Needless to say I'll be watching her every move. Kidding, kidding . . ."

She wasn't kidding. I asked her what Snow had ever done to her, and she said it was a good question.

# 5

*i* never knew a Thanksgiving that took so long to come around. I guess Louis Chen got tired of hearing me repeat those words, because he said: "You know, the way you're talking is getting kind of creepy."

Aunt Mia told me not to get my hopes up. Dad made chain mail, little scraps of knitted electrum with circles of blue crystal peeping through the links. He cut the crystals in deep Vs and the surfaces were dull until you tried to look down to the bottom of them and almost cooked your eyeballs. It wasn't really jewelry—he couldn't sell it, could only give it away. He handed me a piece and told me to hit my hopes right out of the ballpark.

Mom stopped going to Grammy Olivia's coffee hours. "The gloating," she said to Aunt Mia.

Everyone who remembered Snow seemed glad

to hear she'd be back. "So pretty," I kept hearing. "So well behaved." No one said they'd missed her. Take Christina Morris who worked at the bakery—she'd been in Snow's class at school, and when Dad told her Snow might look in on her, she said "Hurray!" just as if she'd been told Miss America was coming to town. It wasn't the kind of reaction you'd give to news about someone who'd really been part of your life. I wanted to hear someone say they'd cried when they found out she wasn't coming back to school. It would've been good to hear that somebody had done what I did last summer when Louis went away to summer camp. I went after him that very same afternoon, through fields and over low bridges in the direction I'd seen the bus take, running, then limping. I got as far as the fire station in Marstow, two towns over, then the sun set and I realized I didn't know where to go next, so I walked back home with stones in my socks and was grounded for two weeks. I wanted somebody to say they'd done something like that because of Snow (who's about a hundred times prettier than Louis, after all) but no one did.

Louis's birthday was on the same day as Connie Ross's, right in the middle of September, and Mom loaned me her blanket-sized U.S. flag in exchange for my promise that I'd guard it with my life. My contribution to the picnic was a few perfectly ripe Bartlett pears and some soft cheese that had a long name and came wrapped in waxy brown paper. I wound the flag around the pears and the cheese, tied the whole package to a stick, and went through the woods with lunch over my shoulder. As I went I made a deal with myself not to talk about Snow or Thanksgiving anymore. Talking wasn't bringing either subject of conversation any closer. Also I was getting angry. Angry about the things people were saying, the way they were making Snow sound like some kind of ornament just passing by . . . not even passing by, but being passed around. Everybody agreed that Snow was valuable, but she was far too valuable to have around for keeps. Nice to look at for an afternoon, but we'll all breathe easier once she's safely back at the museum. I was beginning to hate people because of the way they talked about my sister, because of the way they didn't really want her. Even Miss Fairfax was doing it, telling Dad to just have one afternoon when Snow would be at home to all visitors so as to get all the visiting over with in one go.

We sang "Happy Birthday" and Jerry Fallon started a food fight, running around the tree trunks whooping and throwing slices of luncheon meat. Later, once everything had been hurled or eaten, we washed the cheese and bread crumbs out of our hair and passed out in the sunshine, the six of us on Mom's flag, which we'd spread out on the grass near Spooner's Brook. I made everyone take their shoes off first. Jerry and Sam were back to back, and Connie and Ruth were top to toe, but we all had our arms around and over and under one another, warm skin and frosty violets (Ruth was wearing her mother's perfume). Louis fell asleep with his head on my stomach. Once I was sure the others were asleep I laid my hand on his head. The boy was huffing and puffing the way he does when he's having dreams; it made his hair dance. I didn't sleep myself. I was just resting. Connie stood up and walked away—to pee, I thought. She didn't make any effort to sneak away quietly. She walked normally, her feet crushing leaves.

Sam went next, then Jerry, I think—I'm not sure of the order because I didn't open my eyes—then Ruth, their footsteps promising that they'd be back in a few seconds. They didn't come back. When Louis got up, I opened my eyes. I was on my own beside the brook and the splash of the water was like fast, soft hand claps, keeping time with my heart. I sat up and the flag rolled up around me. I didn't pull it up around my shoulders, it tucked itself around them. I looked over my shoulder, hoping I'd see the others in the distance, perched up in the trees grinning ghoulishly. They weren't there. But as I breathed I felt a hand crumpling my shirt, fingers and thumb spread wide across my back. My eyes were open, and I looked right at him, the owner of the hand. But I couldn't see anyone. He was there all right, but somehow it was like trying to see all of the sky at once. That was nonsense, so I tried to turn and look at him again, but an arm crossed my other shoulder and held me still. He wasn't playing rough, whoever he was; it was more like he was shy, or just teasing me.

I was still trying to decide whether it's smarter to scream before you start getting scared when he touched his lips to the back of my neck. Five times, maybe more, each kiss a little lower down. Slow, light, soft. All I saw was red, white, and blue above us, the flag streaming high as fountain jets. When he stopped, I shuddered and was breathless and warm all over. The flag lay flat and after a few minutes I felt tough enough to run my hands along the cotton, checking, but nothing moved inside it.

It wasn't Louis who kissed me. It was a boy, as far as I could tell. Those arms, still a little unsure of their own strength. I don't know who he was. He smelled of lemon peel, and I don't know any boys who go around smelling of lemon peel. Louis doesn't need to know about it, either. I doubt those kisses were even meant for me. They must belong to Mom. You know when you put on someone else's coat and old train tickets fall out of the pockets? I think maybe it was like that. Not really anything to do with me at all. Mom looked the flag over very closely when I brought it back to her, even held the seams up to the light. Once she was sure there was no damage she said I could borrow it anytime. I said thanks. And thought: *But no, thanks.* We were Whitmans. That was how I liked it—that *n* I sometimes add to my name doesn't mean much after all, it's just a frill—and that must have been how Mom liked it too, because she talks as if Flax Hill is where her memory begins. Whenever we're out of town, she compares everything to Flax Hill. Parks, stores, fountains. If that changed, I'd really have to wonder why.

It was the following Saturday that a man with an un-American accent phoned the house and asked to speak to Boy Novak. "Sorry," I said. "No Novaks around here." I thought it was a prank call, somebody calling from "deepest Transylvania" to remind me that an ancient prophecy was supposed to come true tonight. There'd been a storm going on for hours—a dark sky with lightning jumping across it, and rain coming down so hard you couldn't see exactly who was coming toward you on the street; it turned your friends into tall, damp figures scurrying around on secret business. Dad and Louis had decided it was perfect weather to grab a baseball glove and go play catch in the backyard. For everyone else the weather was right for staying home and making stupid phone calls.

"Who is this?" the man asked, in a hollow, B-movie-sorcerer voice. I told him it was the Queen of Sheba and hung up.

But that was really the way he talked. The next day Gee-Ma Agnes came round for breakfast and brought a pan of hominy pudding with her, brimming with lemons and cream. Phoebe had made it and it was so good that nobody even said anything when I licked my bowl. When Gee-Ma threatened to take me to church, Dad told her I'd go if she could catch me; it must've been the pudding that made him think it was all right to just give away a chunk of your daughter's Sunday like that. Gee-Ma made a grab at me and I ran out of the house and along the riverbank with my hula hoop, a desperate heathen in polka-dotted rubber boots, yelling *Keep laughing, Dad. You're gonna pay for this*. Gee-Ma was a lot faster than I'd expected, but she ran out of steam about ten steps away from a tree I'd planned to climb to escape her.

"I'm gonna pray for your soul, Bird Whitman," she puffed. She bent over and put her hands on her knees, letting her breath find its way back to her.

"Don't chase me, Gee-Ma," I said. "I'm not worth it." I threw my hula hoop into the air a few times until it found a branch to spin around. Then I scrambled up into the heart of that old tree. It was a linden tree, and it didn't mind being climbed—its bark had little pegs in it, pegs that held steady beneath the sole of your foot. There's a lot of privacy up there too, with the green leaves pouring down all around you. I was cold; the mist kept creeping in under my clothes. "It's not natural to flee like that when you're offered a chance to praise the Lord," Gee-Ma said. "You come down from there!"

"I can't, Gee-Ma. I'm stuck. Hey, look at all this mud."

The rainstorm had swollen the water level. I forget how tall water can be until I see it standing above earth, lifting leaves and stones off the grass and floating them away. Gee-Ma stayed back because she didn't dare get wet all the way up to her knees. My hula hoop was close by, but I didn't start swirling it around my ankle until she realized she'd be late for church and went away. That's what the man who'd phoned our house must have seen as he walked under the trees talking to himself in that B-movie voice of his (I heard him before I saw him). He must've been following us. He must've looked up and seen a hot-pink circle working its way from one end of a branch to the other, slowly, like it was searching for something. I knew he'd seen me because he stopped talking to himself. I think he was in the middle of a sentence, but he stopped. A second later he knocked the hula hoop into the mud. At first I thought he'd thrown a stone, but it was a walking stick he struck out with—he struck out more than once, more than twice, and by the time I realized that knocking my hula hoop out of the tree was only the first stage of his plan, he'd hooked the handle of the walking stick around my ankle and was pulling, pulling—

"Who are you?" he asked, real loud, as if he was scared, as if he was in my place and I was in his. I reached up, or down, it was hard to tell because my head slammed against the tree trunk and I saw my feet swinging in the air above me—my body was twisted around the branch and I locked my hands around it and held tight. The wood pushed through my skin, I said *"Vvvahhhh,"* or something like that, my teeth chopping at my tongue, the branch groaned, it wasn't going to hold me, it was coming away from the tree. I'd fall six feet or more. "Don't. Don't. Don't. Please. Please."

He stopped pulling. "Get down here."

I climbed down without answering him, hands and feet slipping in bloodied mud, and my knees gave out as soon as I was back on the ground. He put an arm around my neck and made me get up. We walked backward into the bushes. I was crying, but he didn't care. What he held flat against my hip bone was scarier than a knife—it was a syringe filled with clear liquid. The needle. There was a plastic cap on it, but light flashed along it as I struggled to breathe. "Control yourself," he said. His mouth was right against my ear, and his lips were wet. There was liquor on his breath. Some kids walked past, arguing, laughing. The girls were trying to teach the boys pig Latin.

I turned my head so I was looking right at the man with his hand over my mouth—he pushed my face away from him, but I waited and then turned my head toward him again.

"Ha, looks like Bird lost her dumb hula hoop," Fat Kenneth Young said. I heard a splash—I think he kicked at it.

The man asked me what I was staring at. He was a white man, clean-shaven. Ultra-clean-shaven; not a single cut. He had a round nose and wide-awake blue-green eyes and his white hair went up into a peak above his forehead; if we'd met some other way, I might have looked at him and thought, *Weird, it's a dolphin-man, or a man-dolphin, in a plaid shirt and jeans. He looks nice, maybe Gee-Ma would like him.*

"Please let me go home," I said, in a calm, completely fake voice. "My mom and dad are expecting me and—"

"Shut up," he whispered. "Who are you? I've seen you with Boy. At her job. And you try to boss her around at the grocery store. Queen of Sheba my ass."

(We haven't seen you.)

"I'm Bird."

He said: "You are Bird."

"Yeah. I'm—Boy's my mom, that's why I'm with her a lot."

The other kids' voices faded into the distance, and he let go of me once we were alone again. I never saw what he did with the syringe. I don't think he dropped it. Hands shaking, he fumbled around in the top pocket of his shirt, pulled out a pair of eyeglasses, put them on, and looked at me. Then he took the eyeglasses off and muttered: "Well. What can I do?"

He looked sick to his stomach. He tried to hide it, but he couldn't. His skin turned a little gray and his cheeks puffed out. I could have stood there for hours, watching him turn to stone, watching the gargoyle appear. That was his real face. Or do people only turn ugly for as long as they're looking at something ugly? I played dumb. I said: "Uh . . . what's wrong? What did I say?"

He answered me so quietly I pretty much had to lip-read. "I came to meet with my granddaughter, and you are her."

I dried my eyes on my sleeve and sighed. I didn't want it to be true, would have given a lot for it not to be true, so it had to be true.

He raised his voice. "You are slow or something? You didn't hear me?"

"I heard you."

"Well?"

"Well."

"What has your mother told you about me?"

"Nothing."

He rubbed his chin. "You hungry?"

"What?"

He offered to buy me a cheeseburger. I said I'd

eat at home, but changed my mind and went to the Mitchell Street diner with him after he promised to tell me how to catch rats, and also what Mom had been like as a kid.

"Do you really want to know how to catch rats?"

"Yeah."

"They just want the rats to go away. They believe that they should not have to think about the rats that sneak out of their garbage and into their walls, they should not have to see how those disgusting creatures die. That's what I'm paid for. I'm supposed to catch my rats and hold my tongue and let it all be like magic."

"Well, tell me about it."

"You are not squeamish?"

"Yeah, I am. But I still want to know."

"I shouldn't have treated you this way that I have treated you. I'm sorry."

I didn't believe him and I walked behind him so I'd have fair warning if he went for me again. I guess I wanted to have something to tell Snow.

We took a booth at the Mitchell Street diner. Susie Conlin handed him a menu before she took me to the restroom and soaked my hands in a basin. She dabbed disinfectant on the cuts the linden tree gave me. There were seven. She counted them aloud and made me count along with her. She was my regular babysitter for about a year and a half, so she still talks down to me something awful, and maybe always will. I don't mind her doing it, though. She just likes looking after people. Dad's making her a tiny rainbow stud for the piercing she just got in her nose.

*i ate my cheeseburger* with a knife and fork so it wouldn't taste of disinfectant. But Frank thought I was trying to be ladylike. "Your father teach you that?" He grinned, and I did the same. I just took what was in his grin and gave it right back to him. He choked on a french fry and I passed him a napkin.

When he really started talking, I borrowed a pad and pen from Susie and took notes. Taking notes meant I didn't hear his tone of voice as much.

FRANK NOVAK
- He was flattered that I was writing down what he said. Flattered or he felt he had a message to give. He spoke slowly and repeated himself so I could get it all down.
- He wanted to know if I was going to call the police on him. "Good luck getting them to believe you."
- "You are not adopted?" he asked, hopefully.
- How can he be Mom's dad? There's no trace of her in him, or vice versa. And that's weird, because he's a forceful man. For instance, I couldn't push back

against his accent. My vowels started to copy his—he thought I was making fun of him. Mom would've had to be really careful and deliberate in her decisions not to do anything the way he did it. No moving her hands through the air in an almost musical way as she speaks, no pursing her lips, no excitement, calm, always calm. Maybe he noticed what she was doing. I'll bet he hated that.

- When he talked about rats, his forehead tightened and he looked lost. It was as if the words he was saying didn't mean anything to him, they'd decided to say themselves and he was hoping they'd leave him alone if he just cooperated. He didn't tell me how to catch rats in the end. He kept working up to it, then he'd say: "It's all I know. Maybe you shouldn't say everything you know. Maybe it leaves you empty-headed, eh?"

- I asked him about the syringe, what the liquid in it was. He said: "What syringe?" (What did he do with it? If I'd called the police, would they have found it on him? I went back to the linden tree with Louis a couple of days later and we searched for hours. If he'd dropped it, we would have found it. He didn't seem to know what I was talking about. Acting? I half believe I could dream up a syringe. But only half.)

- He says a rat bit him on the face when he was a boy. Mom was really surprised that he'd told me that. She doesn't know if it's true; that was the first she'd heard of it. He said he used to have to go through trash cans looking for food. And there was a rat in the trash can, and the rat was hungry too; he was taking its food, so it bit him on the face. I tried to dislike him a little bit less after he told me that, because that's the kind of thing that shouldn't happen to anyone. "Where's the scar?" I asked. He laughed. "It healed well. It healed well."
- He read to me from a little suede-covered book. *"The bites of rats are sometimes difficult to recognize. They always attack the parts that are fat, i.e., the cheeks and the heels—"* The book was falling apart onto the tabletop, and the pages he was reading from didn't have any print on them. *"They divide the skin in a straight line, which often has the appearance of having been cut with a knife; so close is the resemblance that it's often difficult to avoid a mistake—"* He said those were the

findings of a French doctor from a long time ago. I just said okay. He said: "Look it up sometime. I'm serious . . . look it up." I said okay.

- Hard to know how to take the things he said about Mom. I don't accept what he said but I can't get past it. He told me Mom is evil. I said: "What do you mean, 'evil'?"
- FN stands for Frank Novak and BW stands for Bird Whitman. (I had to be quick; I think I said more but I can't remember what I said.)
- FN: I'm not talking about powers of darkness or something you can protect yourself from with crosses and holy water. Of course it is difficult to describe, because it seems so ordinary. Seems so, but is not. Evil studies the ordinary and imitates it. Then you can say it was just a little bad temper, we all know what that is. But some people . . . with some people the spite goes so deep, it is a thing beyond personality . . . you don't want to understand me. I'm speaking of a little girl who was born too early. She was so small. It was crazy how small she was. She didn't open her eyes for days after she was born. She kept her eyes closed and shivered and shivered,

like someone was yelling at her that she wasn't going to make it and she was doing all she could to ignore them. Maybe she wasn't meant to live, I don't know. But she wanted to, this baby girl. She struggled. She really struggled. I didn't work for a month. I held her, walked around the house holding her in a blanket. They couldn't do much at the hospital. They didn't have those good machines to help out back then. I remember a nurse told me I should have a Mass said for the baby's soul. A wet nurse came every day—it was the one time in my life I've wished I was a woman, so the wet nurse wouldn't have had to come for my child. The doctor came every other day. I don't know how she pulled through. This is the thing— maybe it wasn't her that pulled through. Maybe it was just that will to exist in the world. I mean, it wasn't the will of someone young, it was the will of . . . something that has had life before and knows that life is good.

- It's not Mom's fault if she was born too early.
- There was so much he wasn't saying I didn't know where to start with the questions.

When I opened my mouth, he held up his hand.

FN: There was a morning I was sure that she was gone. I woke up and she wasn't shivering anymore. You see, I slept sitting up in a chair against the wall, so it couldn't tilt back. I slept that way so I could have her against my chest through the night. To keep her warm, I suppose. To keep her alive. If anything was wrong, I wanted to feel it immediately. So. She wasn't shivering. I lifted her up and she was so much heavier than she had been the night before. She didn't move at all. I put my cheek against her cheek and I cried. I cried so much. And I said *Why?* There was knocking at the outside door as well. I heard it but I didn't answer, I held the dead child. It was afternoon when I looked at her again . . . I'd been crying all that time. I looked at her again and her eyes were open. She was alive again. There was a teardrop on her chin and she was trying to see it.

BW: You think it was the crying that brought her back?

FN: Without question it was the crying. She liked it. She got better after that.

She got strong. The first time I saw her smile—I switched on the wireless set one evening and tried to find some music for us. A woman was being killed in a radio play on one of the stations, and the actress screamed. I thought it'd make Boy nervous, but Santa Claus himself couldn't have gotten a wider smile out of her.

BW: That all?

FN: I could tell you tens of stories about the pain she caused other children before she learned to be scared that I'd catch her at it. Most children get into fights, but it's a bad sign when a child fights dirty, without anyone even showing her how. One girl angered Boy in some way—she said something, I think—this girl had a sore leg; she'd had some small accident days before . . . it was the sore leg that Boy went for, quick as quick. She kicked that sore leg out from under the girl. The happy children, the ones who had friends they could rely on, those children were safe from her. She was drawn to the anxious ones. The ones who had potential for misery. I watched her.

When she ran away from home, I
knew she'd gone to find someone
who was unhappy, and once she'd
found them she'd use her gift to
make it worse.

BW: What do you think Boy would say if
I told her all this?

FN: Don't know. Try it.

- He suddenly became a gentleman and
asked if I wanted the rest of his french
fries. He said he hated waste.

*dad knocked on* the diner window; I saw him and
Frank didn't. He had my hula hoop tucked under
his arm, and when he reached us, he dropped it
and picked me up off my seat. He held me tight
against his chest and said, "Thank God," and
"You're grounded forever," and I heard the hoop
rolling around on the tiled floor.

I said: "I don't get why I'm grounded forever."

"It's directly connected to what happens in a
father's heart when he finds a pink hula hoop just
lying there in the mud. To find that and have no
idea where its owner is—I mean, goddamn it,
Bird."

I thought about it. He was right.

"And then I ask around and nobody remembers
having seen her. And *then* Agnes starts talking
about enemies—"

"This is Flax Hill. I couldn't have gone far."

"Don't you see that that's what made it so scary that no one had seen you? Your mom's been on the phone to every kid in your class. But then Susie called your grammy. And you're grounded forever."

It was funny—I'd kind of expected Frank to be gone when Dad finally put me down, but Frank was still there, dipping his french fries in mayonnaise. He'd probably guessed that Dad wouldn't hit an old man.

"Arturo Whitman," Dad said, and held out his hand.

Frank went right on eating. "I know who you are," he said.

Dad looked at me, looked back at Frank, then suggested that Frank introduce himself. Frank said his name, said it with pride, and Dad grabbed his arm and forced him out of the booth. For a second I thought Frank was going to get beaten around the head with his own walking stick, but Dad pressed it into his hand and told him to get out. "Just go. And if I see you look back at me or my daughter—if you look back at us even once— I'll kick you right into the middle of next week."

Frank said: "Why would I want to look back?" And he did as he was told.

*apparently susie conlin* told Dad to come get me because of Frank's negative energy. She told

307

Dad I was sitting in a booth with an old man who was telling me his life story and stopped talking whenever she walked past. She said I was writing down everything the man said, that I was wincing as I wrote with my bandaged hand, and that I looked really tired. She thought the old man should find somebody else to tell his life story to.

"He didn't hurt you, did he?"

"No."

"If he did—"

"No. It was the tree that cut me."

"Show me what you wrote down."

"He took it with him."

Mom was sarcastic when we got home. "You and your Nancy Drew act. Thanks for coming home," she said, interrupting Dad, who was telling her about Frank and how he didn't think Frank was going to come near us again. She was red-faced and red-eyed. I put her arms around me and held them there until she hugged me.

*also . . . i found out* the worst thing that can happen when you tell someone you love them. I thought that if you love someone and they don't love you back then they're nice to you. Or at least, if you end up feeling terrible, the other person didn't mean for that to happen. But Mom said "I love you" to some man on the phone, a man named Charlie, and he said: "Why?"

I got into the eavesdropping late, but I knew she

was the one who'd called him, because the phone hadn't rung. She was mad at him. She thought he'd told her dad where to find us. "You told that man about me and Bird!" she said. He said he hadn't spoken to Frank Novak in years, and was Bird a boy or a girl, and Mom said: "She's my daughter. My little girl." Then this Charlie person said he had two sons, and a wife. He said he was happy. (I could almost hear Frank Novak saying "The happy ones were safe from her.") That was when Mom told him she loved him. And he asked why.

Mom said: "Charlie? Charlie?" as if the phone line wasn't working properly, but the line was clear. He said he had to go and hung up. Then I had to wait for Mom to hang up—obviously I couldn't hang up before she did. She didn't put the phone down for at least a minute. I stood there listening to the dial tone and began to wonder if this was a trick and she'd left the receiver off the hook in the parlor so she could appear in the hallway and tell me I'd been busted. Then I thought she might be crying into the phone, but her breathing was regular. After she hung up I dashed across the hallway and into bed with my heart going like gangbusters.

Mom: Charlie . . . I love you.

Charlie: Why?

Mom wore sunshades for the next few days. She wore them indoors and at night, and she smiled when Dad teased her. He thought she was acting that way because Snow was coming home.

Dad: I love you, honey.

Mom: And I love you.

She slept all the way through the weekend. She didn't even get up to eat.

I tried to tell Aunt Mia that she should maybe come over or take Mom out somewhere. I'd want someone to tell Louis I was feeling down if for some reason I couldn't tell him myself. But Aunt Mia was avoiding me. When I called her apartment, she said, "Hello?" and then dropped the phone when she heard my voice, and then I had to call back six times before she finally answered. If that isn't avoiding somebody then I don't know what is.

"What's new?" she asked, once she was done denying that she was avoiding me.

"I met my grandfather."

"Oh?"

"Yeah, on Mom's side."

"I figured. Well?"

"Well, we sort of hated each other."

(I'd cried about that. The tears came all of a sudden, when I was jumping rope with Ruth and Paula. Suddenly my feet wouldn't leave the ground and my face and neck felt raw, as if they'd been scraped with rocks. It was the look he'd given me when he understood that I was his granddaughter. It was like a burn. And now that I was safe from it, the syringe scared me even more.)

"It's okay, *cara*. I didn't get along too well with one of my grandfathers, either."

"Yeah, but . . . this was . . . anyway, he said something weird."

Aunt Mia dropped something—a coffee cup, something like that. There was clattering and I heard her curse and scrabble around with a paper towel. Then she said: "To you? He said something weird to you?"

"Yeah. How's your objectivity?"

Aunt Mia said: "Fine, I guess. Why? What did he say?"

"He said that Mom's evil."

I repeated myself after a couple of seconds because Aunt Mia didn't say a word. I wasn't sure she was still there. I'm not always sure about Mom, but Aunt Mia is definitely not evil, and in a way she's my proof that Mom is morally okay. It would've helped if Aunt Mia had laughed or seemed shocked, but she was just quiet. I began to whisper it a third time but she stopped me: "Can you put your mom on the line?"

"I thought you'd never ask. She's sleeping, though. Do I try to wake her up?"

"No. No, let her rest. Just . . . tell her to call me."

"But you're okay, right?"

She called me a sweetheart for asking. It was hard to tell whether or not Mom and Aunt Mia had

311

fallen out. Mom didn't seem to think so, but maybe she'd done something that Aunt Mia was holding a grudge over. I know she went to Aunt Mia's place twice, but both times Aunt Mia wasn't home.

Dad asked if we should be worried about Mia, and Mom got irritated. "Why should we be worried about Mia, Arturo? Because she's not married? Because she works hard at a job she likes?"

Dad let a few seconds go by and then said: "The Mia we know makes a little time for her friends no matter what, that's all."

" 'The Mia we know,' eh? So what are you saying . . . that there's this whole other Mia we don't know?"

There was quite a long discussion about it and Mom didn't realize she'd been tricked out of being irritated until Dad had made some rough sketches to show us which one of Aunt Mia's bookcases could be a door that revolved into a hidden room.

I did what I could to smoke Aunt Mia out . . . I mailed her a copy of the notes I'd taken at the diner. She'd have called if she'd read them, no doubt about it. They must have gotten lost in the mail.

# 6

*i* came home from school on the Tuesday before Thanksgiving and Snow was there, playing Julia's piano. Not a whole piece of music, just tumbling little passages. I peeped around the parlor door and watched her working the piano pedals with her bare feet. The bare feet seemed proof that she was out of the ordinary; it was already so cold that I was wearing socks over two layers of pantyhose. Dad came up behind me and pushed me into the room with her, saying: "C'mon, that's your sister in there."

She looked more colored in person. Maybe it was the way she'd chosen to wear her hair, combed and pinned up on one side of her head so that it all rained down on one shoulder and left the other exposed to the dusty sunlight. She smiled at me and the words I'd been about to say went into hiding.

"Have mercy, Bird Whitman. I may need you to dial it back a notch with the cuteness," she said, and slid off the piano stool. She was three days early. Her voice was a lot more girlish than I'd imagined it, considering the things she'd written to me, but her hugging technique was like Dad's, maybe even a little more intense. She'd brought me a bouquet. Some of them looked like squashed gray-blue poppies. Others were almost roses, their color a stormy purple. Their petals and stamen were all twisted together, but they smelled good. Snow said they were the kind of flowers that only opened up at night; you picked them at night and then they stayed open.

"They're not poison flowers, are they?"

She stared at me. "What?"

"You know . . . like La Belle Capuchine's flowers in your letter . . ."

"Oh! Ha ha. No, no poison."

"And no suitcase, either?"

"Left it at number eleven. I'll be sleeping over there, in that creepy room with the tulle curtains and the sugar plum fairy mobiles. You know, I never even liked ballerinas."

"Huh, well you should've said so."

"I think I started to once, and everybody started saying, 'Uh oh . . . *somebody's* not herself today.' I was outnumbered."

"Oh." So she was outnumbered. That was not a good excuse.

"Come to the mirror." She fixed one of the night flowers behind my ear and stood looking over my shoulder.

"I see it," she said.

I looked at us. "What?" We didn't look as though we were related. Not even cousins.

"That thing you wrote to me about how technically impossible things are always trying so

314

hard to happen to us, and just letting the nearest technically impossible thing happen—"

"Oh . . . yeah, I see it too! Oh, Snow. Think of all the pranks we can play."

The mirror caught a few rays of sunset through the open front door, and the image of us went chestnut-colored at the corners. Snow's hand was on my shoulder and both my own hands were at my sides, but our reflections didn't call that any kind of reunion. The girls in the mirror had their arms around each other, and they smiled at us until we followed their lead.

"Looks like long ago," Snow said. "Like Great-aunt Effie just said: 'I hope you girls don't think you're something new? We've had sisters like you in this family before.' And then she shows us an old, old photo . . . one of those tinted daguerreotypes . . ."

She lay with her head in my lap for most of the afternoon, jumping up every now and again to start a disc spinning on the record player. We talked about Frank Novak and how he'd told me Mom was evil and she said, "You know that's not true, right? I don't know what she is, but evil isn't it." We talked about Ephraim, who was most definitely not her boyfriend and was never going to be.

"So . . . your room at number eleven. What did you want instead of ballerinas?" I asked.

She really considered the question, as if it still

mattered and changes would be made based on the answer she gave.

"Plain pink and white. Deep pink, not cotton-candy pink."

We heard Dad telling someone it was an open house, and Miss Fairfax started walking up the hallway toward us. The pattern of her footsteps is pretty distinctive, elegant, just like her. I know it well from being designated lookout at school. But she turned back when she heard us talking. Others came by with covered dishes and clay pots; they didn't speak to us, just rapped their knuckles on the open door, waved, and left notes on the kitchen table, alongside their offerings.

(*Will return to kiss thine hand at thy earliest convenience, fair maiden—Anon.*

*Welcome back, Snow. Let's catch up soon! Susie Conlin.*

*Hey there, beautiful one, don't you dare leave before you come see us—Mr. and Mrs. Murray.*)

Later in the evening we went to see what there was to eat and I was awestruck. There wasn't an inch of space left on the tabletop, or on any of the counters; it had all been taken over by multicolored crockery. The air smelled roasted. "Uh . . . I've never seen anything like this before," I said, grabbing at a pile of note cards before they slipped onto the floor. But when I looked at Snow, I caught her finishing a yawn.

"Me, either," she said. "Isn't it kind of

everybody?" I didn't answer her. She started reading some of the note cards with a really touched expression, but I'd caught her. She was used to being treated like this. It was nothing to her. I had a moment of hating her, or at least understanding why Mom did. Thankfully it came and went really quickly, like a dizzy spell, or a three-second blizzard. Does she know that she does this to people? Dumb question. This is something we do to her.

*one
two
three*

# 1

*i* don't know who or what anybody is anymore. There are exceptions: My husband is one, and Alecto Fletcher's another. The other day Arturo looked into my eyes and said: "Here I am, with my stupid face. Remember? The face that's so stupid you told me you never wanted to see it again?" His hair's thinned a lot on top, but he's even more lionlike now that he's all bewhiskered, and I just haven't got a single defense against him anymore. I almost spoke about it to Webster. Ted gets cheaper and cheaper all the time; his behavior at restaurants is becoming incredible—how convenient that he falls asleep or has to use the restroom just before the bill arrives. The question "How can you love him?" could sour my friendship with Webster at this point. Because she does love Ted. Fiercely. Wives are uncanny creatures, the day is a boxing ring and we dart around the corners of it, pushing our luck with both hands. We risk becoming so commonplace to the men we've thrown our lots in with who can't see us anymore, and who pat the sofa when they mean to pat our knee. That or we become so incomprehensible that it repulses our husbands, who after all can't be expected to stomach a side dish of passionate misery at every meal, no matter how much variety there is. But husbands are uncanny too. It all seems to come from having to be each other's anchor, bread and butter, constant calm. Emotionally speaking he and I have to remain in some fixed state where we can always be found if necessary. In the midst of arguments I should rightfully have won I've found myself conceding points to him because some appeal is made to this fixed place. A look, a word, a touch. How could anyone enjoy this, the possibility, necessity even, of their being called to heel in this way? It disturbs me that there's a part of my heart or mind, or some spot where the two meet, a spot that isn't mine because I'm a wife. This part isn't really me at all, but a promise I made on a snowy day. A promise to stay and to be with Arturo and to be good to him, and when there's no other way, I have to go to that promise to find my feeling for my husband. We walk the finest of foolish, foolish lines. How can Webster still love Ted? How can anybody love anybody else for more than five minutes?

Alecto Fletcher was the only one I could tell about Charlie and Arturo—without using their names, of course. I said: "Suppose there's a woman who's finding that she's only really started to love somebody now that somebody else has stopped loving her—do you think that's real, or would you say this woman's just trying to make the best of things?"

Alecto picked caviar out of her teeth and said: "Well."

"I'm asking for a friend."

"Were those exact words said: 'I no longer love you'?"

"No."

"No. Hardly anybody ever says it like that, do they? They simply become unkind. Look—for some people love is like a king they swear allegiance to. That kind of person has to be released from one bond before they can begin to forge another. All very conventional behavior, but fiercely interior convention. I'm not trying to imply that such people are wise or that they impress me—I'm one of them, and it's probably the most futile form of integrity going. But if it's a side dish to other forms of integrity, then it's all right. And there are worse scenarios, Boy."

"Worse scenarios than what?"

"Than love not beginning on time, of course."

All right, I don't know what or who anybody is anymore except for Arturo, Alecto, and Clara and John Baxter. Clara and John are a fine couple and that's all there is to it. They put an impenetrable barrier of good manners up against some of Olivia's more insulting inquiries, but didn't bow their heads to pray when grace was said. As we all sat around that table together, Gerald putting away heavy-duty quantities of turkey and stuffing so he didn't have to talk, Vivian clearly wanting to show some warmth toward her sister but ending up just squeaking platitudes at her, John attempting to drink away the feeling of being pretty damn unwelcome, Agnes keeping Snow's left hand prisoner so that the girl had to alternate between use of her knife and use of her fork, as I sat there with that family of mine I reassessed Olivia as a fellow nonswerver. She stood by the decisions she'd taken with Clara because there was nowhere else for her to stand. Clara has a good heart, but goodness is independent from gentleness. Had Olivia exposed a chink in her armor there could've been a bloodbath. Quite rightly so, I guess. That old woman treats my Bird as coldly as she can get away with, stopping just short of making Arturo lose his temper. But the sight and sound of her acting out all that hostility . . . I couldn't sit next to that without wanting to try to shield her somehow. I don't know, just so she could rest for a moment before picking up her battle-ax again. Olivia was young when she sent Clara away, young and probably so brutal that Gerald thought it was better for the child to grow up in Biloxi than stay home and be stepped on. If that's what Gerald thought, who's to say he wasn't right about that? Olivia had raised Vivian, and there Vivian was, a thirty-eight-year-old attorney-at-law who should have had enough poise to keep her from gaping when her brother-in-law told her some of the things he used to do for youthful kicks. John Baxter used to follow middle-aged white ladies down deserted streets at night, walking faster as they walked faster, slowing down if a witness appeared. He found their fear of him hilarious and sad. One woman begged him to leave her alone and tried to make him take her purse. Another woman turned around, walked toward him, put her hand on his arm, and whispered, "How much?" That took the thrill out of the game, and he stopped playing it. Clara, Arturo, and I were the only ones who laughed at that. Snow said, "Uncle John," in a tiny, distressed voice. It was pretty effective, the gasp of distress combined with the white dress and the ardent glance and the shadowy hair all loose around her face.

"I don't get it," Bird said. I told her I'd explain later, and she answered: "No, you won't." She nudged me and pointed her chin in Gerald's direction. My usually amiable father-in-law had stopped chewing and was just holding his food in his mouth. He looked revolted by John and everything John said. But then Gerald had been eating too much.

"Emmett Till," he said, suddenly. "Emmett Till did what he did just one time. Livia, what is it he did . . . right, he whistled. He was a Northerner and he didn't know any better. So he whistled at a Mississippi white woman. She didn't like that, so fetched her gun. But she didn't have to use it;

she had a husband and a brother-in-law, real men who weren't afraid to take on a fourteen-year-old boy. You saw what they did to Emmett Till. You saw the boy's face. Agnes, you cried and said he looked melted—"

(Fourteen years old. So close to Bird's age. Too close.)

Olivia gave Gerald's sleeve a brisk tug, to remind him he was in mixed company and that people were trying to eat. He lowered his voice a little: "But you, John Baxter, you know that the men who killed Emmett Till didn't do a single second of jail time on account of that murder. And you, a Kentucky man yourself, not even a Northerner . . . you say you scared white women for fun. Didn't you value your life? Didn't you see that if the authorities didn't give a damn about you, you had to give that much more of a damn about yourself? I don't know what you think of me, and I don't much care, but I'll thank you not to sit at my table and brag about your stupidity."

Clara laid her knife and fork down, and placed her hands in her lap. She and John made a painfully obvious point of not looking at each other. They seemed more embarrassed for Gerald than insulted on their own behalves. Arturo said: "Now wait a minute, Dad—" but John shook his head. "Your pa was just speaking his mind. I wasn't bragging, Mr. Whitman. It didn't matter too much whether I was deliberately following them or whether I just happened to be going their way, those women would've been just as scared regardless, so why not make a joke out of it? I guess I had some form of death wish, and I knew just how little anyone who looks like me has to do to get killed. I saw the face that Emmett Till was left with. I want you to know that I wasn't bragging."

Clara had shifted her chair so that her shoulder rested against John's, but she still didn't look at him. The two of them kept right on facing Gerald, who muttered something about John still needing to take more time to think before he spoke.

I'd hoped that Bird was too busy reciting Spanish poetry to her father to overhear that particular exchange, but the kid dashed those hopes of mine by suddenly asking me if I had a pen. I said I didn't, and that there was to be no leaving the table in search of one, either. I know I can't keep my daughter from tracking down that picture of Emmett Till's remains lying in their casket—Mia will probably show it to her, if nobody else will—but I can make it harder for Bird's grief to begin. I doubt she'll believe that I share it; not at first, maybe not for a while. It's been thirteen years since the murder, but for Bird the news would be minutes old. I've tried to tell her a few things I've figured out, but I can see that she doesn't get what I'm saying, it's like I'm just bothering her, all she hears is mumbling. The three things I know:

First, I'm with Bird in any Them versus Us situation she or anyone cares to name.

Second, it's not whiteness itself that sets Them against Us, but the worship of whiteness. Same goes if you swap whiteness out for other things— fancy possessions for sure, pedigree, maybe youth too . . . I'm still of two minds about that.

Third, we beat Them (and spare ourselves a lot of tedium and terror) by declining to worship.

Bird needs time. I hope I'll remember thinking this if she ever comes to disbelieve that I love her. No revelation is immediate, not if it's real. I feel that more and more.

When it was time for each of us to say what we were thankful for, Agnes thanked Clara and John for taking such good care of Snow "for us."

Clara didn't raise her voice, but the aftermath was just as if she'd yelled and smashed her wineglass. "For you? We did it for Snow."

Bird nodded at her. She's growing up into a huntress, every line in her clear and strong. She got her eyes from me, and when I talk, she dissects me with my own gaze. That's gratitude for you. Her first period came, and she called me into the bathroom. She was sitting on the can with her knees pressed together and her underpants in her hand, and she showed me the blood with an expression that asked me how she could possibly

be expected to tolerate this level of incon-
venience. I remembered her at six years old; she
came home from her first day at elementary
school and wanted to know who she could speak
to about not having to go there anymore. She was
sure that there was some official type who took
you off the school register if you just went to them
and explained that you didn't like it. I wouldn't
have minded a tender mother-daughter moment
in which I reassured us both that she was still my
little girl, but in reality I had to say "Welcome
to womanhood" quite assertively, maybe even
aggressively, for fear she wouldn't accept it
otherwise. I'm leaving it to Arturo to give her the
talk about fooling around with boys and waiting
until she's sure that the boy respects her. Louis is
well brought up and their friendship strikes me as
genuine, but he's older than she is, and his friends
set each other stupid dares. Those knuckleheads
think they invented pig Latin. About three years
ago Arturo got wistful about not having a son. I
told him we could look into adopting a boy and he
said: "Let me ask you something, Boy. Where do
you get the balls to bluff the way you do?"

At the dinner table John began to tell another
story from the good old days (this one had a
carefully edited sound to it), but Bird reached
across the table and pushed the edge of Vivian's
dinner plate with her fork. "What's that in your
cranberry sauce?"

Vivian hurriedly stabbed at the subject of Bird's inquiry with her fork and flipped it into a paper napkin, but Clara declared: "Hair."

"Hair?" Gerald said, and Vivian looked ready to die. A couple more sizeable clumps fell onto her turkey as her fingers fluttered nervously around her glossy beehive hairdo, and Arturo and I gazed at each other with dread. For my part I was sure this drastic shedding signaled a serious illness, and my memory suddenly opened up an uncomfortable index of all the occasions upon which I hadn't shown her the kindness she deserved.

Olivia was unimpressed. "What is the meaning of this, Vivian?"

Vivian scraped more hair into her napkin, forced a laugh, and said: "Sorry, Mama—I think it's the lye. Too strong, or too regularly applied, something like that. But I'm fine"—she glanced at Arturo and reached around the back of Snow's chair to squeeze his arm—"I'm fine."

"You always did overdo things, Vivian." Olivia gestured to Agnes to pass down the wine carafe, but Clara handed the wine to her mother herself, saying: "You always did preach about hair. So tell us, what did Viv overdo? Was she supposed to pass as white, but only just? Was she supposed to come top of her class every time, but only just?"

Olivia very calmly began to remind Clara that we were having a family dinner and that it was unpleasant for everybody when people spoke out of turn, but Vivian took a gulp of wine, rallied, and said: "No, Mama. I want to know. What did I overdo? It's more than what Clara says. I could go on and on . . ."

Gerald cleared his throat. "That's enough. You listen to me. All your mama and I wanted was for our children to make some kind of difference in people's lives. To serve justice, to teach, to do good—Clara, this includes you. Circumstances— we—well. We've tried hard to make it easier for you to do those things without people slamming doors in your faces."

Arturo sighed and said tonelessly: "Thank you." Gerald turned in his son's direction with a look of puzzled appeal, but Clara spoke first: "Can you really mean it, Pa, that all folks have to do is look the part? Does Viv get no credit at all from you for working damn hard and being good at what she does, plain and simple?" Her tone wasn't aggressive, more idly inquisitive, and she didn't look her father in the eye, but stared at the square of floral wallpaper above his head, clearly not expecting great things of the halting answer he began to give her.

Olivia leaned forward and snapped: "For God's sake, wake up from your dream world, Clara. You go and find out how many colored women are pulling down the salary that Vivian is, and we'll talk about this again."

John began nodding. "You know she's got a point there, Clara."

Olivia half smiled at him and Clara half frowned at him and he said: "Not that passing is the way."

"That statement would carry far greater weight with me if it had come from someone who stood even a remote chance of passing," Olivia said.

(From the moment Clara had first spoken up, Agnes Miller had been sadly humming "Sinner Man," of all songs. *Oh, sinner man . . . where you gonna run to?* Arturo asked her to cut it out and she said: "Cut what out?"

"The humming, Agnes. The humming," Arturo told her. "We don't need it right now."

She stopped, bewildered. "Who was that humming? I didn't like it, either. Oh . . . I see . . . you're sure it was me . . . ? I'm so sorry.")

Olivia looked across the table at Vivian, who'd tied a scarf around her head. "I see now that you must do what you want, Vivian. Stop keeping your hair tidy, if that's what you think is damaging it—I've never had any trouble in that area, but as I say, do what you want to do. I'm your mother and God knows I'd rather have you well than sick. Do you understand?"

Everybody kept still. I'd become aware of my neck swiveling as I looked at each person who spoke. This watchfulness was partly selfish, I was anticipating an episode of plate hurling and wanted to be sure I wasn't caught in the crossfire.

Snow and Bird hadn't moved their heads much—it was their gaze that had been traveling from person to person, on opposite sides of the table. But if my daughter and her sister had noticed each other's expressions, they might've been surprised to find that they both looked exactly like Judgment Day.

Vivian walked around the table to her mother's seat and shyly submitted to being kissed on the forehead. There was also a whispered recital of pet names I never knew she had. Agnes piped up: "I hear they're beginning to say that black is beautiful now."

Olivia gave her friend a deeply cynical look and said: "We'll see. Would anyone like some more of these potatoes? They're very good, Clara."

"Fattening, though . . ." Agnes murmured, but Olivia continued: "I hope you'll let me have the recipe."

"Sure," Clara said, in a faint voice. Maybe she couldn't find the caustic tone she wanted. Brazenness can knock you sideways like that.


*i volunteered to* clear away the plates once everyone was done eating, and Snow got up to help me. Vivian and Agnes and Olivia talked over one another. *Oh no no no, Snow, you're the guest of honor, leave it 'til Phoebe comes tomorrow—* but Clara gave Snow the nod that sent her to the kitchen sink with me.

I meant to ask Snow how she and Bird were getting along. I'd thought they'd be inseparable, but I hadn't really seen them together. I'd seen Bird roaming the woods with her gang of five, and I'd seen Snow out on the terrace of Flax Hill's European-style café (European-style as far as any of us could tell, anyhow), smoking cigarettes, hearing out marriage proposals, and giving them marks out of ten. The girls in the group laughed indulgently, knowing that Snow was too nice to want what wasn't hers, and why not let your boyfriend practice proposing so he'd get it just right for you? The girls' laughter got a little artificial when Snow dropped her lighter and six or seven of the boyfriends vied to pick it up. Bird's fifteen-year-old beau couldn't speak for stammering when he encountered Snow on the porch; yes, of course he did. Here's what I couldn't have foreseen—that I'd be anxious for Snow and her sister to be friends. More specifically, I thought it would be better if Bird liked Snow. I couldn't give a reason for this anxiety; Bird has disliked people before and they've been fine. But like everybody else around here, Bird isn't quite as she was. Maybe the timing of this visit is bad. While Snow's out in the evening, Bird plays Julia's lullabies at low volume and sits cross-legged beside the record player, listening with a vacant expression. Arturo asked me if Snow was aware that Bird had borrowed her records, and I mixed him a drink and handed it to him before I answered. "Don't take this as me bad-mouthing your daughter; I'm not. It's not so easy to tell what Snow is and isn't aware of. She very sweetly keeps those cards close to her chest; I hope you won't deny that."

My husband drained his glass, and when he spoke again, it was about Bird, not Snow. He reminded me of how she'd been deeply interested in the Cinderella story for a few months when she was nine years old, how she'd had one or the other of us read it to her a countless number of times and gone to sleep without expressing approval or disapproval until one night when Arturo closed the storybook and she asked: "Is it a true story? Not the fairy godmother stuff and her dress turning back to rags at midnight—I know that's true. But Cinderella just sweeping up all those ashes every day and never putting them into her stepmother's food or anything—is that true?" He said he knew it was dangerous to say yes, but another part of him thought *So what—she can't prove it isn't true.* Our daughter settled back onto pillows and said pleasantly, "I think they're lying to us, Dad," before switching off her bedside lamp to let him know he was dismissed for the night. He said that the way Bird was listening to Julia's voice reminded him of the way she'd listened to the Cinderella story all those times we'd told it to her. He was understandably concerned, so I told

335

him everything was going to be okay, which was another lie of the Cinderella variety.

The sink was big enough for Snow and me to stand side by side while we soaked and scrubbed all the sauce boats and soup bowls and the swallow-patterned plates. We looked into the dishwater instead of at each other. She trickled water through her fingers.

"Weren't we here together like this years ago? Only I sat up on the counter. It was your birthday and you were stirring things and chopping things and begging a cake to rise."

"That was in the other house."

She brought both her hands down and punched the water, spraying us both with greasy suds. I took a few steps back in case she was about to run amok, but she went still and kept her eyes averted. I wiped my face with a kitchen towel, decided to work the "game of charades" angle, and said, "Angry?" in the same tone of voice I'd have used to ask *Animal, mineral, or vegetable?*

She said: "I'm sorry. Close the door, please. This isn't like me."

When I came back to the sink, she was scrubbing again, elbow deep in dishes.

"Snow. Who told you it isn't like you to get mad?"

She didn't answer, just dragged her sleeve across her face, then returned both hands to the sink.

"You feel I've treated you badly? Snow?"

"Yes, you have."

I'd like to know if Snow has come to feed on adoration, on the gentle tone of voice people take with her. Does everybody who crosses her path have to love her? Capture all hearts and let none go free, is that the way she wants it? But I don't think she knows the answer any more than I do. She's mad that I haven't been able to love her. Maybe she's afraid that I see something in her that she isn't able to see for herself. But the trouble is, I don't see much of anything when I try to see her. She stands near me and I know that someone's there, but when I look, I find another face in the way, and hear another voice, not Snow's at all, but distorted versions of my own face and voice, I think. And even though this screen and I have become aware of each other, the screen rests easy, banking on its history of standing between people and my own aversion to closeness. I've been so afraid of getting closeness wrong, because I don't know how to do it, because I don't know what my mistakes reveal—maybe they reveal very good reasons for my having been unloved as a child, I just don't know.

"Let's make up," I said.

"How? I don't hear you apologizing."

Our reflections rippled in the water, stretching to breaking point, and swam away from each other in pieces, then the pieces shivered together again, stretched to their limit, burst.

"Let's do it the way kids do it," I said.

"The way kids do it?" She was looking at my reflection, not at me.

"You know . . . when you treat a friend badly and you both know it and the only way to get them to forgive you is to let them hurt you."

"What? That wasn't how I made up with my friends," she said with alarm.

"Oh. Maybe it was just a Lower East Side thing." (Maybe it was me who'd taught my classmates that this was the way to make up.) "Anyway. Hit me."

She blinked rapidly. "No."

"I recommend it."

"But I don't want to. So."

"Look . . . the way it was when I was a kid, the person you'd treated badly had to hurt you back, or there were two possibilities. The first was that you continued to like them but you lost respect for them, because in the world of kid think, not taking revenge can be a sign of weakness. The other option, and this is something that continues into adult think, is that the other person's not taking their moment to hurt you made you stop liking them as much. You started to fear them, because it seemed like they were waiting for a better chance, a chance not just to hurt you, but to devastate you. The only way for there to be both liking and respect is if you hit me now and we call it quits. Do you get what I'm saying?"

I could see I'd somehow sold her on the method, but still she hesitated.

"I've never hit anyone before."

I drew her arms up out of the water and brought her right hand down against my cheek. She pulled back sharply, scattering soapsuds. "Okay, it's done," she said.

I shook my head. "Come on. That was nothing."

She tried to run, and knocked a chair over—Arturo called out "Everything okay in there?" and we called back: "Yup!" and "Absolutely!" It was like a two-legged race around the room, a race against nobody, but I wouldn't let her go, I had her by the wrists and I used both her hands to strike at my face until she began doing it for herself. That girl slapped me so hard my ears rang, and she said, "I'm sorry, I'm sorry," even as she hit me. She simmered down, sank onto a chair, and I folded up onto the floor and rested my chin on her knee. According to the clock on the wall five minutes had passed.

"I hate Olivia," she said. I looked up at her.

"I believe you."

"I asked her if she was surprised that you sent me to Boston. I said I bet she'd expected it to be Bird who was sent away. She said, 'Surprised?' and she told me about a white woman who went to Africa back in the thirties. While they were out there, the woman's husband shot a gorilla dead. They didn't realize it was a female gorilla until they saw the baby gorilla she'd been trying to protect. They felt guilty, so they brought the baby gorilla into their home and got an African woman to nurse it—"

"What? These people got an African woman to nurse what? The baby gorilla?"

"Yeah, I said something similar. And I asked Olivia why she was telling me this, and she said her point was that one can waste a lot of time marveling at the decisions of white folks. She said there's nothing any of them do that can surprise her. Then she went right on signing her charity checks. That's Olivia Whitman, can't stop giving. I think she might hate herself, but I can't help her out there. I feel so little love for her. I want to, but just when I'm getting there, she says or does something that makes me go nuts."

I said: "Don't let her see. At her age . . . I don't know. It'd probably finish her off."

Snow had given me a black eye. And Arturo asked me a leading question before I even attempted an explanation. "Did you fall over?" That was what he asked. Yeah, yeah, that's exactly what happened. It became an odd little running joke between Snow and me for the next few days. As she passed me, she'd whisper into my ear: "Did you fall over?"

And then there's Mia. Mia and what she's been doing behind my back. She only came clean when I phoned her and told her about the rat catcher. I couldn't work out who'd told him where we were. Olivia and Agnes and Gerald didn't know his name, and even if they did, what would their motive have been? For half of a sleepless night I thought it had to be Arturo. Arturo knew the rat catcher's name. Arturo could have tracked him down. This thing he has about completing things, having the whole gang there for the head count—

Mia interrupted me. "We need to talk," she said. "I've got an all-nighter to pull, but I'll come over when it gets light."

She was true to her word. She arrived as I was making coffee, slouched in a chair in front of the stove, too decaffeinated to stand. The first coffee of the morning is never, ever, ready quickly enough. You die before it's ready and then your ghost pours the resurrection potion out of the moka pot. Snow was there with me, smoking her breakfast cigarette and telling me something about her job. Her tone suggested she wasn't looking forward to getting back to work; I wasn't one hundred percent sure what she was saying. I was merely making listening noises. I do remember that she said she'd helped Bird get ready for school. It's been a long while since Bird's requested help getting ready for school. I don't know what tasks would be involved in helping her get ready at this stage of her advanced ability to comb her own hair, get her own books together, and eat her own cereal, so I thought it was a good sign that she'd allowed Snow to think she was helping. Mia was carrying a red folder. She passed it to me, kissed Snow, and asked her, "Remember me?" Snow's smile was perfectly vague and perfectly tender, and she said: "Of course."

"And how's your Aunt Clara?"

"She's back in Boston now, and doing just fine, thank you."

She left us; she had errands to run. Agnes wanted her to buy fuchsia wool.

Mia stopped smiling as soon as she'd gone. "Give me a break," she said. "That girl cannot be for real."

I pinched the bridge of my nose. "I don't know. Maybe this is actually as sincere as she gets."

"I'll take that under advisement. What happened?" She brushed my bangs to the left. "Don't tell me Arturo . . . ?"

"No, Mia. But if I ever want to make him cry, I'll tell him 'people' think he has the makings of a fine wife beater. I tripped over a chair. I know, I know. Why is my life so exciting?"

Mia's folder contained a single sheet of paper. It was a xeroxed birth certificate. Name: Frances Amelia Novak. Date of birth: November 1, 1902. Place of birth: Greenpoint, Brooklyn.

"Where'd you get this?"

She lifted her coffee cup to her mouth and set it down again. "I went looking for your mom, Boy."

"Why would you do that?"

342

"That doesn't matter as much as the fact that I found her. I found her."

"It was you who brought the rat catcher after me."

"I told him where to find you, yes. Sit down, Boy. Sit down and hear me out. I thought he deserved the chance to tell you what I'm about to tell you. He had one last chance and he didn't take it and he's not going to bother you anymore."

Frances Amelia Novak. Date of birth: November 1, 1902. "I've got to get to work. Tell me later."

"No, now. You need to know this now. Mrs. Fletcher will understand."

Mia was bleary-eyed from her all-nighter, and when she jerked her head, three neon pins escaped her hair and scuttled across the floor. I still wanted to trust her. "Start with why you did this."

"Okay. I wanted something to write about. The way you're looking at me, people have looked at me that way before. One guy called me a bloodsucker. That's not it. It's more like my mind's stacked with all these incongruous items, other people's stories that I've been telling pieces of. And the people don't come back for their stories, but that doesn't make them mine. The Mia Cabrini pawnshop, I call it sometimes. But since the termination . . . my termination, I should say, but that sounds like the termination of myself, doesn't it . . . I've got to write something. That or get a hole drilled in my skull to let the fog out."

I poured us both more coffee. It was cold and thick. "It would've been better for you to write about the termination itself. Maybe it'd help you. I'm not just saying that because you're using me."

She didn't flinch. "I don't think it would have been better. I want to describe what someone goes through when they refuse to be a mother, or when they realize they just can't do it. I mean, okay, so I knew what it was for me. I knew that I was afraid of yet another relationship in which I care about someone a hell of a lot more than they care about me. For that to play out between me and a kid, for all our lives . . . I don't regret the termination. I know I cried all over you about it being my last shot at having a kid, but I think I've done all my crying over this. I hate that my life is teaching me that I can only be loved if I put my love out of reach and just drift above people until they love my remoteness. I'm not just talking about romances, but about friendships too. Whoa, Mia, you're too intense. I get a lot of that. So I know that I won't be loved the way I need to be. I know that's not going to happen in my life. I've got other stuff to do, I can just get on and do that other stuff. But say I go ahead and print that, it's just a sob story, easy enough for most readers to think they understand. If I'm going to talk about this thing, I don't want to be confirming anybody's theories about the way life goes—not even my own. So I was thinking. I was thinking, maybe I could do a well-disguised piece about Olivia Whitman. She sent Clara away. But then she raised her other two. I wondered if I could write about you and Snow for a second, but Snow isn't your kid anyway. And then I thought about your nameless mother, and I thought she might be dead. But if she was alive . . ."

"Is she?"

Mia leaned forward in her chair. "Boy, don't you get it? When I started searching, I started with the rat catcher. I thought I could find your mother through him, and that turned out to be true. I searched public records for anything connected to Frank Novak and Francis Novak and Frantisek Novak and I found a few, but none that led me to that address on Rutgers Street that my pal mailed that money to years ago. I went down to New York for two weeks and pestered poor innocent Francises and Frantiseks. I stood outside the brownstone you grew up in, trying to switch on X-ray vision. I looked up your birth certificate—"

"I haven't got a birth certificate." I'd been proud of that, having to enroll at high school with an affidavit sworn by the rat catcher that he was my father and that I'd been born on the date he said I'd been born on.

"It's on record that you have. But this is stuff you could've looked up if you'd wanted to . . . anyhow, your birth certificate says your mother is Frances Novak and your father is unnamed. The

Frank Novak who raised you doesn't officially exist."

"Doesn't exist?"

"Not officially."

I cackled. I couldn't help it. She didn't know what she was saying.

"Keep hearing me out. I'm not just talking out of my ass here. I did a lot of work on this and I can show you all the paperwork. That's why I haven't been around much. Maybe you thought I was moping. Maybe I hardly crossed your mind. Anyhow, my earlier searches came to nothing because I'd been looking for men. Frances Amelia Novak was born in Brooklyn in 1902. Her father, Sandor, was a Hungarian immigrant, a concert cellist turned delivery-truck driver, and her mother, Dinah, was an Irish-American seamstress who made these quilts . . . I went to see one of them at the folk art museum, the tiny one in Midtown. It was art, what your grandma made. Frances was a scamp with a knockout smile—"

Mia was showing me a series of xeroxed photographs. Oh, God.

"And she was super, super smart. It was a pretty mixed neighborhood—linguistically, I mean—the warmest reception a colored messenger boy would get around there in those days were questions like 'Do you think this is Harlem?' But Frances picked up snippets of Czech and Dutch from the neighbors, as well as speaking Magyar, her father's first language, fluently. She brought out the best side of her more idealistic teachers, made them feel that she had just the kind of intellect they'd got into teaching to help develop. She'd ask for additional reading and extra assignments. You'd think the other kids would've hated her, but they were glad for her, voted her Most Likely to Succeed. She made it into Barnard on a scholarship, got her BS in her chosen field of psychology, embarked on postgraduate research, maybe with a view to becoming a faculty member . . . that's what she told her friends, anyway. She knew that the first female member of the psych faculty had been taken on less than five years ago, and they'd taken her on as an unpaid lecturer. She knew that she'd need more than just a flair for the subject, more than just curiosity, she'd need to be utterly single-minded in her pursuit of a faculty position, and the research itself meant more to her than that. She was interested in sexuality. More specifically, she was interested in proving that homosexuality isn't a mental illness. But she never finished her paper—"

"How do you know what she thought and what she was interested in?"

"I met four of her former girlfriends for coffee, and they all brought letters with them. Letters she'd written to them when they were all at Barnard together. I'd thought the friendships were platonic, but the letters get pretty raunchy in places, and all three of the ex-girlfriends said, 'Yes, yes, we were true friends, but we were lovers as well, you know'—these serene intellectual women who only really get bashful about abstract theory. They brought me photos too. Look at her. Apparently impressionable young woman after impressionable young woman would just up and leave their boyfriends for her. I know she's your mother, but you get the appeal, right? I don't know when Frances started expressing a preference for females, but it was most certainly by the time she was in the final year of her BS studies."

I shuffled through all the photos of my glamorously disheveled bluestocking mother, hair as long as Lady Godiva's at a time when short hair was all the rage. She had the look of someone who sings inside themselves, silently and continually; at least I hope that's what people mean when they say someone has a twinkle in their eye. Hers was there even when she was playing possessive, her arms tangled around the woman on her lap. "What happened to her, Mia?"

"This is exactly what Frances's girlfriends wanted to know. They all showed up hoping I could tell them. She was twenty-nine and that was supposed to be the year she got her doctorate, but she skipped campus and the apartment on Morningside that she shared with two other women. She was there on a Tuesday—spotted in the library—she asked one of the women I met with to loan her some money, but her friend was just as broke as she was. Then on Wednesday she didn't show up to a talk she'd agreed to give to some undergraduates. She'd never done anything like that; she was the kind who showed up to lectures even when she was ill. Nobody seems to remember her as being particularly highly strung, either. By Friday her friends were making active efforts to track her down. Then other friends suggested she didn't want to be tracked down, that she was just working hard on her paper. But working where? She hadn't returned to the Morningside apartment since Tuesday evening. Her roommates wanted to call the police but everybody said they were overreacting. Her parents ended up reporting her missing in April 1933."

"I was born in November 1933," I volunteered.

"Yeah."

"So what have you found out?"

Mia looked out of the window and braced herself, then looked back at me. "Frank told me this himself. Frances was raped. It was an acquaintance of hers; a male friend's younger brother. He was an undergrad at Columbia who thought that all lesbianism meant was that you were holding out for the man who really got you excited. Frances had warned him to stop airing

349

this view. He'd also, I don't know, grabbed at a friend of hers and called her a tease and so on. Frances had issued her warning to this guy in front of other people and I guess that had humiliated him and—don't let me rationalize what he did anymore, Boy. He caught her coming out of the library that night in February, seemed contrite, told her he was just a boy trying to grow into a man and that his motto was live and let live, and he urged her to visit a speakeasy he'd heard about. And she went with him, to show him there was no longer any quarrel between them. He bought her three drinks. They went for a drive along the Hudson. He said, 'What do you say we drive all night?' She said sure. Being in motion helped her get a lot of good thinking done. His parents were out of town and he drove up to their house in Westchester, drove into the garage, shut the doors, and broke her life in two."

"What was his name?"

"Steven."

"Steven what?"

"Steven Hamilton."

"Is he alive?"

"Screw him. I didn't check. It's Frances I followed, and she didn't encounter him again."

"So where did she go?"

"There was a women's shelter she knew of, run by a Harlem heiress out of her own home. Mainly for nonwhite women, but they didn't automatically turn you away if you were white. She stayed there for three months under the name Francine Stone, but they eventually asked her to leave. She was . . . uh, demoralizing the other women who 'had suffered their own violations but were determined to continue their lives as women in spite of them,' I think the note said. Frances understood and admired that, but it wasn't her way. Her distress had hardened. You know how Frank says he became Frank? He says he looked in the mirror one morning when he was still Frances, and this man she'd never seen before was just standing there, looking back. Frances washed her face and fixed her hair and looked again, and the man was still there, wearing an exact copy of her skirt and sweater. He said one word to her to announce his arrival. What he did was, he flicked the surface of his side of the mirror with his finger and thumb and he said: 'Hi.' After that he acted just like a normal reflection; otherwise she would've felt like she had to go to a psychiatrist and complain about him. Once she'd established that he was there to stay, she named him Frank and stopped off at a barbershop and got a short back and sides—she felt that haircut suited Frank's personality. She went around in heavy boots, and a high-collared shirt . . . maybe you'll remember the rat catcher's collared shirts and the way he'd wear them even in the summer, to hide the fact that he didn't have an Adam's apple . . .

she took to speaking in an artificially deep, gruff voice. The people around her didn't know what to do about her and frankly they didn't like her. To them it was as if she'd been bitten by something vile and that in some way she was becoming the thing that had bitten her. She left the shelter, found a room that she shared with a girl on a strict twelve-hour basis—from six in the morning to six in the evening the room was Frank's, and from six in the evening to six in the morning the room belonged to the other girl and Frank had to get out."

"I take it the roommate was a hooker?"

"Maybe. However it was she made her living, she knew all kinds of people, and hooked Frank up with a physician who was willing to turn criminal for a reasonable fee. Frank made two appointments, and ended up breaking them both. He was afraid of dying on the physician's table. He'd heard stories, and he wanted to live. He worked jobs that didn't require documentation—an extermination company that had a high turnover of illegal immigrant employees turned out to be the job he lasted longest at, but it was a job he lost when he had you. You were premature and he said he had to take a lot of time off. He remembered his father's rat-catching methods and started working for himself—"

"Stop calling her 'him.' You're telling me my mother has been desperately ill for decades and

I'm fighting like hell to take it in, but you've got to stop calling her 'him.'"

"I don't know that I can. As it stands right now he's been Frank longer than he was Frances. It's gone beyond alter egos. Boy, I've been reading medical monographs about people whose alleged alter egos have different blood types from theirs—one guy's alter ego was diabetic, and he wasn't—or he was the alter ego and the diabetic was the 'true' personality—who's to say? When those kinds of biological facts start coming in, you have to ask if becoming someone else is more than some delusion or some dysfunction of the mind. What I mean to say is that Frank's personality is pretty awful—he tried to hit me when I told him I was going to tell this story, but he wasn't fast enough—but he's awfully sane. Well, maybe not when it comes to thinking of names. He says he almost named you Pup."

"Mia."

She took my hands, and kissed them. "Boy."

"Please don't write about this. Find someone else to write about."

"I'm sorry, *cara*. I don't expect you to understand this, but I have to tell. You know, Bird sent me something in the mail a few days ago. Some notes she'd made while Frank was talking to her over lunch."

"What?"

"He said some stuff to her that's probably going

to upset you—no, he didn't threaten her. I think he was actually trying to tell. Trying to tell her what he had agreed to come down here and tell you."

"I'll be the judge of that," I said.

"I'm sorry it's like this. You've got a daughter who has to know and a friend who would do anything for you apart from not telling. This can't be what you signed up for." She squeezed my hand, and I squeezed back.

"Do you think Frances is gone forever?"

"Boy . . . you know I can't answer that . . . I never met her."

I don't know why that was a comfort, but it was.

# 2

*r* eading Bird's notes took the comfort away. Frank's claim that I'm evil doesn't shock me so much, partly because I've questioned myself on the very same subject before. It's not my actions that raise the questions, but my inaction, the way I've consciously and consistently avoided chances to reduce other people's unhappiness. I call it a side effect of growing up in a building full of families and thin walls and floors: We all heard everything and did nothing. I heard love going wrong for people, so wrong. The silence for weeks when Mrs. Phillips next door miscarried. Then the weeks of noise that followed—Mr. Phillips came home later and later, and Mrs. Phillips waited up for him, playing records until the small hours, switching off the gramophone and sobbing when he came in through the door. Mr. Kendall on the other side of us kept spending the rent money; his wife kept faking surprise at this. Every month Mrs. Kendall asked, "How could you, Fred? How *could* you? What are we going to do?" and you could hear her hatred and her boredom; it stayed in her voice even as he hit her. For a few months there was a pretty glamorous-looking couple upstairs—down on their luck, I guess. I remember them particularly because I never found out either of their names, only heard him calling her whore, whore, WHORE. Of course they must have heard the rat catcher knocking me around too. We all got a little less human so we could keep living together.

No, these are the words that kissed my equilibrium good-bye:

*It was the one time in my life I wished I was a woman.*

There it was, in my daughter's handwriting. Frances had wanted to come back.

I couldn't sleep. Arturo snored blissfully beside me until I put a stop to that.

"Arturo. Arturo. Wake up."

He gasped and waved his arms. "What? What is it? Fire?"

355

"No. I need to know how to break a spell. Any ideas?"

"Break a spell, you say?"

"Yeah. How?"

"Woman, how the hell should I know? Let me sleep."

"Quit yelling."

"I'm not yelling."

"Sounds like yelling to me."

He stuck his head underneath his pillow; I got up. Dawn broke calmly and filled the house with its glow. And Alecto Fletcher answered the phone when I called her.

"Oh. I knew it was you. Who else could be so disrespectful of an old woman's need for rest?"

"I won't keep you long, Alecto. I just wondered if you knew how to break a spell."

"That's right, ask the crone; she'll know. Are we talking about a magic spell?"

"Um. Not in origin, but in effect maybe."

"And you're asking for a friend . . ."

"My friends just don't know how to behave."

"Your friend already asked me herself. Sid Fairfax came over yesterday with a fairly interesting book of art monographs and the very same question you've just called me to ask. I'm worried about her too. It's plain to see that she loathes this town, but she's told herself she can't leave because she loves her mother and she can't be happy if her mother is unhappy."

"I didn't know any of that. I thought she was staying because she's in love with Kazim."

"Yes, we'd be in love with Mr. Bey, wouldn't we, if we dared to be? Agnes Miller allows herself to flirt with him; perhaps we should too."

"What can I say? He's an actual Prince Charming. But what'd you tell Sidonie?"

"I told her that magic spells only work until the person under the spell is really and honestly tired of it. It ends when continuing becomes simply too ghastly a prospect."

"I'm not sure I . . ."

"Pester your subject, Boy. Pester this person, whoever it is. Make the enchantment inconvenient for them, find myriad ways to expose their contentment as false, show them that the contentment is part of the spell, engineered to make it last longer. Do you see?"

"I take it you've broken a lot of spells, Alecto?"

"I'm speaking more from the experience of having been under them."

"May you live forever."

"Yes, you'd like that, wouldn't you? So you could phone me at five in the morning forever."

*i made cocoa,* took a cupful out onto the porch and closed my eyes as the sun climbed the sky. I pretended that the light was patting my black eye in a friendly, investigative way, trying to see if early light alone could heal it. I'd pretended this a

357

number of times back in New York. It was the quickest way to feel cared for after you'd taken a battering. With my eyes closed, I returned to the apartment on Rutgers Street, tried to find something, anything, maternal in what I remembered of the rat catcher. There was nothing. I saw his sneer again. His sneer and his fists. His eyes I couldn't remember so well; I rarely let him look into my eyes, I'd kept him out no matter what. *Okay, scratch maternal. How about feminine?* Maybe a few moments too fleeting to articulate, but that's men for you—it was like that with Arturo too. Through the keyhole of the rat catcher's bedroom door I once saw him place his hand on his girlfriend's calf and slide upward to the top of her thigh. Could I file that under feminine? Yes and no. It was the touch of a lover. Slow and sure. Taking pleasure, promising more. She bent over him and nipped at his earlobe and they laughed a little and moaned a little and I backed away from that keyhole in a hurry.

*snow came up* the garden path and asked if there was any cocoa going spare. I said yes and made a fresh batch, ignoring her protests that she hadn't intended to put me to any trouble.

"Why are you up so early?"

"I just wanted to walk around without seeing anybody," she said, studying the porch floor. I thought she looked a little fatigued, so I made her take a vitamin tablet and tried to enact a talking cure.

"You go home tomorrow, don't you?"

"Yes, ma'am."

"And do you go back to work right away?"

"No, I don't have a case until next week."

There was a skin on my cocoa, and a thicker one on hers, but she was drinking around the edges of it.

"A case?"

"I knew you weren't listening the other morning."

"I'm sorry, honey." Honey. I'd never called anybody honey in my life before then.

She smiled. "Don't be. It's dirty work, Boy. I've been following men's wives and taking note of their indiscretions. It pays well because it's valuable to the clients. It makes their divorces significantly cheaper."

You never really feel your jaw until it drops. I think it was the crispness of her words just as much as the worldliness of what she was saying. Should a diaphanous butterfly ever perch on my finger and provide analysis of the day's stock market activity I won't bat an eyelash.

She looked up (we were directly beneath Bird's window) and continued in a whisper: "I don't know if I can stick it out for much longer. You're taking photos of a couple from across the street, you're sitting next to them in some bar, eavesdropping for incriminating details, sometimes the guy will get up and go to the restroom and the unfaithful wife will turn around and just start *talking* to you. People in love are so trusting. They'll say, 'Hey, don't worry, your prince will come,' and I'm all no no no, don't talk to me, I'm stalking you. One woman . . . I liked her, and it was sad to hand in the stuff I'd got on her . . . she started telling me about her life with her lover. It was all moonshine, I knew who her husband was, and where their home was, and where she sent her kids for their education. But she told me the man she was with was her husband and they had four boys he took fishing every Sunday, and between the boys and work they only had one date night a month so they had to make it special, and I just started shaking. I keep going to Isidor—that's my boss—to tell him I'm quitting, but then he pays me . . ."

I sniggered, and then we were both laughing.

"Don't go home tomorrow, Snow. Stay awhile, okay?"

She hesitated.

"Isidor might fire you, but if the job makes you shake, is it really right for you? Visit awhile longer. Please."

"It's not because of Isidor. It's that kiddie bedroom. But I guess I only have to sleep there."

# 3

*O*n Saturday morning I had a long talk with Arturo about Frances and the rat catcher and what I meant to do. He laughed at me and then he forbade me and then he warned me. I walked out of the room and he followed me into the next room. Then he walked out of the room and I followed him into the next room, and not for a second did either of us stop talking. We split a sandwich for lunch and he conceded that if he were in my place he'd want to meet Frances too. If there's still anything left of her. If she wants to meet us. I think he was just getting hoarse. Plus he knows this terrain. He's been handling the difference between the mother you want and the mother you get for years, managing the discrepancy like a pro, making it look easy.

(Charlie would've been full of useless pity, I think. It's so stupid to compare, or even to think of him at all.)

"But just for a week." For some reason Arturo tapped his watch. "Bird can't miss too much school. One week for now and then we'll talk."

"Right," I said, remembering that Snow had thought she was only visiting Clara and John for a week. I kissed him and went upstairs before he could begin to remember that too. I packed a bag—books and records, things I thought Frances might get curious about or find offensive enough that she'd wake up just to challenge them—and I knocked on Bird's bedroom door. She wasn't in there, just a scattering of spiders hanging in midair, waiting for me to close the door again so they could continue on to their secret destinations. Arturo was back in his studio by the time I went downstairs, but Mia had arrived, with her suitcase, as agreed. She hadn't seen Bird, either, but she had a lot of complaints and suggestions to make. This trip would seriously disrupt her work on the article, we could engage a suitable doctor from here, and so on, and so on.

"Hold that last thought while we go grab Snow."

"Her too?"

Snow didn't answer when we knocked, but Agnes had said she was in there, so we went in. She was lying facedown on her spangled blue bed. Her hands were pressed over her ears, and when we first entered the room, we couldn't hear why (Mia looked around at all the mobiles and wall stencils and gave a silent whistle), but I stood beside her bed and heard singing. A clear, mellow voice with a hint of a ragtime pitch, as if the singer felt such emotion that the melody came out uneven.

*All I do is dream of you is dream of you the whole night through . . .*

Julia.

Snow's lips were moving; she was involuntarily singing along. Mia grabbed my arm, then searched the tops of the shelves and the dresser for a record player. When she couldn't find one, she knelt down beside Snow and tried to lift the girl up. I went to the window. I didn't especially want to, but that was the direction the singing seemed to be coming from. The bedroom overlooked Olivia's garden, which looked empty until I flung the window open and saw movement behind the hedge. The singing stopped. I ran down into the garden and out of the front gate and caught Bird about a millisecond before she vanished into the woods. I caught her by her ear, and I yanked hard.

"So you're a mimic, huh?"

"It's not a crime!"

"So you're trying to drive your sister crazy?"

"I'm trying to see if she's a phony or not."

"And if you manage to drive her out of her mind that means she's not a phony? I'm going to twist this ear right off of your head, Bird Whitman."

I guess I must've sounded like I meant it, because she screamed with such fear that I instantly let her go. Mia and Snow came running toward us, and Bird wrapped her arm around a tree trunk as if depending upon its aid. Maybe she was given my eyes so that I can never stay mad at her. But you can't let a thirteen-year-old just walk around with the ability to sound much too much like a dead woman.

"How long have you been doing this?"

She shrugged, and I turned to Snow.

"That was the third time," Snow said. "But Boy, don't kill her, or threaten to. She—she didn't know what she was doing." I think it took a lot for her to say that. Not that her sister appreciated it.

"Yes, I did know what I was doing," Bird insisted.

"You will never do anything like that ever again. And you will go pack a bag immediately," I told her.

She lifted her chin. "Where are you sending me? Can I write a note to Louis first?"

"We're going to New York for a few days." I looked at Snow and Mia. "All of us. We're going to go look at a quilt your great-grandmother on my side made, Bird. It's an important quilt. It's in a museum. I don't know why I started with the quilt. Really we're going down there to go see somebody. She needs us, I think. I'll explain more on the bus. And we need her. You, Bird, you've always got to know, and we'd better find you a way to do something other than devilry with that. And you, Mia, you've got to tell, and Snow— well, you're a pretty face and more. As for me, I'll do whatever else there is to be done. And yes, you can write a note to Louis. But get a move on. The bus we want leaves in an hour."

Bird bolted into our house, but Snow tucked

her arm through mine and whispered to me that she didn't want to come with us, she didn't think she could help, she wanted to go back to Twelve Bridges. I linked my other arm through Mia's and the three of us walked slowly up and down the street, talking about Frances.

Olivia Whitman walked out of her house and into the road as Mia was driving us to the bus station. So we had to stop the car. She gestured for Mia to roll down the window, and when she was obeyed, Olivia said, "Where are you taking my grandchildren?" She tried to sound imperious, but she just sounded old.

Snow looked out of the other window and bit her lip. Bird almost startled the life out of Olivia by planting a noisy kiss on her cheek.

I told her to wait there, and that we'd be back for her, and Olivia stood aside and let Mia drive on.

# acknowledgments

Thank you, Marina Endicott; thank you, Jin Auh; thank you, Tracy Bohan; thank you, Megan Lynch; thank you, Dr. Cieplak; thank you, Kate Harvey. And Ronnie Vuine—thank you.

**Center Point Large Print**
600 Brooks Road / PO Box 1
Thorndike ME 04986-0001 USA

**(207) 568-3717**

**US & Canada:**
**1 800 929-9108**
**www.centerpointlargeprint.com**

LARGE TYPE
Oyeyemi, Helen.
Boy, snow, bird